MOJO HAND

By Greg Kihn from Tom Doherty Associates

Horror Show
Shade of Pale
Big Rock Beat
Mojo Hand

to Nancy —

MOJO HAND

Rock on!

GREG KIHN

[signature] 11/26/99

FORGE®

A TOM DOHERTY ASSOCIATES BOOK
NEW YORK

A Forge Book
Published by Tom Doherty Associates, LLC
175 Fifth Avenue
New York, NY 10010

Forge is a registered trademark of Tom Doherty Associates, LLC.

Library of Congress Cataloging-in Publication Data

Kihn, Greg.
    Mojo hand / Greg Kihn.
        p.   cm.
    ISBN 0-312-87246-1
    I. Title.
PS3561.I363M64   1999
813'.54—dc21   99-26643

First Edition: November 1999

Printed in the United States of America

0 9 8 7 6 5 4 3 2 1

This book is dedicated to my dad, Stan the man.

AUTHOR'S NOTE

For decades, blues fans have speculated on the life and death of Robert Johnson. The legend says he sold his soul to the devil in exchange for his talent. There are those who believe he was poisoned by a jealous husband at a gig. Others believe he met his fate at the crossroads, the devil collecting on his debt. Some believe all of it, while others believe nothing at all.

STATE OF MISSISSIPPI

MISSISSIPPI STATE DEPARTMENT OF HEALTH
VITAL RECORDS

BUREAU OF VITAL STATISTICS   **STANDARD CERTIFICATE OF DEATH**   State File No. 13704

MISSISSIPPI STATE BOARD OF HEALTH

1. PLACE OF DEATH

County _Leflore_   Registered No. _____

Voting Precinct _____ or Village _____

or City _Greenwood (outside)_   No. _____ St., _____ Ward
(If death occurred in a hospital or institution, give its NAME instead of street and number)

Length of residence in city or town where death occurred? _yrs._ _mos._ _ds._ How long in U. S., if of foreign birth? _yrs._ _mos._ _ds._

2. FULL NAME _Robert L. Johnson_   (Write or Print Name Plainly)

(a) Residence: No. _Greenwood Miss._ St., _____ Ward. _____
(Usual place of abode)   (If nonresident give city or town and State)

PERSONAL AND STATISTICAL PARTICULARS	MEDICAL CERTIFICATE OF DEATH

3. SEX _M_   **4. COLOR OR RACE** _B_   **5. Single, Married, Widowed, or Divorced (write the word)** _single_

21. DATE OF DEATH (month, day and year) _8-16-38_

22. I HEREBY CERTIFY, That I attended deceased from _____ 19____ to _____ 19____

I last saw h____ alive on _____ 19____ Death is said to have occurred on the date stated above, at _____ m.

5a. If married, widowed, or divorced HUSBAND of (or) WIFE of _____

The principal cause of death and related causes of importance in order of onset were as follows: Date of onset

6. DATE OF BIRTH (month, day, and year) _____

7. AGE Years _26_   Months ____   Days ____   If LESS than 1 day, ____ hrs. or ____ min.

8. Trade, profession, or particular kind of work done, as spinner, sawyer, bookkeeper, etc. _Musician_

Contributory causes of importance not related to principal cause: _____ _2-28_

9. Industry or business in which work was done, as silk mill, saw mill, bank, etc. _____

No Doctor

10. Date deceased last worked at this occupation (month and year) _1938_

11. Total time (years) spent in this occupation _10_

Name of operation (if any was done) _____ Date _____

What test confirmed diagnosis? _____ Was there an autopsy? _____

12. BIRTHPLACE (city or town) (State or country) _Hazlehurst Miss_

13. NAME _Norah Johnson_

14. BIRTHPLACE (city or town) (State or country) _D.K._

15. MAIDEN NAME _Julia Major_

16. BIRTHPLACE (city or town) (State or country) _Miss_

23. If death was due to external causes (violence) fill in also the following: Accident, suicide, or homicide? _____

Date of injury _____ 19____

Where did injury occur? _____
(Specify city or town, county, and State)

Specify whether injury occurred in industry, in home, or in public place _____

17. INFORMANT (and Address) _Jim Moore_

Manner of injury _____

Nature of injury _____

18. BURIAL, CREMATION, OR REMOVAL Place _Zion Church_ Date _8-17_, _1938_

24. Was disease or injury in any way related to occupation of deceased? _____ If so, specify _____

19. UNDERTAKER (and Address) _Family_

(Signed) _____ M. D.

(Address) _____

20. FILED _8-18-38_, 19__ _Cornelia J. Jordan_ Registrar.

THIS IS TO CERTIFY THAT THE ABOVE IS A TRUE AND CORRECT COPY OF THE CERTIFICATE ON FILE IN THIS OFFICE

F. E. Thompson Jr. MD
F. E. Thompson, Jr., M.D., M.P.H.
STATE HEALTH OFFICER

Nita Cox Gunter
Nita Cox Gunter
STATE REGISTRAR

WARNING: A REPRODUCTION OF THIS DOCUMENT RENDERS IT VOID AND INVALID. DO NOT ACCEPT UNLESS EMBOSSED SEAL OF THE MISSISSIPPI STATE BOARD OF HEALTH IS PRESENT. IT IS ILLEGAL TO ALTER OR COUNTERFEIT THIS DOCUMENT.

☙ ONE ☙

The blues descended on Vincent Shives like the ashes of some distant fire. It drifted in the air until it fell on his shoulders, carrying the memory of magnificent flames. He walked ghostly through the swamp, albino skin glowing in the platinum radiance of a full moon. He'd been followed for a while by some teenagers who called after him until they realized where he was going. Then they dropped off fast. That had been over an hour ago.

Though it was a muggy summer night he wore a black overcoat and gloves. Black, thick, tinted wraparound prescription glasses covered his sensitive eyes, giving him an odd, comic-book-spy appearance. In the moonlight his skin appeared nearly translucent. Blue veins squirmed beneath an unhealthy-looking hide the color of the dead. Long white hair swung like limp pasta on either side of his gaunt face, framing it like a cheap Italian dinner.

Vince stayed on the path.

He walked purposefully, sliding one storklike leg in front of the other, black boots clomping in the soft mud. His feet made subdued sucking sounds. From somewhere in the night mournful loon cries echoed across the black, still water. To Vince the music of the loons sounded like slide guitar. He even thought he recognized the song: "Gris-Gris Gumbo Ya-Ya."

The summer humidity played tricks with the sounds, reflecting certain frequencies, making them almost sound like human voices. Once he was reminded of the song, the lyrics danced around his head as he walked. "Gris-gris gumbo ya-ya . . . Hey now, gumbo yay-yay . . ."

Vince walked through a copse of trees into a clearing. Ida John's voodoo shack was not outwardly marked by any sign, and the windows were covered with yellowed newspaper. The glow of an oil lamp illuminated the paper from inside. It stood alone at the edge of the water, a sagging pier jutted out into the swamp.

The music played in Vincent's head. "Gris-gris gumbo ya-ya . . . Hey now, gumbo yay-yay."

He strode past the rotting corpse of a chicken, humming with flies, hanging from a tree limb. Vincent Shives did not hesitate. He mounted the wooden step and knocked three times on the front door. Loose screen rattled. The sounds of the hot, muggy Louisiana night clung to his back, hanging there for a moment like a diseased monkey. The loons sang another chorus. Vince shook it off and turned the doorknob.

The music in his head faded as he stepped into the low-ceilinged room. He coughed to announce his presence.

Several hurricane lamps flickered. Dust particles hung in the air, visible in the shafts of moonlight leaking between the newspaper panels. The dust swirled in the eddies and currents when he moved. The cloying scent of incense covered a much worse smell, something putrid, discernible above the sandalwood. Vince pushed his glasses up and squinted. His pink eyes adjusted to the light.

Shelves holding bizarre and wildly esoteric merchandise lined the walls. There were hundreds of hand-labeled bottles containing powders and potions. Two bleached skulls grinned. A dusty glass case featured a collection of bones arranged according to size. Dried toads stood at attention.

The curtain behind the counter parted and an ancient black woman stepped through. She stared through the lifeless air at Vincent.

"I came, Ida John. Just like you said."

Ida John nodded. She brought a cardboard shoe box up from below the counter and placed it in front of him. Vince looked at it with keen interest.

"Go ahead. Open it," she said with a cracked voice. Vince thought he recognized a slight accent.

Daintily, he removed his gloves. They were the tight-fitting black leather automotive-type gloves that professional drivers wore. His naked hands were moist and incredibly pale after the opaque black of the gloves. He flexed his fingers self-consciously.

The old woman watched him, her eyes challenging. Vince avoided looking at them. He carefully lifted the lid of the box and looked inside. There, resting like a piece of sculpture amid some tissue paper, was a severed human hand. It appeared mummified, brown skin dry and leathery, even cracked in some places. It gave off a strange, cadaverous odor which bloomed up into Vince's face when he removed the lid. But Vince did not wince. He thought the thing was beautiful. Suppressing a smile, he reached in carefully and picked it up. It seemed surprisingly light in his hand. He held it high in the light of a hanging lamp and examined it. "Looks like the real thing."

The bone, yellowed with age, had been crudely cut just above the wrist and jutted out a grotesque one or two inches. Vince wondered whose hand it had been. It didn't matter, of course, but then, it did. What mattered most was the power.

"How much?" he asked.

The old woman cocked her head, birdlike, and eyed him suspiciously.

She didn't like this white man—he was bad juju. Albinos were bad luck, everybody knew that. And in her heart she didn't want to sell the thing to him. She didn't want him to own the power. The Hand of Glory could be the most powerful force in the universe, if you knew how to use it. How could this white devil know?

She searched his face with her aged, discolored eyes and wondered what terrible twist of fate had brought this albino to her door. She'd been careful to cut some of the fingernails off the hand and save the clippings in a jar so that the magic of the mojo could not be used against her. Ida always kept a little of what she sold. She assured herself that whatever she passed into the unsuspecting world would not come back to haunt her. That was just common sense. She'd spent a lifetime unleashing all sorts of terrible forces on people, always strangers, and she knew the precautions. Magic fed on hatred and revenge. Ida understood that above all.

And this white man vexed her.

"Real Mojo Hand cost money," she said hoarsely. "Maybe you want a fake one? Then you go see Madame Oomph. This one real. This one . . . very strong."

"How much?"

"Five thousand."

Vince stared at the hand. *Where did the old crone get it?* It looked pretty old. The muscle tissue had fused and dried up like beef jerky, and the fingers were slightly curled inward. Underneath the chipped nails he noticed some black dirt, as if the thing had crawled from the grave by itself. The skin was so discolored that he couldn't tell if the person had been black or white.

"Negro?" he asked.

Ida nodded so imperceptibly that Vince nearly missed it.

"Good." Vince felt the itching, burning power of the Mojo Hand as he held it. It tingled. And suddenly Vince felt bold.

He had to have it. The Hand of Glory was a powerful talisman, known among believers to be uncommonly effective. Its magic was the strongest money could buy. Vince knew that any crime could be committed with the Mojo Hand, and the owner would never be caught or punished. It had the power to make a person *uncatchable*. And there were other, darker powers, but Vince had no illusions about tapping those. Yet.

The secret was knowing how to unlock the energy. Vince felt electrified with the possibilities and absolutely sure he could make the hand work for him. The old woman glared, but he didn't notice. Vince reverently placed the hand back in the box. Finally he looked at Ida John.

"Five thousand? Is that what you said?" That seemed high, higher than he'd expected. Vince had already resigned himself to meet any reasonable price.

The old woman put the lid back on the box and pulled it toward her. She motioned for Vince to stand back. "Maybe I won't sell it to you."

"What?"

"Maybe I sell it to somebody else. You bad juju. I can tell. Very bad juju." She continued to speak in clipped sentences, her accent sour and thick-lipped. "Too white. A white devil. That's what you are. Very bad juju. White man with the Mojo Hand. Very bad juju." She shook her head vigorously.

Vincent Shives removed a large roll of hundred-dollar bills from his pocket and counted out fifty of them. He put the money on the counter in front of the old woman and waited.

Vincent watched her attention flicker from the money to his face and back. A heartbeat later, her bony hand reached out and snatched up the cash like a lizard. The deal was consummated.

She counted it quickly by touch, but she knew he would not cheat her. No one cheated Ida John.

Ida knew Vince feared her. He feared because he believed. And believers were the most dangerous people in the world.

She'd gone against instinct this time, but the money had seduced her. What did she care what this pale spook did with the Mojo Hand? He was just another lost soul, one in an endless stream of weak and ignorant pilgrims who came to her. She hadn't liked anything about this transaction, but it was over now, the money warming in her hand.

Now she wanted to get Vince out as soon as possible. She wanted him far away, with his dead man's skin and his evil pink eyes. She cursed herself for being greedy, and turned her back on him.

Vince wasted no time collecting the box under his arm and moving toward the door. The hand shifted inside its cardboard coffin. The dead fingers scratched the sides of the box, and the ghostly weight shifted again. Vincent stepped to the door, trying not to hurry, but hurrying anyway. He could feel Ida John's stare across his shoulder blades. Like the yoke of oppression.

"Bad juju!" she called out behind him. "Don't come back here!"

In a moment Vince was outside and gone. She watched him disappear into the swamp. "White devil," she muttered. She crossed herself and made a series of hand signals in the direction he had gone.

 TWO

The Cheshire Cat Club in Chicago had no backstage toilet, so Beau Young and Oakland Slim were forced to use the seriously unsavory public rest room. Oakland Slim drew accolades from everyone.

"My man! How's it goin', Slim?"

"Brutha! Nice stream!"

Oakland Slim and Beau were side by side in front of a long metal trough, trying not to breathe. The sound of Slim's urine hitting the metal was like hard rain on a Texas shack. It drowned out the comments of Slim's adoring public.

"Piss like a racehorse, Slim!"

"Hang on a second, bro," Slim said. His foghorn voice reverberated in the concrete rest room, impossibly low and gravelly.

Slim leaned back, enjoying his release. He turned to Beau and smiled. "You know, that preshow urination is often the most important urination of the day."

Beau nodded.

"Muddy Waters told me that, and you can take it to the bank. It's the last thing I do every night before I go onstage."

Beau nodded again.

"Don't want to have to cut the set short or be doin' any long drum solos."

Oakland Slim eased his two-hundred-pound body away from the trough and zipped up the pants to his blue, double-knit, flare-legged leisure suit. Slim dressed at the height of fashion for a bluesman in

1977—pastel leisure suit, wide collar, shiny black shirt, and square-toed Italian boots. His huge brown baby face beamed beneath a modest Afro. For a man in his mid-fifties, Slim kept up with styles. He turned to the fan, another black man in his fifties, and winked.

"I'd best not shake hands with you yet. Wait till I wash and dry 'em."

The fan nodded. "Yeah, sure. I can dig it. Hey, Slim, remember me? I saw you in Detroit. We had a couple drinks."

Slim bent his prodigious form over the tiny sink and meticulously washed his hands. He spoke into the porcelain. "Detroit? You gotta be more specific, man. I play about two hundred dates a year. I see Detroit a couple times."

"Well, it was a club."

Slim chuckled. "That don't do much to narrow it down." He dried his hands with a paper towel and tossed it into a bin. "I'll shake your hand now."

The fan thrust his hand out and Slim gripped it manfully. Slim knew how to deal with fans. "I gotta go tune up. I'll catch you later."

"Thanks, man."

Slim turned to Beau. "Let's blow this stinkburger."

They left the rest room and made their way backstage. Slim exchanged greetings with people every step of the way. "That's the way it is when you're a blues legend," he told Beau. "Gotta be nice to people or they'll stop payin' the bills."

Beau didn't reply verbally. Often Slim's conversations didn't require a response, just a nod or a grunt. Beau did both. Slim continued. "Personally, I like a club where my shoes stick to the floor. It's my kinda scene."

Beau laughed. Now away from the rest room he was able to breathe freely again. "Well, you got it here." His boots made smacking sounds as he walked.

"You in tune?"

"Uh-huh. I'm ready to rock."

"Tell the band. It's show time."

Beau led the musicians onstage. As the youngest and the only white guy in the band, he was constantly on trial. Beau kept his head in every song, ready to take a solo at a moment's notice. More often than not that was all the notice he got from Slim and the band. The bass player, a tall, thin preacher-faced man, never let Beau rest. He threw Beau the musician's medicine ball whenever he got the chance. For some reason, he thought Beau would crumble, but he never did.

Beau held his own with the veterans. Even the surly bass player had to admire that. The white kid was smooth for a rock and roller.

Rockers rubbed blues guys the wrong way. They took the sacred music and mucked it up with heavy guitar tones and stupid lyrics, and worst of all, they made money off it. That was just plain wrong. Slim could rant for hours about rock guitarists ripping off Muddy Waters riffs. It was an old story. Rock and roll, the blues' bastard child, stepping in to take all the money again. Some guys resented it.

But Beau had paid some dues. In the late sixties he'd been in a band with a hit record, the Stone Savages, later known as Beau and the Savages. Actually it was 1.5 hit records, but Beau wasn't counting anymore. The Stone Savages etched a footnote in rock history with their teeth and fingernails, leaving their crudely carved initials in the stone right next to other 1.5-hit wonders like the Strawberry Alarm Clock and the Electric Prunes. If it hadn't been for some extremely poor money management, and Beau's falling prey to every occupational hazard known to musicians, he might have been a star. But in the end it had been mostly drugs, sex, and rock and roll itself that had conspired against him.

When the band stopped making money, and the gigs dried up, Beau went home to the wife and son he'd left behind. But after seven hard years on the road Beau's parenting skills left much to be desired. He could roll a joint much better than he could change a diaper. The marriage began to crumble about the same time Beau got heavy into coke.

Two years later, Beau couldn't remember if he'd started drinking because his wife had left him, or whether she had left him because he'd started drinking. Beau *had* to drink to take the edge off the blow. It became the only way he could live. When he finally came out of the daze, his career and marriage had both crashed and burned. Beau started jamming with some blues bands.

Blues felt good, it felt right. It was honest. No bullshit. Ninety percent improv. He dug the way the music could flex and stretch to meet his moods. Riffing on a blues progression had a Zen-like simplicity that was at once easy and profoundly difficult. The element that Beau most liked about it was the presence of *soul*. The intangible. His inner pain and heartbreak actually made the music sound better. When the torment inside seemed to make his fingers bend notes that had no musical name, Beau felt alive. He lived completely in the moment, the only place he wanted to be anymore.

He cut his shoulder-length brown hair to a modest Beatles length and started combing it back and to the side. He began wearing white shirts and dark vests onstage. Beau did everything but change his name in order to belong. He'd found a musical home.

Beau was still handsome, though his years of unbridled partying had begun to show a little. He battled nightly to keep his addictions under control and his hands on the guitar. "You can't get high while you're playin'," he said. But of course, once he did, having someone hold a lit joint to his lips while he riffed away. But the concept was sound, and it worked most of the time. As long as he was playing he wasn't drinking or snorting, and that was good. Beau considered these little truths to be sacred. It had been ten months now.

Music came first and everything else second. That attitude kept a generation of musicians sane. ,

Then came disco.

Overnight the world went crazy for dancing. Blues became obsolete. Gigs dried up, interest waned. By 1977 the blues was gasping for breath in a marketplace that had left all but the fanatics behind. Constricted by lack of airplay and lost in the shuffle for record-store display space, great blues musicians found themselves struggling to make a living.

Hip young blacks considered blues "nigger music" and dug the new funk and jazz. Dressing cool and looking good became more important than the gritty, backcountry soul of the blues. Black power didn't mean blues, it meant liberation. Blues was the music of oppression, of slavery, of bad times. The slick urban style of Superfly made people like Muddy Waters look primitive by comparison. Even a legend like Oakland Slim was scuffling. Beau saw it firsthand.

Oakland Slim had played harp behind many of the great bluesmen, from Howlin' Wolf to Muddy Waters. His first solo disc in 1954, "Catfish Blues," was a national hit and led to a string of 45 rpm singles and long-playing albums. Race records. Slim's solo on "Rocket Ship Mary" by Art "Spiderman" Spivey was considered by many to be the greatest harmonica solo ever recorded.

Beau knew and respected Oakland Slim's track record and felt flattered to be asked to join the band after jamming one Friday night at the Old Waldorf in San Francisco. Slim and Beau became fast, though somewhat unlikely, friends.

The nightclub was packed with men and women drinking hard liquor and smoking unfiltered cigarettes. The band took the stage and plugged into their amps.

Oakland Slim counted off the first song and threw the band into gear with a shake of his meaty hip. The song took off like a slingshot ball bearing. Slim drove the band, taking the song to task, whipping its flanks until he felt it leap forward.

No matter what tempo the band played, Slim always seemed to be a fraction of a beat ahead of or behind them, working the musical throttle, directing energy. When things were right Slim could push and pull the limits of the rhythm section until they transcended just playing music. They were talking directly to God, or the devil, depending on whom you asked.

Slim cupped the harmonica like a loving King Kong caressing Fay Wray with his giant lips. He sucked and blew and coaxed unbelievable tones from the standard Hohner Marine Band harmonica, key of A. The band played in E. Oakland Slim liked to be on the "suck side" of the major chord. That way he could bend the notes from in front, the same way Sonny Boy Williamson and Little Walter used to play.

People celebrated the music like they were gettin' religion for the last time. Shouts of encouragement broke in sonic waves over the band, but neither Slim nor Beau heard them. They were in a tunnel now.

As the lead guitarist, Beau stood close by, stinging outrageous blues riffs in the gaps between the bars. A cigarette dangled from his lips. A lock of brown hair fell across his brow. He kept a look of blithe determination on his strong yet pleasing face.

Slim and Beau worked together like musical soulmates. The interplay between the harmonica and guitar created magic. They rocked the way nature rocks.

Acutely aware of Oakland Slim's legendary status, Beau was respectfully careful not to step on his lines, a trait that endeared him to the blues corps d'elite.

Slim pushed the band harder. His gruff vocals crackled through the PA. He punctuated his phrases with harp riffs and shouts. Beau seemed to know just where to come in, and where not to. He'd studied all of Oakland Slim's early albums, some of them classics. A few were hard to find, but Beau had hunted each one down until he had them all, knew them all, and loved them all.

Beau knew that like so many of Slim's contemporaries, the old man had never made any big money on his records. Slim lived from month to month on his live-gig money. Consequently, Oakland Slim gigged a lot. He'd become a blues gypsy, traveling the country with a weathered suitcase and a satchel of harmonicas, working with pickup bands when he couldn't afford to bring his own musicians. Slim kept rhythm sections all over the country. He had an East Coast band, a West Coast band, a southern band, and a Chicago band. Fifty-six years of age and stocky, he preferred polyester clothes and mystery novels, John D. MacDonald in particular. He always had a dog-eared paperback stuffed in his pocket.

Slim had inner demons Beau couldn't comprehend.

Even though Beau and Slim came from different musical universes, they were partners now. Beau was grateful to leave the shallow life of the pop musician behind to play at the side of a legend. He had a melodic and sexy style, like B. B. King, but with a hard edge like Albert King. He could bend notes like the Doppler effect on a lonesome train whistle miles away.

After spending the major portion of his adult life on the road playing rock and roll, Beau was back where he had started: the blues, something he'd been searching for since he bought his first Robert Johnson album, *King of the Delta Blues Singers* on Columbia Records.

"It's cookin' tonight, baby!" the drummer shouted. "Sock it to me!" Beau leaned back and flashed the man a grin. Tonight did seem special. Oakland Slim let everyone take a solo.

Beau remembered Slim explaining it all the first night. Slim spoke eloquently in a deep voice Beau thought sounded like a cross between those of James Earl Jones and Willie Dixon. "There's two levels the pros play at. The first level is for the audience—a competent reading, dig? Entertaining, showy, that's cool. You'd expect that. The second level is for other musicians. That's when we kick it up a notch."

Slim operated exclusively on the second level tonight. He encouraged Beau to stretch his breaks too, and to push each riff into new territory. They improvised with abandon while the people danced, drank, and shouted. Slim's ample body contorted as he blew his heart out into the six-inch wood-and-metal box of reeds.

Beau worked hard playing the music, while Slim, Beau realized, *Slim was the music.* And the feeling intoxicated. At times like these, for the musicians, playing becomes a spiritual adventure.

The Cheshire Cat Club attracted outcasts and loners, the very people the blues was all about. It was the music of the bottom. Vincent Shives did his best to blend in. Of course that seemed impossible when you looked like he did. His white skin seemed fluorescent in the black light. He dressed entirely in black. Surprisingly, no one paid him any attention. The blues scene was like that—people left you alone. Vincent was ignored by everyone, including the bartender when he tried to flag a drink. He kept moving, staying to the corners and the shadows, watching the musicians closely. To the other people in the club, Vince was just another geek, another lone wolf blues freak. The Cheshire Cat pulled people like that.

The band played on, near the end of their set.

They churned an up-tempo twelve-bar jump blues, a red-hot shuffle. The back beat cut through the room like an electric sledgehammer, sending shivers up the spines of the patrons. Slim closed tight on the microphone, crowding it, making a hard-edged distortion that spat the words of the song through the speakers. No one did Muddy Waters like Oakland Slim.

He sang, "I got my mojo workin', but it just don't work on you. . . ."

Cigarette smoke drifted across the stage into Slim's sweaty face as he sucked air through his harp. He held it directly against the diaphragm and it overmodulated perfectly into the PA. Through the sound system it almost sounded like a full horn section.

Everyone knew the song. Slim shouted the lyrics like a preacher on Sunday morning. "I'm goin' down to Louisiana, gonna get me a mojo hand. . . ."

They were locked in a timeless groove, not thinking about what they were doing. The music just came out, raw and unrefined, each phrase perfect. Straight from the soul. Slim's voice rattled the glass. "I got a Gypsy woman, givin' me advice. . . ."

Vincent listened to the words, his pale ears burning.

Slim led the crowd into the final chorus, using the call-and-answer technique to drive the point home, and Vince found himself mouthing the words along with everyone else.

"Got my mojo workin'!" Slim shouted.

"Got my mojo workin'!" the audience answered. The chant carried its own hook, as if it were yet another song. With the audience involved, it changed complexion. It was an anthem now, and people knew damn well how to respond.

"Got my mojo workin'!"

"Got my mojo workin'!"

The audience took up the chant and carried it home, shouting, stomping, and pounding the tables, exactly the kind of magic that made you want to get up and howl at the moon. Vince felt liberated.

Oakland Slim gave the band a little signal, hardly more than a look, and they knew it was time to end the song. Four measures later they walked the bass line back to the E chord and hit a crescendo. The last note lasted a full ten seconds and brought the house down.

Slim leaned into the mike and said casually, "Hey, it's been great. Thank you and good night."

The applause was solid and sustained. The band waved and walked offstage, emotionally drained. Two encores followed, both up-tempo shuffles, and the band waved good-bye for the last time. They'd been playing for three and a half hours.

Vince watched them vanish, one by one, through the stage door.

Backstage at the Cheshire Cat was the same as backstage anywhere—a narrow hallway, covered with musicians' graffiti, leading to a dank little smoke-filled room. The musicians crowded together in their area and congratulated each other. There were only a few chairs, so some of the guys had to stand. Oakland Slim always got a chair. He was venerated by the other musicians. He'd won their respect over a lifetime of gigs, one song at a time.

Slim sat back, wiped the sweat off his face with a limp handkerchief, and opened a beer. Beau slid in next to him and slapped him wetly on the back. "Killer solo on 'Mojo'!" he said.

"Thanks, kid. You ain't too shabby either . . . for a white boy."

The other band members chuckled automatically. Same old joke. Beau just shrugged; he'd heard it too many times. He was the lone white face in the room. As usual. No big thing.

The stage manager, a stylish, older wide-faced man named Slick, stuck his head in the room and caught Slim's attention. "Art Spivey's here. I thought you might want to know."

Oakland Slim lit up. "Art Spivey? The Spiderman?"

"He's at the door."

"Art 'Spiderman' Spivey? The king of the slide guitar?" Beau asked.

Slim nodded. He was rolling his eyes and shaking his leg. "Oh, yeah. Me and Art's been tight since Eisenhower. Played together all the time back in the old days. He was the best, the all-time best. That man could burn. Everybody kissed his ass, he was the sweetest thing in creation. Muddy Waters used to sit and watch him all night."

Slim's eyes went down, his voice modulated lower, and he leaned in to Beau. "Course, now he's got the palsy."

Beau listened, trying to understand everything Slim said, although sometimes that wasn't easy. Slim's speech pattern was as grooved and dark as the humid summer night. He spoke slowly and breathed a lot in between phrases. Beau waited for a further explanation. When none came, he asked. "The palsy?"

"Yup. Can't hardly move his fingers anymore. It's a goddamn shame, ain't it? Arthur was the king."

At that moment, Art "Spiderman" Spivey walked in. He was rail thin, with a face like a leather hatchet. A shiny, threadbare gray-blue suit hung off him sadly. He swayed slightly while he shook Slim's hand. He looked about a hundred years old.

"Well, well. Spiderman! How're ya doin', old man?"

"Who you callin' old, you fat sumbitch!"

"You're still as ugly as ever!"

"I'm a mile past ugly. How's the world been treatin' ya?"

Spiderman grinned broadly. The lines on his face cracked into a thousand deep valleys when he smiled. "Fine. Just fine. You giggin'?"

"All the time."

"Damn, I wish I could get a gig. God, how I wish I could just play one more gig. Just one, can you dig that? And you know where it would be? Henry's Swank House! That's where! You remember Henry's?"

Slim laughed and grabbed Art's chicken-wing arm. "Of course! Henry's! That was such a fine place! We used to have sooooo much fun there, my Lord. I remember Annie Fanny, and her sister Roweena. All them freaks."

Art accepted a drink from someone, a shot of straight bourbon, and knocked it back in one practiced motion. He handed the glass back to the guy who had given it to him and whistled low. "Yassss . . . Could I get another, brother?"

Slim laughed.

"I got a thirst so great, I swear it throws a shadow!" Art rasped.

"I can believe that!" someone behind them said.

One of the other musicians relinquished his seat and pulled the chair up for Art. The wizened master guitarist sat down with a groan. Another round of drinks went past as the two old men told each other how good it was to be alive. Beau stood by quietly.

A few minutes later, Oakland Slim introduced Beau to Art Spivey. Beau had been waiting patiently. He grinned and shook Art's gnarly hand.

The Spiderman coughed a deep rattle and spat into a brown handkerchief. "I heard about you. A white boy on guitar, a rock and roller even. That's really somethin'." He winked at Slim. "I never woulda believed it till I seen him play, but that boy's good. He's got potential. Who woulda thought, back in the fifties, that young white dudes would be playin' the blues . . . and right up there alongside the black gunslingers! Damn! Times sure done changed."

Slim cooled him out. "Ain't no big thing anymore. The kid works out fine, and he plays real good. Hell, nowadays most of the audience is white, anyway."

Beau shook Art's weathered brown hand. He smiled at the old man and said, "I'm just trying to learn."

Art laughed a phlegmy cackle that sounded painful to Beau's ears. "There ain't nothin' *to* learn. Just feel it. That's the blues."

Slim nodded at Beau, then turned back to Art. "He's got feel, don't you worry about that."

"Well good for you, son. You keep it up." Art winked and smiled. Rotten teeth flashed. "Y'all got something good happenin' here."

Beau hardly had time to thank him when Art said, "Did you hear about Red Tunney?"

"What happened?"

"He got killed. Somebody slashed him. Opened him up like a can of tomato soup. It was in all the papers. Didn't you know?"

Slim shook his head. "I been on the road. You know how it is."

The Spiderman continued. "Ripped him open. It happened in Saint Lou, where he was livin' with his daughter. Damn, it was pitiful. A good man like that. Remember the time we played with him up in Milwaukee? He was a hell of a piano player, top-notch. Piano Red."

Oakland Slim sat back in his chair and let his stomach expand. His leisure-suit jacket hung on the chair behind him. He'd rolled his sleeves up to the elbow. He rocked back and forth slowly while he talked. Slim enjoyed good conversation and was an avid listener. "That's a shame. He died in Saint Louis? Well, well, there ain't too many of us left, are there?"

Art Spivey shook his head. "No sir. I heard that. We're a dyin' breed. Last of the Mohicans. Think about it. Howlin' Wolf's dead. Little Walter, Sonny Boy, Freddie King, T-Bone Walker, they're all gone. There's hardly any of us left, and the ones that are"—he stopped and looked at Beau—"are takin' it in the butt."

Slim nodded in agreement. "I heard Frank Sinatra got fifty million dollars, and you and me ain't got doodly-squat. Can you believe that shit?"

Spiderman tapped his knee, and Beau could see his hands tremble. "And now the ones that are left are gettin' killed! You know, pretty soon there won't be no one left to play the blues but these young white boys." He looked at Beau. "We're losin' a great musical heritage. The blues is a national treasure, man. Somebody should do something about it."

Beau spoke up for the first time. "What about the government? Doesn't anybody care? Maybe the Library of Congress could help out."

"Library of Congress? Ha! You gotta be kiddin'. Library of my ass," said the Spiderman.

"We've been all through this, Beau," Slim added, his voice full of resignation. "Nobody wants to help. It's a waste of time. Nobody cares what happens to the blues because it's black man's music. Race records. It's low-down and dirty. It's too real for the dickheads."

"Far too real," Art agreed. "But whatcha gonna do? That's the way things are. I'm just glad that some guys, like this old turkey, are still doin' it."

"Praise the Lord."

Art frowned. "Keep the Lord out of this, old man. It's blasphemy."

Slim remembered that Art had been a part-time preacher earlier in life, before booze and blues. He remained sensitive to impiety from anyone, even his oldest friends.

"Didn't I read where Red Tunney got some songs in a movie?" Slim asked.

Art Spivey lit a Lucky Strike. "Shit, he didn't make nothin' on that, he sold his publishing long ago, writer's share and all."

"Speaking of publishing, how about yours?"

Art exhaled and coughed. "I made a real good deal for it a few years ago, got some cash up front . . . but hell, that old stuff ain't worth a damn."

Slim eyed him suspiciously. "You never know. I'm tryin' to hold on to mine, maybe someday—"

"Maybe someday you'll win the lottery!"

Slim smiled slyly. "Someday that stuff is gonna be worth money. Mark my words."

The conversation turned to old friends, lost loves, squandered money, and great gigs, and before long the room began to thin out. Guys were packing up and going home. Slick came in and announced that it was closing time. Beau, Slim, and Art Spivey walked out the side door to the tiny parking lot, their hard shoes crunching through the broken glass. Beau and Slim had their own transportation, Slim's rented Lincoln Town Car, and offered to drop Art off somewhere. At first he declined, saying he'd catch a cab. Slim pointed out that Art couldn't afford a cab and insisted that he ride with them. After a few weak arguments, he reluctantly agreed.

They dropped him off in front of the Roosevelt Hotel, a true flophouse on the South Side. It was a depressing old building in the middle of a depressing old neighborhood in the heart of wino country. The Roosevelt was last stop for many a wayfaring stranger.

He thanked Slim and left the car, walking slowly toward the door. Slim pulled away from the curb and shook his head. "No wonder he tried to weasel out of the ride. He didn't want us to know he lived here. He was embarrassed."

Art made his way up the steps and into the gloomy, piss-stained vestibule. He fumbled for his keys to the outer door and cussed. He wasn't as fast as he wanted to be. Ten minutes later he was at the door to his room, which he unlocked with much less effort. He stepped inside.

The room was incredibly dreary and run-down. It seemed to speak for its endless stream of occupants—*this is it, the end of the road*. The bed was a sagging nightmare of stained sheets and old blankets. The one small sink, which stood out from the wall, dripped and stank. The entire place reeked of cheap booze and stale cigarette smoke. An archaic radiator stood beneath the window, its paint peeling, revealing at least five layers of color beneath. Five levels of decomposition, five redecorations, five hopeful attempts at legitimacy. Art knew that this layer would be the last. There would be no more trying to mask the truth anymore. No paint jobs left for the Roosevelt, only the wrecking ball.

He took two steps in and began to pull off his coat. Suddenly a figure leapt from the dark, springing at him with violent force.

Art was knocked to the floor like a rotted tree in a thunderstorm. Two of Art's ribs cracked and drove the breath from his withered lungs.

The assailant rose up above him, and then Art saw it, something strange, something that made his flesh crawl. At that moment Art knew he was going to die.

Something that resembled a claw came up and hovered over the old man's face for a split second, then descended into his chest. Something dug into his lung and pierced the thin membranes there, pulling down and out through his intestines, gouging wetly until it snagged on his belt. He gasped for air as he felt the skin ripping away and sensed the terrible depth and trauma of his injury. It felt a mortal blow. Art let it happen without protest. There was nothing left to do but wonder why.

Art thought, *There must be some kind of mistake, there must be. None of this makes any sense.* He was more surprised than anything, dying there in his room, with confusion as his final emotion.

The figure lingered over Art, squatting apelike, and silently ripped at him again. Blood began to flow onto the filthy floor, pooling around some cigarette butts and dust balls. Art stopped breathing.

After making sure the old man's heart had stopped, the killer rose, wiped the weapon as best he could on Art's coat, and stood stationary in the darkness. He stared down at Art's lifeless, shocked face.

Outside, across the street, a neon sign advertising "Live Girls" flashed off and on in the night. Its blue light filtered through the dirty glass into dead eyes. One word reflected up from the street below—"Live."

Beau woke up in his hotel room to Oakland Slim pounding on the door. He opened it a crack and peeked through the chain, and from the first moment that he saw him, Beau knew something was terribly wrong. "It's Art. They killed him."

"What?"

"Spiderman's dead. Somebody killed him last night in his room. It musta happened right after we dropped him off!"

Beau tried to wake up. He rubbed his eyes. "He got killed?"

"I ain't kiddin', he's dead. Some crazy sumbitch stabbed him in his room. He didn't have a chance."

"But why?"

"Who knows. That Roosevelt is a shit hole. It's full of junkies and winos, any one of 'em coulda done it. Hell, down there they kill you for a pair of shoes!"

Beau started getting dressed. "I don't think Art had a decent pair of shoes."

"Amen to that. I can't figure it. It must have been a psycho or a druggie."

"It's hard to believe," muttered Beau, now jump-started into a state of full wakefulness.

Slim looked Beau squarely in the face, his voice as sober and weighty as Beau had ever heard it. The full consequence of the words pushed down on him. "The cops wouldn't tell me anything . . . except that he got ripped up real bad. They said it looked like he got mauled. Mauled, for God's sake!"

"Well, Art Spivey couldn't have had too many enemies, right? The man was flat broke. It musta been a fluke. He was in the wrong place at the wrong time."

Slim went over to the window and looked out. "Who'd want to kill Art Spivey? It just doesn't make any sense. Something's goin' on here."

✋ THREE ✋

Vincent Shives sat in his filthy apartment and played a 1951 National Steel Dobro guitar—his beautiful baby, his magic carpet, an extension of his soul. He'd stolen it from a dead man, but he feared no curse. If anything, the dead man would have wanted him to have it. The guitar was good juju.

Original National Steels were rare, the same timeless model that most of the great bluesmen used. It had a distinctive throaty, metallic sound, unlike any other stringed instrument. He hunched over it, concentrating on the silver slide on his finger. The room resonated with the stinging notes of each bottleneck riff.

Nobody alive had ever heard Vince play. Nobody knew how good he was. He could mimic the style of any blues guitarist perfectly. Slide guitar was his specialty, but he wasn't married to it. Vincent Shives could do it all, only nobody knew it. He'd been careful all his life to keep his playing a deep, personal secret. The side of him nobody would ever see. The open, raw, exposed side only the blues can reveal. The world would hear Vincent Shives, king of all blues, when he was ready. And not a moment before.

He walked across the floor and put an Art Spivey record on the turntable. He sat down and began to play along flawlessly. Anyone listening might have thought that the guitar on the record was in stereo, doubled electronically, that's how close to the original he played. He performed with an eerie, monklike fanaticism, his mind as taut and focused as a high-powered rifle.

Music filled the room, and Vince played his heart out, matching Art Spivey note for note. On the floor was an open package from the *Bluesworthy* mail-order service. Now that Art Spivey was gone from this earth, Vincent had to absorb all the music that had come out of him. He had to become Art Spivey.

With robotic precision, he faithfully reproduced the Spiderman's every subtlety and nuance. His obsessive devotion to the Spiderman's music compelled him to play for hours without pause. He played until his fingers blistered, then bled.

He ate and slept little. At the end of the third day he put the guitar away and never again listened to Art "Spiderman" Spivey. He didn't have to. He had absorbed the man's soul and inspiration.

He kept the Mojo Hand within reach, in the shoe box with the lid off, where he could look at it. Sometimes he thought he'd seen something . . . something fantastic. He thought he'd seen it move. When that happened, he stopped playing and picked it up. He couldn't be sure, but it may have changed positions very slightly. The fingers seemed a fraction of an inch more bent. He stared at it, wondering if his eyes were playing tricks on him. In the end he felt fairly sure it was all an optical illusion. The more he looked, the less likely it seemed that the thing had moved at all. He decided it was in exactly the same position it had always been.

The hours spent meditating in this manner had become the centerpiece of Vince's life. Holding the Mojo Hand, he thought about where it might have come from. He visualized it attached to the body of his idol, the greatest bluesman of all time, the phantom Robert Johnson. Vince could see it sliding up and down the neck of that big old Kalamazoo guitar he'd seen in photographs. He watched with his mind's eye as it stretched and danced across the fretboard. Then he focused back on the dead thing he held in his hand.

✋ FOUR ✋

The sun in Golden Gate Park spread yellow light like melted butter across the popcorn shoulders of people attending the San Francisco Blues Festival. Blues fans had been streaming into the park since early morning, and the smell of barbecue hung heavy in the air.

By the time Oakland Slim took the stage there were over ten thousand blues aficionados on the gently sloping field. They sat on blankets and lawn chairs, drinking beer and shouting for their favorites. The dizzying mix of lifestyles was fascinating: bikers, hippies, straights, gays, old couples, and college kids. They joined together over the music. Pot smoke wafted through the crowd.

Oakland Slim was well known in the Bay Area. His fans cheered when he walked onto the stage. The old man had won these people over decades ago. He got a standing ovation before he even played a note. Not a bad way to start a set. Beau took a sideman's post, standing slightly behind Slim. Beau remembered gigs like this, playing with the Stone Savages right here in this same park ten years ago. Only then it had been the Panhandle and Beau had been psychedelic. Beau had to remind himself that it was 1977, not 1967, and the Summer of Love had long passed.

Slim couldn't wait to get started. He jumped right into his "I'm a Man/Mannish Boy" medley as soon as the introduction had been made. With its anthemlike groove and an undeniable beat, "I'm a Man/Mannish Boy" was an inspired choice to kick things off for their set at the festival. A good outdoor song.

The crowd, galvanized by the cadence of the venerable Willie Dixon tune, rose as one and began to move. Everyone knew the words.

People down in front were dancing, waving their hands in the air. Slim's harp work slashed razor sharp. He ripped into his solos with a freshness Beau hadn't heard before. The methodical beat pounded home the message as the band just kept hitting it harder and harder.

Slim shouted the lyrics: "I got a black cat's bone, and a mojo too!"

Slim and Beau traded riffs, bending and pushing until the song broke through the ceiling and became pure energy. Every ear in the field focused on the sound. When Slim brought it down, someone in the front row shouted, "Get primitive, man!"

"I'm a Man/Mannish Boy" lasted a full fifteen minutes. Beau's incendiary guitar solo on the third break went from a whisper to a scream in the space of one twelve-bar progression. He started low, on his midrange pickup, and let it build and simmer like a pot full of bubbling barbecue sauce. He kept building until the tension reached a peak—then he let it explode and kicked in all three pickups. Dynamics, Fender Telecaster style—Beau's specialty. Sweet stuff, too. A good guitarist at work in his element is a beautiful thing. And Beau was beautiful.

Slim added a series of raunchy harp fills that sounded like a tenor sax. Beau filled in the blanks. Slim's voice shouted a lusty Pentecostal melody: "Ain't that a man? Ain't that a man?"

Beau smiled like a lunatic with a boner when Slim blew his signature riff in the key of E. Beau had heard it coming. Every harmonica player Beau had ever known had a favorite phrase that he'd come back to all the time. He'd usually end a solo with it, and that little turnaround would become his trademark. Since the number of riffs you can play on the standard Hohner Marine Band mouth organ is severely limited by the number of holes, most guys just repeated the same phrases played different ways with different variations. But Slim worked *between* the notes. Only musicians could dig it. Today, spurred by the other blues greats in the crowd, Oakland Slim blew his lungs out. The song ended in a rave-up crescendo with Slim shouting, "Ain't that a man? Ain't that a man?" The crowd went apeshit, stomping its approval.

Slim counted off the second song before the applause died down. Beau couldn't stop grinning. He'd just learned some valuable stuff. *A quick launch always plays well outdoors.* The crowd really got into it. In a flash the place was rockin' like a huge outdoor nightclub, only without the smoke and jerk-offs.

The sound system did the rest. It was almost easy.

Vincent Shives moved among the crowd, silent and ominous. His radioactive face loomed blank as he hovered on the fringes. He instinctively kept shifting, wanting not to be noticed. Behind tinted glasses his pink eyes absorbed everything. He watched Oakland Slim. He moved closer to the stage to see the white kid guitarist's fingers, watching to steal some tricks. For a few minutes he stood spitting distance to the monitors before moving on.

I can play that, he thought. *I can play all that. Ain't no one here who can touch me. I got the power. These people think this is some hot stuff, well, they ain't seen nothin' yet. I'll bet they think that joker up there onstage can play, but it just ain't so. When I come out, they won't believe it. When the king is dead—long will live the king. Suck it up, man. You just wait.*

Vince's ratlike eyes squinted at Beau. *That white boy is askin' for it. What does he think he's doin'? What right does he have to play the blues? At least these old assholes have seen some pain, but what kind of pain has that cracker seen? Go ahead, ride your ax, you turkey, your time will come.*

You think you know pain?
You really want to know pain?
I am the king of pain.

In the daylight, from the stage, Beau could see the audience clearly. For a change there were no stage lights to blind his eyes, no dark club full of smoky silhouettes. He scanned the crowd for interesting faces.

Vince's white hair and black overcoat were more conspicuous in the summer throng than back at the Cheshire Cat Club. Beau noticed the gaunt, frowning albino who stared up at the stage. He watched him move through the layers of people slowly, stalking. Something about the guy's face made him uneasy.

For a moment Beau lost concentration and scrambled to mentally refocus on the task at hand, playing music. Beau believed that the one thing all professional musicians had in common was the ability to tune everything out when they play and concentrate solely on the music. Maybe that's why most musicians were incorrigible as youths, he thought, always off in another world when authority addressed them. Later in life, that social handicap became an attribute, an occupational peculiarity. Beau snapped back into the song. The gaunt stranger retreated.

Beau looked over at Oakland Slim to see if he'd noticed the albino, but Slim had his eyes closed, blowing hard. A bomb could go off and it wouldn't faze him. Slim just hunched over and wailed, engrossed in song. After a lifetime of playing music, he pretty much had it down.

The set picked up from there. They finished up sixty minutes later to a wildly cheering, totally appreciative audience. Slim introduced everyone in the band and thanked Bill Graham, the security people, the audience, and God, in that order.

He left the stage in triumph. People congratulated him all the way back to the hospitality tent. The carnival-like atmosphere out in front of the massive speakers carried over backstage, where most of the performers sat around drinking and jamming. Slim put his guitar away, popped open a beer, and went to find his old friend B. Bobby Bostic, the festival headliner.

B. Bobby Bostic was not your average bluesman. He drove a Cadillac and lived in a four-bedroom house in Mill Valley, California. His concerts always sold out and he toured the world constantly. He'd been nominated for a Grammy. His records, and there had been more than fifty spanning five decades, usually sold well, and he'd even managed a couple of Top 40 hits. He had a high school diploma and intended to write his autobiography. He lived with two white women twenty-five years younger than he. He was incorporated. All the big English rock bands recorded his songs. He owned stocks. He had Keith Richards's home phone number.

B. Bobby was big-time. The rest of the blues community looked up to him like a god. To Beau he might as well have been Elvis. *The Kang.* But how could a guy sing the blues and sleep in a waterbed with satin sheets?

Slim said it didn't matter. "The blues is inside, it's all feelin'. You can't talk about it, you can't describe it, it's an intangible. Dig this—the richest man in the world can have the blues. Don't matter. It's in the soul, man. Sometimes it can get backed up like a bad toilet. That's when you gotta flush it out."

OK.

Slim had known B. Bobby Bostic for decades. They shared graduate-level educations at the university of tough breaks. They were both orphans. Both were dogged survivors. The only difference was that B. Bobby's ship had come in and he was making money. Slim stayed back on the chitlins circuit. The two had stayed in touch over the years, at times as close as brothers. It was B. Bobby who'd recommended Slim to the festival booker. Slim owed him for that.

Slim needed the gig. He always needed the gig. The name of the game in the seventies was exposure, especially to the ever expanding young white audience. Live gig money equaled Slim's livelihood.

Slim wasn't envious of B. Bobby. He figured the man deserved all he got, and then some. The success of one could only help them all, he said.

Slim found B. Bobby's dressing room, a huge Winnebago motor home. He strode up to the side door and knocked. From inside he could hear Bobby's distinctive baritone voice booming like a rusty cannon.

"Bullshit! All real bluesmen never practice. They live the music."

"But . . . you must have spent many hours rehearsing when you were young," a female voice said. "People don't just wake up one day with the ability to play like that."

There was a resonant chuckle. "Not unless they make a deal with the devil! Hell no! I never rehearsed, I just played. There's a big difference. When you got the blues, they crawl around inside you like big cockroaches until you can't stand it no more, then the music just comes oozin' out! Hell, I never wanted to play the blues—nobody in his right mind would. I was chosen. My mother wanted me to be a man of the cloth."

"You didn't choose to play the blues?"

Bobby took a deep breath and boomed out one of his favorite lines: "I did not choose to play the blues. It's plain to see, the blues chose me!"

B. Bobby Bostic's road manager heard Slim knocking and opened the door. He recognized Oakland Slim and motioned for him to come in. "Bobby's doin' an interview for *Bluesworthy* magazine. He should be done in a couple minutes," he whispered.

Bobby saw Slim and jumped up to embrace him. He turned to the attractive young white woman who was conducting the interview and said, "Here's the man you should be talkin' to. He's forgotten more about music than most people will ever know!"

"Aw, shucks."

"See? See what I mean? 'Aw, shucks.' Who says that anymore? Only this man here. Miss Annie Sweeny, meet the fabulous Jerome Butts, better known as Oakland Slim. This man is a living fossil."

Slim nodded at Annie. She said a polite hello and tried to get back to her conversation with Bobby. "Mr. Bostic? I only have a few more questions and my time is short."

"Go right ahead, honey."

Annie Sweeny fought to keep her interviews focused and professional. At least this guy wasn't a macho pig like some of the guys she'd had the misfortune to interview. At least he wasn't trying to get her between the sheets. Unfortunately, the music business in 1977 seemed full of guys who expected any woman backstage to tumble with them at the snap of their fingers. In contrast, B. Bobby Bostic was cordial and polite.

He didn't stare at Annie's long-legged twenty-six-year-old body or her flawless face. Even when her long brown hair fell across one eye, Veronica Lake style, he kept his attention on the questions.

Annie didn't know her looks were distracting. She didn't try to be beautiful, she just was.

Annie had parlayed a degree in journalism and a genuine affection for the blues into a career. After a few years at *Rolling Stone* magazine, she accepted a job working for her father's blues magazine. She'd grown up listening to his incredible record collection and had encyclopedic knowledge of the music. She shared her father's passion. Annie never looked back.

Thirty minutes into the interview, Slim's entrance reminded her of another question. "What about the future of the blues?"

"The future? Well, right now it's hard to say," he answered. "We're dyin' off like the dinosaurs, you know. People ask you why the dinosaurs disappeared—was it a comet? Ice age? Nah! They died of broken hearts, every damn one of 'em."

Annie smiled. Bobby's prose sparkled like wet diamonds. *That's why so many of his songs stand the test of time,* she thought.

"Broken hearts?" Annie said.

"Yeah. They had the blues inside 'em, and it had to come out."

Slim said, "You're confusing the girl, Bubba."

B. Bobby Bostic laughed. "Confuse Annie Sweeny? Doubtful, Jerome. Her daddy had the best blues collection on the West Coast. You remember Jake Sweeny, God rest his soul. The man was a scholar. Did a lot for the blues. When he passed away he left the whole shootin' match, including the magazine, the mail-order business, and one mutha of a record collection to young Annie here. I think she's doin' a hell of a job." He turned to Annie, who blushed. "Y'all doubled in size since last year, right? You still doin' that mail-order rare stuff? Jake always made a good dollar on that."

Annie nodded.

Bobby turned back to Slim. "Kinda tough for a young white chick, don't you think? So give her some credit. She ain't as confused as you are, Jerome. She knows a thing or two."

Annie couldn't help but blush. She hadn't expected Bobby's endorsement.

Bobby continued. "What I'm tryin' to say, in answer to Ms. Sweeny's last question, is that I know what all those brokenhearted dinosaurs knew, that it's the soul that makes blues great. Not technique. And that's what the future is all about."

Slim shook his head. "Brilliant."

"Thank you. Next question."

Annie cleared her throat. "When you write a song, do you start with a guitar riff or a lyric?"

"Neither. I start with the magic."

Just then, the road manager interrupted. "I'll have to terminate the interview now. It's time for Mr. Bostic to go to work."

"Of course." Anne turned off her cassette recorder and put away her notebook. "Thanks for the time, Mr. Bostic. It was a pleasure meeting you too, Mr. ahh . . ."

"My friends call me Slim."

Anne stood, slender and lithe in worn, tight jeans. She wore a small white tank top and red cowboy boots. She shook hands with everyone and left the trailer quickly. Slim watched her climb down the metal steps. "Pretty young white girls writin' about the blues? My, how things have changed."

"If you ask me, it's an improvement. Last interview I did, the guy looked like Jerry Garcia."

"Who's Jerry Garcia?"

"Never mind. Say, after the show you got any plans?" Bobby asked.

Slim shook his head.

The road manager held Bobby's suit jacket for him and he slipped into it. Then he adjusted Bobby's tie and handed him his guitar.

"Good. I'm taking you out for some Italian food, OK?"

"No barbecue?"

"All that pork is bad for your heart, you should know that. What's wrong with you, Jerome?" Bobby strapped on the guitar. "You got that white boy on guitar? I heard he was good."

"Didn't you catch our set? We had a good show today."

"I never watch the opening band, you know that. It's bad luck. But I heard some kind of moanin' through the PA just a minute ago. Was that you? Christ, I thought it was the Rollin' Stones!"

Everyone had a laugh at that. Slim took no offense. The road manager handed Bobby a glass of amber fluid, which he drank in a single swallow. "Ahh, that's good!" He winked at Slim. "Medicinal purposes only."

As Bobby walked toward the stage, his band fell in line behind him. Pausing at the foot of the stairs that led to the stage, he looked back over his shoulder at Slim and said, "Dinner tonight, don't forget, and bring the kid if you want. It'll be more fun. We need some young blood around here anyway. I can't hang with you old dudes anymore. I like to party on occasion."

Slim smiled. "You want to party? OK, we'll party."

"The world's been goin' downhill since the word 'party' became a verb," Bobby replied. He turned to a woman who'd been standing nearby, a bleached blonde in her mid-thirties dressed in turquoise stretch pants and a yellow tube top. "Honey, take care of this man. He's my friend Oakland Slim. He probably ain't had no poontang in twenty years."

The blonde raised an eyebrow. "Don't look at me, old man. I only work here, remember?"

B. Bobby and his band laughed uproariously at that, glad for the quick tension breaker as they walked onstage. It kept them loose.

"You're too smart for me, girl. But seriously, this man's lost. See if you can find him a seat down front—he wants to see a *real* show. Get him up close enough 'cause he wants to watch my fingers! Maybe he'll learn somethin'."

The girl looked disapprovingly at Slim.

Bobby said, "This here's Yolanda, she's my special friend. Her and her sister Belva take care of me. She's what you might call my private secretary . . . very private. She's also my valet and she can cook. Course I had to show her how to make crab cakes—you remember my crab cakes, don'tcha?"

B. Bobby was from Baltimore, and like all good Baltimoreans he knew how to make a good crab cake. He only used Old Bay seasoning, which he had stockpiled at his house. "My mother taught me."

"Your mother made the best crab cakes in creation. I can testify to that. She knew how to steam crabs too, hot and spicy. God, they were good! Steamed crabs and National Bohemian beer."

"It's a religious experience."

Bobby turned and headed up the steps for the stage. Yolanda took Slim by the arm and led him to the VIP section, directly in front of the stage, where they watched as B. Bobby Bostic put on the show of his life. He blew people away. "Gotta play every show like it's your last," he told the crowd.

Annie Sweeny spoke briefly with one of the photographers and wandered back to the hospitality tent. She stood in line waiting for a cold drink, and noticed Beau Young staring at her. She looked away quickly, not wanting to make eye contact with a strange man backstage. The last thing she wanted was to get hit on by yet another deadbeat musician. She'd had her fill.

Beau noticed her right away; attractive, no wedding ring, flying solo. She seemed wholesome in a way that appealed to him instantly. She had natural beauty, not like the usual stage-door bimbos he met. She seemed to carry a certain backstage dignity. Instead of spandex and platform shoes, she wore jeans and cowboy boots. He noticed that her laminated pass said "All Access."

Her dark hair moved with a life of its own when she walked, and her slender hands fluttered expressively when she spoke. Beau watched her order a soft drink. Her tan face sported a smattering of freckles across high cheekbones. Annie's nipples showed through the white cotton of her tank top. Beau tried not to stare.

She turned and kept her back to him while the bartender drew her a foamy root beer in a plastic cup. When she turned around again she almost walked right into Beau, who was now standing directly behind her. "Sorry," he said. "Almost caused an accident there."

Annie looked at Beau and didn't smile. "Excuse me," she said.

Beau just stood there, an idiot's smile on his face.

Annie spoke again, a little louder, a little more pointedly. "Excuse me. Would you mind getting out of my way? I've got a job to do here."

"A job? What kind of job?"

Annie sidestepped away from Beau. She didn't want to be goaded into conversation. Besides, she really did have a job to do. She ignored his question, pretending not to hear it.

"Can I meet you?" he asked.

Annie shrugged. This guy was incorrigible. "You already have," she replied flatly. "Now if you don't mind, I have to get to the stage."

"Are you a singer?" he asked quickly, before she could escape.

"No, I'm a journalist," she answered, a little exasperated. "Please don't ask me any more questions. I'm working."

Beau watched her walk away and strongly considered following her, but didn't. His first impression hadn't been exactly storybook. Annie's image seemed as indistinct as a Matisse watercolor, her colors soft and unfocused, yet all the more alluring because of it. He was determined to get closer.

On her way to the stage, a burly biker approached her and said something. From where Beau stood he could see that Annie was clearly shocked by the big guy's amorous and probably obnoxious advance. Beau started walking briskly toward Annie.

The biker came on as strong as ammonia. "Suckyerpussy," he slurred drunkenly. He said it fast, as if it were all one word, smeared together by alcohol and a festering case of advanced horniness.

His belly rolled over the strained waistband of his jeans, protruding under the dirty T-shirt he wore. Beau could see that the guy was huge, and probably used to getting his way. Annie looked horrified. "Come on, baby, suckyerpussy . . . best you ever had."

She veered away from him, but he grabbed her arm, his greasy fingers pinching her skin like a pair of pliers.

"Don't be shy, darlin', I got a tongue like a water moccasin. All the little girls are crazy about it. Suckyerpussy. How 'bout it?"

She pulled her arm away. "No!"

Beau slid up next to Annie and put his arm around her. "She's with me, man," he said bravely.

"Well, whoop-dee-do! I'm real impressed," the biker spat. "I eat punks like you for breakfast."

Beau smiled like a man going into bankruptcy court. "It's OK, man. I'm a musician. I play guitar for Oakland Slim."

The biker squinted at him. "Yeah? How do I know?"

"It's true. You wouldn't hurt a musician, would ya?"

"I don't know. I'll have to think about that."

Beau led her away before the biker could react. Annie bristled. "I don't need you to deal with guys like that. I can take care of myself," she said tersely. "Now don't go believing you're some kind of knight in shining armor and I'm going to get all gooey and fall into your arms for saving me, 'cause I'm not."

Beau made a sour face. "Hey, I was just trying to help. Sorry. I wasn't tryin' to—"

"Good," she cut him off. "I don't like guys who come on too strong. Like him."

Beau laughed. "Look, it's over, all right? I'm sorry I butted in. My name is Beau Young and I actually do play guitar with Oakland Slim. That wasn't just a story."

"I heard. I just met Oakland Slim when I was interviewing B. Bobby Bostic."

"I'm heading over to the main stage right now to watch the show with him. Wanna go with me?" Beau smiled a huge, goofy smile and wiggled his eyebrows up and down, like Groucho Marx.

Annie considered her options. Sometimes it was better to humor a guy than go against the grain and dump him on the spot. That could be unpleasant, not to mention time-consuming. After all, she had a job to do. Besides, Beau was kind of cute.

"I'm not going to be able to get rid of you, am I?" Annie replied with a sigh.

Beau shook his head. "Nope, and I sure would be honored if you accompanied me, ma'am." Suddenly he sounded like John-Boy Walton.

Annie shrugged. Their eyes met and held for a moment. Something in Beau's smile warmed her. "All right. But don't get any ideas," she said.

"I don't have ideas. I leave that up to the pros. I promise I'll be good." Beau changed the subject. "B. Bobby Bostic and Oakland Slim are very close. They played together for years. Slim worships Bobby and all the success he's had. They're like brothers. If you're doin' a story on Bobby, you might want to talk to Slim."

Beau and Annie found Slim, and they watched Bobby's performance together. Beau couldn't believe it when Slim told him that they would be hanging out with Bobby later. Beau felt like a king, watching a great show, sitting with a pretty girl, and rubbing shoulders with blues royalty. He asked Annie if she would be interested in join-ing them for dinner, but she politely declined. She had a deadline to meet, and Bobby hadn't invited her, she explained. "You go on ahead and have a great time. Tell me about it later," she said.

Beau looked hopeful. "Later? You mean there's going to be a later?"

"Maybe. But don't get your hopes up. The jury's still out on you." Annie smiled. The lovely lines of her face stretched. Freckles showed. When Beau asked for her phone number she impulsively scribbled it down on a scrap of paper and pressed it into his palm.

That night, Bobby, Yolanda, and Belva took them to Vanessi's Restaurant on Broadway. The parking attendant knew Bobby and gave his Caddy a prime spot. They crossed the busy boulevard into the heart of San Francisco nightlife. Down the street the strip clubs competed for attention with neon beyond reason. A few doors up, bass-heavy reggae throbbed out of the Stone. Across the street, Pearl Harbor and the Explosions were rockin' the Mabuhay Gar-dens. The drag show raged at Finocchio's. The sidewalks were full of punks, hippies, Rastas, bikers, cross-dressers, and tourists.

Bobby threaded through the unbelievable street scene to the restaurant door, leading his little group like holy men through the streets of Calcutta. Once inside, Bobby began to tip everyone with a pocket. After a few interesting minutes in the bar, they were tucked into a corner table.

It was the best food Beau had eaten in years, with enough garlic to steam artichokes with his breath. The meal started with a table-side Caesar salad. Time slowed to a crawl. Bobby ordered for all of them after looking into their eyes to ascertain what each really wanted. It was Bobby's opinion that Beau really had to have seafood cannelloni, that his soul yearned for it, and that if he ate enough of it this night, his life would change for the better.

When the main course arrived, Beau realized that Bobby was completely right. The stuff tasted marvelous and turned out to be the perfect choice for him. Slim was advised to consume shrimp scampi, and he happily complied. B. Bobby Bostic held court for hours, plying them with alcohol, entertaining them with bawdy poetry, jokes, and rude remarks. Beau noticed that the girls remained quiet and pleasant throughout the evening and seemed to know a lot about music. They fawned over Bobby like geishas, pouring his drinks, fussing with his suit, adjusting his tie. Bobby obviously loved the attention. He'd punctuate his monologues with, "Ain't that right, girls?" and they would agree. Dressed as millionaire trailer trash, they sat on either side of Bobby like exotic bookends. Big hoop earrings rattled when their heads moved.

The two blues legends talked musicians' talk deep into the night. Beau listened. Bobby seemed to know everybody in show business and had the dirt on everything. He loved gossip and dispensed it freely, usually with a wink and a word of advice. He told them about his investments, lectured them on tax shelters, gourmet food, sports, the economy, and growing tomatoes. Beau couldn't help but be impressed. Bobby sounded like an expert on hundreds of subjects. Self-educated, he was a voracious reader who sucked up every word he could find. The conversation inevitably turned back to the blues. Bobby pontificated on the spirit and substance of the blues as he broke into his third bottle of wine, which he interfaced boldly with shots of Canadian Club.

"You know, around the world, American culture is still loved and imitated, no matter how much our politicians screw it up. The blues are everywhere, can you dig that? Most people out there don't even know who Jimmy Carter is, but they all know the words to 'Hound Dog.' Hell, I found blues clubs in faraway places like Helsinki, Hong Kong, even Russia. Last month I jammed with a Dutch blues band over in Amsterdam at the Paradisio, and those cats couldn't speak a word of English, not one blessed word. They sang, 'I got de bloos, oh baby, I got de bloos.' It was hilarious. But you know what? We still connected. The image of the ugly American is everywhere, man. But the ugly American sure ain't no musician, I'll tell you that."

Beau listened, occasionally burping up garlic, and imagined the places Bobby had been, the people he'd played for.

Bobby bought all the waiters and waitresses a drink, gave them all his autograph, and left a huge tip. Without exception, each one hugged him gratefully as he left. If it wasn't for his drinking problem, the man could have run for president, Beau thought.

✋ FIVE ✋

B. Bobby Bostic bade good night to his friends and drove his El Dorado across the Golden Gate Bridge. Considering all the alcohol sloshing around in his stomach, he drove incredibly well, never showing the slightest hint of intoxication. Yolanda sat in the front seat with him, her sister Belva in the back. The radio played a set of white English blues bands doing variants of double-time boogie, stuff that Bobby had put on the map. It was a clear night and the lights of San Francisco glimmered behind them with postcard intensity.

"Damn fine evening, wouldn't you say, girls?"

"Damn fine," echoed Belva and Yolanda, in unison.

From Route 101, he took the Mill Valley exit and drove carefully into the dark, tree-lined streets. The last thing he needed now was to get stopped by the cops, one crowd he could never quite impress. For a man with a drinking problem, the cops were a constant threat, dogging him, trying to catch him driving under the influence. Bobby had been caught several times, and the cops knew his car. One more DUI and Bobby would go to jail. He kept one eye on the rearview mirror. No cops in sight. *Good.*

Ten minutes later Bobby made his final turn onto the road where he lived, a winding two-lane blacktop up in the hills. It seemed quiet. The rest of the neighborhood appeared to be asleep. In this part of Marin County there were no sidewalks or streetlights.

He parked the car in his driveway, and the two women got out unsteadily and wobbled toward the house. Yolanda went to open the front door with Belva two steps behind. Bobby called after them: "I'll just be a minute, babes, you go on in."

He walked around to the trunk and inserted the key. It popped open with a loud click that seemed to quiet the chorus of crickets and frogs for a moment. The driveway was unlit. Bobby couldn't possibly have seen the movement in the trees at the side of the blacktop.

He was humming a Sinatra tune while he felt around inside the trunk for his guitar case. *Damn, that was fun,* he thought. *Slim and the kid had a blast. Where's that guitar? Christ, I hope I didn't leave it somewhere. I gotta cut back on the booze. I'm getting to be like an old woman, forgettin' everything that ain't written down. It's dark out here. I can't see a thing. Tomorrow I'm gonna get some security lights so I don't break my neck.*

Bobby found the handle of the guitar case, pulled it out of the cavernous trunk, and slammed the trunk closed. He was suddenly overcome with an overwhelming urge to urinate, something he'd been holding inside all the way home. In Bobby's mind, the true test of a man's worth was whether he could whip out his dick and pee on his own property any old time he wanted. *Hell,* he thought, *it's my land. I'll piss where I want.* He staggered over to some shoulder-high shrubs and unzipped his fly.

Oh, God that feels good! Oh yaz, so fine, so very fine, to bleed my lizard on a natural vine.

Bobby let his eyes close for a few seconds as he savored the act, grooving on the sound of his urine splashing the ground like the flow from a garden hose.

Something moved behind him.

He thought he heard a step. His first reaction was to squeeze out the last few drops, then stuff that big black boa constrictor back in his pants. But Bobby moved slowly.

It's just an animal, Bobby thought, *that's all. Critters. There's nobody around at this hour. I'm cool, just having a little fertilizin' party on my own property, ain't nothin' wrong with that.*

Bobby kept his cool, finished his pee, shook his trouser snake, and put it back in his pants. He was about to zip up when he heard rustling behind him, closer this time. As he turned to see what it was, something hit him in the side, just above the kidney. He felt a sharp pain and was surprised to feel his shirt becoming wet. He saw nothing—no person, no weapon, just darkness.

Bobby's hand went down to his wound and came away covered with something dark and sticky. "What the hell?!"

He felt like a swimmer under a shark attack. He heard movement around him, shuffling, some feet on the blacktop. He braced himself. *I don't believe this. Somebody's trying to mug me!* his mind screamed. *It's gonna take more than a few cuts to slow B. Bobby Bostic down. I've got a few surprises of my own for this sumbitch. Damn! Now I'm mad.*

Bobby felt another slash. This time he raised his left arm and it took the brunt of the blow but paid a heavy price. Something hooked the skin just below the wrist and ripped laterally across his body, opening up a huge tear in his arm that ended at the elbow joint.

"Shit! What you doin'?!" he screamed, a streak of rage and desperation in his voice, like when he shouted, "Can I get a witness?" into the mike.

The phantom slipped away, back into the darkness a few steps. Bobby was shocked and angry. His two wounds began to seriously hurt, the pain getting more unbearable by the second. He felt a great amount of blood run from his torso onto the ground. He nearly slipped in it. He spun around, ready to defend himself in any direction.

"You crazy asshole! Where are you?" Bobby shouted.

No one answered.

Bobby took two quick steps toward his car, toward the passenger's-side door closest to the glove compartment, where he kept a loaded snub-nosed .38 Smith & Wesson Police Chief's Special. He'd never actually fired the stainless-steel five-shot revolver. He only kept it for protection, something he desperately needed now. He intended to jerk the door open—*did I lock it?*—pull out the gun, and start shooting.

Bobby got as far as the door, his good hand closing desperately around the handle, thumb working overtime like a miniature flesh piston, trying to get the door open.

Open up! Open, damn you! His hand was slippery. More blood. *Just a few more seconds now, just a few more heartbeats and I'll blow this punk away.*

Bobby began to believe that he could actually make it to the gun when the slasher struck again. The door clicked open but too late. Bobby fought for his life now.

"Hey! Back off, man! I'll blow your damn brains out!"

The darkness moved. Bobby could make out a vague shape. It was a man, a man with what looked like a claw in his hand. *What the hell?* He squinted, straining to see so he could defend himself. Something glinted in the darkness.

The man from the dark lunged at him again like a fencer. He felt another blow at his side, near the first laceration, and reeled as if he'd been hit by a baseball bat. *Is that the way it feels to get stabbed? God, it feels like a mule kick.*

The two wounds in his torso joined. Life streamed out of him at a frightful pace. He wondered if he would live long enough to get the gun out. It all happened so fast. Bobby couldn't keep up. He seemed to be moving in slow motion, while the attacker moved like lightning.

Then, in one horrible second, it all came clear. *I'm gonna die. This guy is out to kill me.* Bobby caught a glimpse as the figure spun away, a millisecond of lucidity in which he thought he saw a claw dripping blood at the end of the phantom's arm. *A demon! A devil!*

Confusion and terror swept Bobby's soul. He tried to move away from the attacker. He raised his arm again to block the next blow, but he was no match for the swift, silent stranger. Again the slasher struck, gouging at his shoulder, and at this point the pain became debilitating. Something sharp and wide hooked a tendon two inches above his heart and ripped it out like a rubber band. A severed artery squirted blood into Bobby's face. He staggered back and tried to see, but the night was so black, so disorienting, and the slasher was so fast. Bobby flailed wildly, but the slasher moved with him, letting the old man lead in the dance and matching him step for step. The phantom lunged again, and Bobby didn't even react this time. He went down, his face smacking into the cold asphalt. A gold tooth skittered away.

Blood collected around him in a quickly expanding puddle, making red mud where it came into contact with the dirt at the driveway's edge. B. Bobby Bostic said good-bye to this world and everything in it and aimed his soul toward heaven.

 SIX

Vincent Shives tossed and turned in a cheap motel room near San Francisco International Airport. The mustard-colored walls met the avocado carpet like two garbage trucks colliding. A water stain on the ceiling resembled a map of Australia. The sound of a faucet dripping ticked away time. The floor and dresser were littered with empty beer cans and cigarette butts.

The moon shone dimly through the faded curtains next to his bed. Vince suffered in his sleep. Personal demons picked and clawed at his soul, slowly trying to chip it away like waterlogged concrete. He hadn't slept well in decades.

He opened his eyes suddenly, sure that he'd heard something. The sound of traffic on Route 101 filtered through his head like distant surf. He listened closely, ears straining to pick up the slightest sound. Then he heard it again. Soft scratching, like an insect. A big, slow insect.

He pulled back the covers and sat up. He'd been sweating in his sleep, and his shorts and undershirt clung to his bony frame. He held his breath and listened again, but this time he heard nothing. He lay back down again and closed his eyes. The sound came again, like something rustling, stirring in the darkness. Rats, maybe. Vince could deal with rats. He thought about getting up and drinking another beer, then realized he'd already drained all twelve of the Coors he'd bought earlier.

He resigned himself to lying there, eyes closed. If he couldn't sleep, he could pretend to sleep. Vince had fooled himself like this before, lying coffin still with his eyes clamped shut until daybreak.

Down below his bed the shoe box was bathed in moonlight. A shaft of ghostly luminescent silver hit it dead on. Of all the places in the room for the thin arc of light from outside to illuminate, it found the box.

Something stirred.

The lid moved. It inched back slowly in the hollow moonlight and two fingers appeared over the edge. The hand was alive, and moving.

It climbed out of the box like a great ungodly spider, quick and confident with impossible movements. The reanimated dead fingers carefully felt their way along like an insect, pausing here and there to raise and tremble, as if sniffing the air. It moved across the worn shag carpet and made contact with the bedcover.

It climbed up the side of the bed, noiselessly making its way toward Vince's head. He kept his eyes firmly closed, hoping that Morpheus would come and save him from his insomnia. The dead hand deftly alighted on his chest. The slight weight of its dehydrated, mummified flesh hardly made him stir. He remained still, his chest rising and falling with the hand riding it like an alien cowboy.

The leathery fingers felt their way to his neck. The pale skin pulsated with the rhythm of Vince's tortured breathing.

The thumb and forefinger closed around his windpipe, and the pressure made Vince come alive suddenly. He sat up, alarmed. The hand grasped firmly to his neck, and the ancient, dirty fingernails dug relentlessly into his flesh. Vince tried to pull it loose but it clung tenaciously. His eyes filled with horror as he tried to suck enough air for a scream. None came. The hand was in control, pinching off the oxygen supply and throwing Vince into a panic. He jumped up off the bed and frantically tried to shake it off, but it would not let go. Vince gasped for breath.

Get it off! Get it off!

His own hands tore at the thing, trying to dislodge it from his throat. But the more he struggled, the tighter it grasped. The hideous hand seemed as strong as Satan's claw. Vince wanted to scream, to explode and cry hysterically, to release the terrible fear that suffocated his soul. He struggled in the darkness, his heart pounding, losing strength from lack of oxygen. He wished he had a knife, a huge butcher knife, so he could thrust it into his own neck, through the hand, impaling it. He would have killed himself to be rid of it.

Get it off! Get it off!

Vince fell, striking his head against the floor. He arched his back, pounding his skull into the threadbare rug with a violence that shook the furniture. Again he smashed against the floor, then the wall, then the headboard, then the floor again. He shook and rolled like an animal, his neck collapsing inward and his eyes bulging. The seizure continued, a mad fit, a hopeless scramble, and Vince became dizzy.

He tried to stand again, but couldn't. His brain, starving for air, began to short-circuit itself, and he saw stars and tiny explosions in front of his eyes. Vince felt himself blacking out, falling numbly into the void. His face met the rug, and fibers of dirty industrial synthetics wormed into his nostrils. Then, abruptly, the struggle ended, and he slumped on his side, curling into a fetal position.

When the morning came, sunlight forced its way into the room and across his face.

Vince's eyes jerked open. How long had he been there? He put his hands to his neck and felt nothing! There was nothing there! He breathed in short, panicked bursts, gulping air, and willed himself to stand. The legs that wobbled and bent under his weight were not his legs. They were much too weak to be his. He stumbled for the mirror in the tiny bathroom and gazed at his horrified face.

Nothing!

He felt his neck, letting his fingertips caress and search for discoloration, for bruising, for any kind of physical damage.

Nothing!

He slowly walked back into the room and looked at the shoe box. It remained next to the bed as if nothing had been disturbed. Vince moved toward it, fearing what he would find. Vince knew that if the box was empty, if the hand was gone or moved, then something incredibly bizarre had happened. But if the Mojo Hand was still there, then everything would be OK. He would know that it had all been a dream.

Vince faced the consequences. Either he was losing his mind or the magic was much stronger than he had imagined. *It's there. I know it's there,* he thought. *I'm not crazy. The hand will be there when I open the lid. I know it will. It has to be. The hand is not yet alive. It's a talisman, not a monster.*

He cautiously put his fingers on the top, took a breath, and prayed for reality. He half expected the thing to jump out at him and grab his wrist. Abruptly he flipped back the lid, which spun to the floor. He looked inside, his heart pounding wildly.

It was still there. In the same position.

Relief washed over him like ice water.

 SEVEN

"You're not doin' any coke are you?" The accusing tone of Beau's ex-wife oscillated through the phone lines. It was early for him, around ten o'clock in the morning.

Beau stared into the mouthpiece for a moment, then slowly brought it back to his face. "No. I'm not doin' any coke."

"How long has it been?"

Beau sighed. "I don't know. Ten weeks I think. Something like that."

"Are you sure you're not doin' any coke?"

"I really don't need this, Gayle. No, I'm not snortin' blow. I've had a couple drinks, that's about it."

"You shouldn't be drinking either. The coke goes with the booze. You start drinkin' and your judgment gets cloudy. Honestly, Beau . . . when are you gonna get your act together? You're not in your twenties anymore. You better grow up. And fast. Little Woody's been askin' when you're gonna be back."

"I just got back in town. I'll come over and spend some time with him this afternoon. Is he there?"

"He's outside playing."

"I miss him." Beau sighed, regretting his decision to pick up the phone. Gayle still used his last name, and that plus his monthly child support were all that remained of his marriage to her. She got half the songwriting royalties on his one and only top-ten hit, recorded a decade ago. When they'd met, the former Miss Gayle Mimi, aka

Gayle Ann Perko, was a bright young Hollywood starlet. Her acting
career ended when she met Beau. He despised Tinseltown and
whisked her away to San Francisco. Although Gayle never said anything about it, Beau thought she secretly hated him for making her
give up her career.

Beau visited as often as he could, but Gayle didn't make it easy.
The guilt of his not spending enough quality time with Woody, their
six-year-old son, was a weapon she used often. Beau felt particularly
vulnerable there.

"How come the child-support payment is late?"

"I sent it in last week."

"That's not what the DA says. They haven't received it yet. You
know, you won't be able to renew your driver's license until you pay
the arrears."

"Oh, that's a great law. So I won't be able to drive to work to
make money to pay the child support. Where's the logic in that?" As
soon as the words left Beau's mouth he knew he'd made a mistake.
Gayle didn't like to be challenged. "I'm sorry. I didn't mean that.
It's early, that's all. I just woke up. My brain ain't workin' yet."

"You sound congested." Gayle's voice carried with it the tone of
an inquisition.

Beau paused, cleared his throat. "I take it you assume I was up all
night doin' lines? Well, I wasn't. I went out to dinner with Slim and
B. Bobby Bostic. I'm clean. I've been clean. I'm gonna stay clean. I
wish you'd believe me. Jeez, all I had was some wine with dinner."

Gayle's voice modulated to another key. "B. Bobby Bostic? You
were with B. Bobby Bostic last night?"

"Yeah. Why?" There followed an ominous silence. "Gayle?
What is it?"

"You haven't seen the papers yet, or the TV news, have you? B.
Bobby Bostic was murdered last night."

The TV in Beau's room didn't work very well. It took a few
moments to warm up. At peak efficiency it only got four stations, six
if you counted the two snowy UHF channels. A ghostly double
image swam on the screen. The voice became audible in midsen-
tence: ". . . was killed last night in front of his house in Marin

County. Police have no clues in the case, and anyone with any information should call Detective George Jones of the Marin County Sheriff's Department."

He flipped the channel. A new voice took over: "Last night, blues guitarist B. Bobby Bostic was killed at his Marin County home, the victim of an apparent homicide. He was discovered by his secretary at two A.M. after a night of celebration following his successful performance at the San Francisco Blues Festival. Mr. Bostic was pronounced dead at Marin County General Hospital. He is best remembered for his 1970 hit 'If Your Love Has Gone.' Police are baffled by the case and say they have no leads at this time. Anyone with information regarding this incident is urged to call Detective George Jones, Marin County Sheriff's Department. Mr. Bostic was sixty-two years old."

Beau sat up in bed. "Holy shit." His hand reached for the phone, and it rang as soon as he touched it. "Hello?"

Oakland Slim's voice crackled through the line. "You hear about Bobby?"

"Yeah . . ."

"I'm comin' over."

Twenty minutes later Slim stood at Beau's door, his bronze face ashen. A bizarre feeling of déjà vu swept over both of them.

Slim said, "I just can't believe it! We were with him last night. It's just like the Spiderman all over again. Something's goin' on, man. There's something really, really wrong about this."

Beau said nothing. He felt numb. Death seemed to follow them around like a bad black dog. Beau's mind roiled with thoughts of conspiracy. Slim looked at him as if he could read his mind.

"Somebody's killin' all the great bluesmen."

"You're our man on this one, Detective Jones, nobody here can figure out a damn thing," a deputy sheriff said as he walked Detective George Jones through the murder scene. Bobby Bostic's house was besieged by cops. The morning sun illuminated a grisly setting. They followed a stream of blood up the driveway. It looked as if somebody had kicked over a can of red paint.

"Call me George."

It was his first homicide in California—B. Bobby Bostic, a famous blues musician, ripped apart and spread across his own driveway as if he'd been attacked by wolves. George looked at the earthly remains of Mr. Bostic with a detached, clinical eye.

"I'll bet you saw worse than this in New York every night," the deputy said.

George smiled a wan half smile, part cynical, part resigned professional courtesy. "That's why I moved out here to California."

"I heard you won the lottery or somethin'. That true?"

George adjusted the collar of his styleless short-sleeved white shirt. The twisted black tie hung askew; his beer belly protruded. George hooked his thumbs inside the waistband of his pants and tried to stuff his shirt back in. "Yeah. I hit a few numbers, won some money, quit the force, and moved out here."

"Why are you back workin' homicide?"

"I got bored."

Standing over the body of B. Bobby Bostic, George put on his game face and began to work. There seemed an inordinate amount of blood, as if the killer had wanted to make sure Bobby lost as much as possible. There were some footprints, but they were faint and hard to cast. The signs of the struggle were well preserved. It looked like the victim had put up quite a fight. The gravel had been displaced here and there, and there were slide marks and splatters of blood. Lots of blood. A loaded .38 lay in the car.

George looked up. "Coroner's ready?"

The deputy nodded. A dour Asian man wearing a blue suit stepped forward, clipboard in hand, a pen in his mouth. Behind him, photographers swarmed around the body, snapping pictures from every angle. Flashes popped intermittently while George asked the obvious questions. "Cause of death?"

"Loss of blood resulting from wounds of an unknown nature. Looks like he punctured a lung as well. I'll know more after the autopsy."

George pointed to the shredded flesh on Bobby's chest. "These wounds are unique. An animal maybe?"

The coroner shrugged. "Unlikely, since an animal leaves certain

patterns inconsistent with what I've seen here so far. Look at this."
He pointed to the parallel ribbons of flesh, spaced about an inch
apart, each bordered by a deep red gash and caked with dried blood.
"See? These aren't signs of mastication, and that's not a typical pattern. An animal would remove portions of flesh. The wounds would
be irregular. These are definitely parallel blade marks, and from the
looks of it, very sharp blades."

George squatted down next to the body, scrutinizing every
detail. He saw the long lacerations on the arms and wondered what
Bobby had been trying to fight off. "Pretty nasty. What do you
think? Razor? Scalpel, maybe?"

"Something like that." The coroner pointed at the open chest.
"Note how the wounds are evenly spaced. I have no idea what kind
of weapon did this, something homemade probably. It's certainly
nothing I've seen before."

George noticed that Bobby's zipper was down. "What do you
make of this?" he asked the coroner, pointing to it.

"His fly is down."

"Maybe he stopped to piss." George paused and looked over at
the bushes. "Perhaps over there"—he pointed—"and someone surprised him."

The coroner nodded. "Yes, that could be."

"The man parks the car," George continued. "The girls go
inside. He stops and pees. The killer surprises him with some weird-
ass weapon. He struggles and dies."

"I suppose that's one way it could have happened."

George pointed to the footprints. "Maybe we can get a decent
impression cast from one of these further up the driveway."

George searched the bushes and found the spot where Bobby
had drained his weasel. In the shrubs nearby he spotted three wads
of pink chewing gum and a cigarette butt. He carefully put them in
a plastic Baggie. *A pro wouldn't leave this.*

George made a list of his observations in a battered black notebook. Bobby wasn't robbed. His guitar still sat on the blacktop near
the car. The killer had hidden in the bushes in the dark waiting for
Bobby to come home. George touched Bobby's car-door handle.

He closed his eyes and imagined the killer waiting, then springing forward from the deep shadows. But he couldn't visualize the weapon.

Oakland Slim drove across the Golden Gate Bridge. Beau sat in the shotgun seat trying not to enjoy the scenery. Their black mood filled the car like stinky air-conditioning.

Slim said, "First it was Tunney, then the Spiderman, and now Bobby." He blew air through the gaps in his teeth. "Some crazy peckerwood is killin' all the kings of the blues. Think about it. There's only a few left anyway. And if he gets away with it . . . Shit, the blues is already on the endangered-species list. That would be the final nail in the coffin. You can count the remaining blues giants on one hand. And that number is dwindlin' fast. We gotta do something about it, man. This is worse than anyone thinks."

"We'll tell the cops."

Slim snorted. "The cops probably don't care. Except for Bobby, all these guys were basically penniless. Just another old black man stabbed to death. Happens every day."

They arrived at Bobby's house, parked the car, and threaded their way through the crowd to someone who looked like he was in charge. "We're lookin' for Detective Jones."

"He's over there. The heavyset guy in the brown shoes with his eyes closed." George seemed to be in a trance.

Slim and Beau walked over and waited until George opened his eyes. "Detective Jones?"

"That's me." George blinked and squinted at Slim. "Who are you?"

Slim stuck out his hand. "I'm Jerome Butts, better known as Oakland Slim. I'm a musician, a friend of Bobby's. We were with him last night."

"You know who killed him?"

Slim glanced at Beau, a worried look in his eye. "I think I might have an idea."

George nodded. "We can talk in the house."

George led Slim and Beau into B. Bobby Bostic's house. It was a large, classic two-story California ranch home. Inside, it smelled like leather. Yolanda and Belva sobbed quietly in another room. Their sedation had yet to kick in. The living room looked like something Elvis might've decorated during one of his jungle-room fantasies. They all sat down on a huge fake leopard skin sectional couch. Gold records and framed photographs lined the walls. A padded turquoise vinyl minibar stood in one corner. George looked around the room, then at Slim. "What do you know?"

"Well, first off, I happen to know that there's been two other murders like this one, both involving old blues musicians. Guys I know. They been gettin' slashed. Bobby was slashed, right?"

"I never said that." George had his notebook out and was trying to jump-start his ballpoint pen against the back cover. After several hard circles, it began to write.

Slim leaned forward and looked into George's face. "I bet he was mauled just like Art Spivey. A most egregious end to such a great man. My point is, I think there's a maniac out there who's killing all the old blues greats. I think he follows 'em around until he finds the right time, and then . . ."

George thrust out his lower lip and drummed his pen against the table. "Where did these other murders take place?"

"One's in Chicago and one's in St. Louis."

"I got no jurisdiction out of state."

"If you could just check, I'm sure—"

George cut him off. "When was the last time you saw Mr. Bostic alive?"

"Last night about eleven o'clock. We went to dinner at Vanessi's."

"So you were with him just before he died. Did he say anything that might shed some light on this?"

"Yeah, we were talkin' about Red Tunney and Arthur Spivey, the other two guys who were murdered. That's what I'm tryin' to tell you. I think it's the same guy who killed them. He has a thing for legendary musicians. The guys they call the kings of the blues."

George kept a poker face. "I appreciate your conspiracy theory, Mr. Butts, but I can't get involved in investigations out of state. I'm just concerned with this case for now. What else can you tell me about Mr. Bostic?"

"He didn't have any enemies and he didn't owe money. There's no motive for something like this. See what I mean? It's gotta be a psycho."

Beau cleared his throat. "It was the same way with Art Spivey. There was no motive there, either."

George turned to face Beau. "I didn't get your name."

"I'm Beau Young. I play guitar for Oakland Slim, I mean Mr. Butts. I was there last night at dinner and I was also there the night before Art Spivey died. In fact we were the last people to see either one of them."

"Is that so? Well, it looks to me like you guys could be potential suspects in both murders."

Beau looked astonished. "Why would we come to you then? Wouldn't that be stupid?"

The expression on George's face was one of mild amusement. "Maybe you're nuts. I don't know. Either way, I'm gonna take you back to headquarters for questioning."

"Bobby was my friend, man," Slim said.

"Are you at least gonna check out those other murders?"

George tapped his pen against his leg. "I'll see what I can do."

Beau looked up to see Annie Sweeny enter the room. His mouth dropped open. Annie saw him, and for a second the worried look on her face softened and turned to surprise. She waved timidly.

"Detective Jones? I'm Annie Sweeny from *Bluesworthy* magazine. They said I might be able to talk to you."

"I'm sorry, ma'am. I already issued a statement to the press. I don't have time now."

"Oh, that's not what I wanted to ask you about. I thought you might be able to say something about the possibility of a conspiracy. It seems like there've been too many murders in the blues community lately to be just a coincidence."

George rolled his eyes. "Not you too. Look, I have a lot of detective work to do on this case before I can start sniffin' around in places I have no authority. If my investigation leads me there, fine. But right now I'm focused on the murder of B. Bobby Bostic."

Annie looked at Beau. Their eye contact was strong. "Is that why you're here?"

"Yeah. Me and Slim have a theory. We thought we should talk to the cops about it."

George Jones stood. He snapped his notebook shut and smiled. "OK, show's over."

As Beau and Slim walked out of the house, Beau heard a voice call, "Hey, man!"

He turned to see a tall, thin man with long hair tied in a ponytail. "Hey! Wait up a second." The man wore a lab coat and glasses. His face was cratered by acne scars. His smile revealed clean but crooked teeth. He hurried over to Beau and stuck out his hand. "Pleased to meet you. I'm Stu Kweeder, deputy assistant medical examiner. You're Beau Young, right?"

They shook hands. "Yeah?"

"I'm a big fan of yours. I saw you guys about twenty times back in the old Fillmore days. Beau and the Savages. I got all your old albums, man. You guys were great."

Beau smiled politely. "That was a long time ago."

Stu shrugged. "I guess so. Back then I was still in school. Now I work for the coroner's office."

Slim looked at Beau. "I play guitar with Oakland Slim now. I'm doing a blues thing."

Stu pumped Oakland Slim's hand. "Cool, man. Blues, huh? That's a far cry from the Savages."

"Like night and day."

"Hey, could I have your autograph?"

Beau smiled sheepishly. "I guess so."

"You still keep in touch with Dean and the other guys?"

Beau shook his head. "I've kinda lost track. Dean's in L.A. doing movie sound tracks, I think. Tom's around. Travis disappeared from the face of the earth."

"What a trip. You guys were my favorite all-time band. I wish I had my albums with me so you could sign 'em." Stu handed Beau a piece of medical examiner's report paper and a pen. Beau signed it on the blank side and handed it back. Stu admired the autograph. "By the way, what are you doing here?"

"We were friends of Bobby."

Stu looked back at the driveway. "That's too bad, man."

"Did you see the body?"

Stu laughed. "See it? I wrapped it. I'm the one who does all the actual work around here. My boss gets all the credit, though."

"What killed him?"

"Massive blood loss. He got shredded up real bad. I have no idea what could do that. Maybe the Wolfman. Hey, you want to see it?"

"What? The body?"

Stu looked around and lowered his voice. "Yeah. But not here." He reached into his breast pocket and withdrew a card. He jotted a phone number down on the back and handed it to Beau. "Here's my card. My home phone's on the back. Call me anytime. I can get you in anytime after six o'clock. That's when all the suits leave."

Beau fingered the card. "Thanks. You know, I might want to take you up on that. Let me give you my number too, in case something turns up. We're trying to find out who did this." Beau tore off a piece of the card and wrote his number.

"I work nights a lot. It's peaceful down there when everyone's gone and it's just me and the dead people. Dead people make good company. They never complain."

"You're weird."

Stu gave the thumbs-up sign. "Rock on, dude."

Beau parked his white 1967 Dodge Dart in front of his ex-wife's house in Oakland. Sun sparkled through the trees and splattered his windshield with full-spectrum light. Gayle and Woody sat on the steps playing with colored chalk. When Woody saw his dad he raced to the car. "Daddy! Daddy!"

"How're ya doin', champ!" Beau stepped out and picked up his son. They hugged each other fiercely. "I missed you."

"I missed you too, Dad. Can we go to the zoo and the pinball place?"

Gayle said, "Do you have to take him there? I'd rather he not go there."

Beau tried to smile. "If you don't want him to play pinball, I won't take him."

Woody wiggled in Beau's arms. "Please? You said!"

Beau eased Woody to the ground. "Jeez, you're gettin' heavy."

"Please?"

"Mommy said no."

Gayle stood and wiped her hands on her jeans. She was still slim, her face still pretty. She wore no makeup and her hair hung long down her back. "Don't make it sound like I'm the bad guy."

"I'm not making you the bad guy."

"Well, to him it seems like Mommy is the one who's not letting him go play pinball."

Beau sighed. "But . . . that's what's happening, isn't it?"

Gayle put her hands on her hips. "That's not what's happening at all! You just don't get it, do you?"

"I guess not."

"What I mean to say is, I don't think it's healthy for a little boy of six to be hanging out playing pinball with a bunch of sleazy adults."

Beau opened his mouth. He sensed the confrontation and chose his words carefully. "There aren't any sleazy adults. Mostly it's other kids. But that's beside the point. You say don't take him and I won't take him. I have no problem with that."

"The point is you tell him he can go, and then I have to tell him he can't. Honestly, can you see what I'm driving at? You're always the good guy. You don't think. You tell him he can go all these places without consulting me first. Then he gets his hopes up."

Woody jumped between them. "Sleazy adults! Sleazy adults!"

Gayle shook her head. "See? See what you started?"

"Sleazy adults! I wanna see the sleazy adults! Are they really sleazy, Daddy?"

Beau knelt down on one knee and put his arm around Woody. "Let me tell you something, big guy. There aren't any sleazy adults. Mommy's just kidding."

Gayle glared at Beau. "So it's agreed? No pinball?"

Beau nodded. "Whatever you say."

Gayle reached in the back pocket of her jeans and produced some folded papers. "My lawyer sent me these."

She handed Beau the bills from her lawyer. Beau looked pained. "I wish he wouldn't do that. He's just charging more and more money on his bill. Every time he answers the phone, every time he reads a message, every time he even thinks about your case, he charges. These legal fees are killin' me. And the ironic thing about it is that it's all money that could've gone to you. Why don't we just tell the lawyers to stop and just deal with it between you and me?"

"Because I don't trust you. I have to insure my son's financial support. You're unreliable."

"But that's fifteen thousand dollars I've given him that I could've given to you."

"I don't want to talk about it." She stepped away from him, toward the steps. From inside the house, Beau could smell spaghetti sauce cooking. "Take him to the zoo. No pinball. No junk food. Be back by six. No later. I'm making his favorite spaghetti for dinner."

"Bisghetti! I love bisghetti."

"Lets go see some elephants."

Beau spent the day walking through the zoo with Woody. When he returned him to Gayle's house, her mood was still tepid. Preoccupied with the murders, Beau managed to stay clear of further confrontations with Gayle. In fact, he didn't say anything, which he'd come to learn was his best tactic. He hugged Woody and said good-bye.

Beau met Slim for a fried squid sandwich and a beer at Spenger's Seafood Grotto, in the shadow of the freeway ramp at the foot of University Avenue in Berkeley. The smell of San Francisco Bay hung like moldy rigging in the air. Seagulls patrolled the parking lot.

Inside, Spenger's was all dark wood, mirrors, and mounted trophy fish. The main room was dominated by a huge mahogany bar, a favorite among artists and musicians. Beau found Slim at the raw bar. Beau ordered a dozen oysters and six shrimp. They sat in a booth along the south wall. Beau spoke first, as soon as he sat down. "It might be somebody who hates the blues, or maybe hates blacks."

"Yeah," Slim said, "the blacks and the blues. You know, it might be some kind of a psycho who thinks that he can rub out the entire art form by killing the masters."

Beau grunted, poking his tiny fork at the grayish open oyster. He spooned a little horseradish onto the shivering glob. "Maybe it's a racist thing."

"Whoever did this had to travel. It took a lot of planning and some money. That doesn't sound like a racial-hatred thing to me. I mean, I could be wrong, but why would he travel across the country to track down one particular black guy?"

Beau dipped a shrimp in cocktail sauce and put it in his mouth. He chewed slowly, thinking. "The king is dead."

"Long live the king," finished Slim.

They ate in silence for several minutes. Slim said, "People call someone the king of something because he's a pioneer. Art Spivey was the king of the slide guitar because he could play it like no one else. He contributed something to it, right? So what if this guy thinks he's supposed to be the king of the blues? And he's warped enough to think that just by murdering the rest of the field, he'll be crowned the undisputed king?"

Beau nodded. "That's a scary thought."

Slim left the bar and Beau stayed on for one last beer. As he was about to leave he felt a slap on his back. He turned to face Tom Finnick, the bass player in his old band, the Savages.

"Beau! You old turd! How's it hangin'?"

"Like a salami in the deli window, man. How's life with you?"

Tom put his arm around Beau and whispered in his ear. "How long has it been, man? Five, six years? Well, let me tell you some-thing, I am wired in, baby. I'm doin' phenomenal. I got the main connection, babe. The mutha lode."

"What do you mean?"

"Let me buy you a drink and I'll explain."

Fifteen minutes later, Beau had heard Tom's story from the moment the band broke up until he walked into Spenger's. It went something like this: Tom survived some bad times and was now a successful coke dealer. "I'm rollin' in dough. I got chicks. I got clothes. I tell ya, man, I'm cruisin'. Tootski?"

"I quit doin' coke."

"Really? That's a shame. 'Cause this stuff is flake."

"Sorry, man. I'm tryin' to stay straight."

Tom shrugged. "Hey, that's cool. Tell you what, though . . ."

Tom surreptitiously slipped a small white paper bindle into the breast pocket of Beau's shirt. "For later. In case you change your mind. This stuff is tits. Pure as the driven snow. You'll thank me."

"I can't. . . ." Beau lifted it out.

Tom made a face. "Put it in your pocket, man. There's narcs all over this place."

"You take it."

Tom raised his hands. "I don't want it. It's yours. I gave it to you."

Beau looked around nervously. "Well . . . I . . ."

"Give it to a friend."

"But . . ."

Tom hugged Beau. "We're blood brothers, man. Don't look a gift horse in the mouth."

"I can't take it."

"Don't insult me." Tom disengaged himself and rocked back on his heels. "How about a joint? At least you'll smoke a joint with me, right? You're not that straight, are ya?"

Beau laughed. "How many joints did we smoke back in the sixties?"

"About a million. Whoee! We were rebels, man! I remember all those gigs we played, every one of them. That was the best time of my life. Bar none. I really miss it."

"You gotta move on, man."

"Yeah, I guess so. But it sure was a groove, wasn't it?"

Beau's eyes glistened. "That it was, my friend. That it most certainly was."

Tom walked with Beau to the end of the parking lot and lit the joint. They smoked together, like old times. Beau enjoyed the mellow buzz. He told Tom all about his blues gig with Oakland Slim. Tom whistled. "I always knew you could do it. You were a hell of a guitar player back in the old days. You're probably even better now."

Beau coughed. "Thanks, man. I try."

"It was the biz that screwed us, not the music."

Beau suddenly remembered a defining moment of his youth, the time he met Brian Jones backstage at the Monterey Pop Festival in 1967. The magic of that meeting stayed with him over the years, as long as he kept it secret. Somehow, he knew if he ever told anyone, the spell would be broken. Brian was dead now, and Beau couldn't help but think that Brian had taken the memory of their meeting to his grave. And so Beau kept his silence. He remembered Brian's words. "It's all bullshit, man."

"Huh?"

"The music business, it's all bullshit." Beau recalled the rest of Brian's monologue. It rushed into his mind like new water into a just-flushed toilet. "If you think about it, you'll fuck it up, man. So just do it without thinking. That's the whole key."

Beau drove to the Marina, then up to the observation point at the south anchorage of the Golden Gate Bridge. The Dodge Dart shimmied up the hill. It's push-button transmission vibrated in the dash like an electric football game. He got out of the car and walked to the edge. Waves crashed far beneath him. A crisp wind blew the tendrils of fog between the towers and into the mouth of the bay. Traffic was light on the bridge. Behind him the city bled neon. Foam hissed in the darkness below. The ancient energy soothed him. He put his hand in his pocket and pulled out the folded paper bindle of coke.

He thought about Bobby. He thought about Art Spivey. He thought about Gayle and Woody. He thought about Annie. His mind was so knotted that he was unaware of his hands unconsciously unfolding the bindle. He gently bent the paper back and stared down. A gram of pure white powder glistened like crushed diamonds. Beau's nose twitched. He felt a tightness in the back of his throat. He touched a fingertip to the coke and brought it to his tongue. The bitter flavor made him shudder.

He looked around to make sure nobody could see. The bridge hung lonely in the night. The rust-colored cables swooped up into the fog and disappeared.

He slowly lifted the bindle up to his face, his nostrils flaring like a bloodhound's. He opened the bindle all the way and brought it closer to his nose. He froze for a second, the pearly coke gleaming seductively in his hand, then blew as hard as he could. The coke exploded into the wind and vanished. He let the paper go and it sailed over the edge.

"Bye-bye, Miss Peruvian Pie."

Beau trembled for a second, then took a deep breath and stood tall. He looked out into the night, across the waters, standing on the edge of the country, facing west. It was as far as you could go, the place where the pioneers had had to stop. The end of the line. Lights flickered on the bridge. He turned and faced the continent of North America. In there, he thought, somewhere in that big country is a monster.

And it's coming. It's getting closer.

Not content to stay on the outskirts of their lives any longer, the evil power grew. Beau could feel it getting closer. The abstract fear that he had felt a week ago now became palpable. It threatened him directly. Something terrible was out there stalking them. Beau shivered.

The wind blew through his jacket and swept his hair up into wild bunches. It rang in his ears and brought miniature tears to the corners of his eyes.

Beau made a decision.

✋ EIGHT ✋

In a small storefront business in a distressed Chicago neighborhood, King Washington sat at a gray metal desk. The walls of his office were covered with faded pictures of him with various show business personalities, mostly blues musicians, a large black man standing among smaller black men. He wasn't nearly as rotund as he used to be, but he was still a big person, over six feet five inches tall and heavy.

His image smiled, the shadow of a happier time, a time of promise and enterprise. He'd been the most aggressive among them, those other faces in the pictures, a natural businessman and leader.

Abandoned by his real mother and raised by aunts and uncles, King Washington grew up a wheeler and a dealer in the neighborhood. Streetwise and devious, he rose to power like a holy man, among the lesser driven, always out for himself, always working the angles. King let his eyes wander over the pictures, having made this mental journey ten thousand times. He saw nothing but the dusty frames.

The man in the photographs stared back, in his twenties a successful producer of rhythm and blues records, in his thirties the president of his own record company, in his forties a powerful music publisher. After that, the pictures became infrequent. There'd been considerably less celebration in the years that followed, mostly accounting and collecting. Many of the men he'd done business with over the years wound up hating him. He'd burned the brave and honest ones, taken undue advantage of the ignorant, and ruined the weak.

Now, at age sixty, with his empire in decline, King Washington was fat and ugly; fat with the spoils of a lifetime of corruption in the music business and ugly with the loss of integrity. He ruled over the ruins of his life like a mad warlord, always greedy for more of what he already had. Power and money were his only friends now, and even they had begun to desert him.

Boxes of records lined the floor and reached halfway up the walls. Dirty and unorganized in every way, the room reflected the mind of its principal occupant. He'd fired his secretary and most of the other employees, and now he did everything himself, or tried to. The truth was, nothing much got done.

He held the telephone to his ear.

King Washington stretched as he sat back in his chair, his oversized feet resting on the middle of the desk. He smoked a moderately priced cigar, one end moist and slimy and the other smoldering. It sent up an acrid blue cloud. His brown-stained fingers played absently with the stinky stogie as he spoke.

The afternoon light faded through the store window, sliced into a thousand dim slashes by the Venetian blinds. The dusty glass gave it a textured, grainy hue, and the cigar smoke hung suspended in front of Washington like a louvered ghost. He rubbed his leathery face with a free hand and coughed. There was an order form for one hundred Art Spivey records on the desktop in front of him. He tapped it with a finger. Wet flecks of saliva-soaked cigar tobacco dotted the page.

He nodded his head rhythmically while he listened to the voice on the other end of the line. When he spoke, his voice was deep and brusque. "Yes. Yes, but I'll need payment in full, up front, do you understand? And by the way, since my inventory is limited on this particular item, I'm gonna have to raise the price."

Two thousand miles away, Annie Sweeny winced. She'd expected it to happen eventually, but that didn't make it any easier to accept. The old bastard was going to up the price on the Spiderman's records. Art Spivey was not even cold in the grave yet, and already people were trying to make money off of him.

Annie sighed. She'd resigned herself to having to deal with people like King Washington when she took over her father's business.

She'd fenced with the unlikable old snake many times for his blues records. King was from the old school, Annie constantly reminded herself, screw thy neighbor, screw thy friend, hell, screw 'em all.

You don't survive in the record business in Chicago for thirty years without being tough as nails. Annie knew that. Still, she was surprised at the speed of the thing, at how incredibly fast King Washington adjusted to the market. Supply and demand, King Washington style.

"Raise the price? Why do you want to go and do that? The poor guy's only been dead a few weeks. . . . Jeez."

"Hey, I'm not in business to take care of little white girls like you. I got a guy in Japan that wants to buy the whole goddamn warehouse. I'm doin' you a favor and you don't even appreciate it. Do you want the records or not?"

Annie wanted to scream, but didn't. "OK. Slow down. I never said I didn't want 'em. I just want to know how much it's gonna cost me. I'm almost afraid to ask. How much more do you want?"

"Seven dollars."

"Per record? Seven more per record? That's kind of steep. . . ."

"Take it or leave it, kid." He shifted his cigar, now losing definition between his yellowed teeth.

Annie had no choice. There was no other place to get Art Spivey records. She did a little mental arithmetic and realized that after her own modest markup and shipping costs, these records would be the most expensive items she'd ever handled. "OK. I'll take it. I think it's too much, but I'll take it. Give me three boxes of B. Bobby Bostic *Boogie Classics* too."

"You want the greatest hits?"

"Yeah. Three boxes of *Boogie Classics*, one box of greatest hits, and four Art Spivey."

"You can expect delivery in six weeks."

"I need them sooner." Annie sounded exasperated.

"Well, send your own truck, honey. Six weeks, that's it, and I can't even guarantee that. I'm backed up over here and no one's liftin' a finger to help me out. I've got serious labor problems. If you want it any faster you're gonna have to pay. Five bucks a case."

"What's that get me?"

"Three weeks, tops. That's five bucks in addition to what you're already payin', you understand that, don't ya? You get the merchandise in three weeks, otherwise it's six. Best I can do."

Annie rolled her eyes. She would not pay the extra—it felt like highway robbery. She made a snap decision to take her chances on the six weeks. "Never mind. Just give me what I ordered. Ship it the usual way."

"Certified check or money order only. No personal checks. In advance. I start processing the order as soon as I get the dough."

"Can't you start today?" Annie tried not to whine. Washington ignored her and kept right on talking.

"Oh yeah, and another thing"—King Washington puffed away on his cigar—"Bostic's goin' up too."

"Oh, for God's sake! What else is going up?"

Washington chuckled. "Everything."

Back in Chicago, on King Washington's end of the line, the weather was changing. Outside his office it began to rain, the droplets streaking his filthy window at an angle. He poured a shot of whiskey onto the dried remains of the last shot. He drank it quickly, followed by another hasty application.

He finished making out the order slip for Annie Sweeny and put it on top of a pile of other order slips, most of them for Art Spivey. The B. Bobby Bostic windfall had yet to begin. Soon, though.

He stood up and walked to the window, but as he rose from his desk, some unopened mail fell on the floor. The top letter was from the law office of Oakland Slim's attorney. He glanced at the envelope. *That damn Oakland Slim again. It never ends. When's that old asshole gonna give up?*

King bent over and picked it up. There was no reason to open it. He knew the contents: demands for accounting, audits, records, unpaid royalties, unpaid publishing moneys, that kind of stuff. Oakland Slim claimed King Washington owed him a small fortune. He threatened legal action. It wouldn't be the first time King had faced litigation. In the old days, he would have paid a call on some of his Mafia buddies. Many a crybaby musician had given up all his bullshit claims once some bones were broken.

The name of King Washington had meant something in Chicago then. Now was a different story. King Washington had mounting gambling debts. He'd been procrastinating.

Through the window he watched some kids run down the street, chasing a mongrel dog. The terrified dog ran as if his life depended on it. King Washington laughed. He'd been on both sides of that scenario, and it was much better not being the dog.

"Damn you, Oakland Slim! You get nothin'!" He threw his half-chewed cigar on the floor. It joined several others already residing there. His face looked as dark as grave dirt. "That son of a bitch is worth more dead than alive anyway."

Detective George Jones, recently of the New York City Police Department, Homicide, took a sip of his coffee and considered lighting another Tiparillo, but it would been his fifth of the day and he had promised himself he would cut down. His square, flat face scowled beneath a military flattop of steel gray bristle.

He didn't really have to work—he could get by comfortably on the money he'd won in the lottery—but George needed to work. And this case needed him. Back in New York, George had been the guy they called for all the weird cases, the stuff nobody else could solve. Cases that had no answer. George Jones had a sixth sense when it came to homicide detection. There were those who called him psychic, but George, a devout skeptic, called it intuition and luck. The net result was the same. George had an uncanny batting average when it came to solving bizarre murder cases. The more bizarre, the better. George found answers and made connections others couldn't. People noticed. When he hit the lottery and made all that money, some said old George had strange powers. Things changed. George got pissed and retired. He moved to Larkspur, California. Boredom and an invitation from the Marin County Sheriff's Department pulled him back into police work. And now he faced another bizarre murder case.

"You workin' alone on this?" a voice said. Captain Pulholtz stood over him.

"Ah, yeah . . . for now. Really ain't much of anything to investigate so far. But I'll keep you posted."

"You know, George, we feel pretty lucky to have you here, a famous New York homicide cop and all. None of us could do squat with this one. Frankly, I'm glad you're around."

George smiled, but it spread reluctantly across his mouth like a cat stretching on a pillow. "I can't let you say that. Ain't true. Man, this is dirty work. Anybody could do it if they really got into it. The problem is, who'd want to get into it?"

Another officer passed George's desk and handed him a large manila envelope. "Autopsy results you wanted."

George opened the envelope and read the first page with interest, then the second page.

 NINE

Annie Sweeny sighed, making a sound like distant ocean surf.
It gave her a few extra seconds to think before she spoke. When she
did speak, her voice carried a soft vulnerability Beau hadn't heard in
it before. Annie said, "I don't like any of this. It really scares me."
Her voice was nearly a whisper.

It made Beau think of his ex-wife, of the way her voice had been
soft in the beginning. Gayle had been just a teenager when he'd met
her, and they'd been married nine years. Annie was the first woman
besides Gayle in whom he'd felt that softness. It sent a pang through
his heart. "Scares me too. I'm convinced there's somebody out
there doing this. One guy. One lone psycho."

Annie looked doubtful. They sat at a window table in a tiny
sushi bar in San Francisco's Japantown. Outside, a heavy mist
swirled like cigarette smoke. Traffic was backed up in Nihon Machi.
Inside, koto music played softly. "What if you're wrong?"

Beau said, "What if I'm right?"

Annie looked beautiful in a worn brown leather jacket and short
suede skirt. Her supple legs whispered against each other, the black
panty hose electric with static possibilities as she shifted in her chair.

They stared at each other for a moment, both looking as if they
might speak. Beau shook his head. His eyes were sad. "Things sure
got shitty fast."

"What do you mean?"

"I saw an old friend yesterday. It got me thinkin'. Ten years ago, in '67, things were so much better, you know? Back in the early days of the Haight. People were different. They really cared about each other. It was beautiful. I really loved it back then. I felt like I was caught up in something bigger, something wonderful. I had this great sense of destiny." He laughed, but it was a bitter, cynical laugh. "We thought we could change the world. That was the last time I felt truly alive. Monterey, Woodstock, the Fillmore. We thought our music would never die. We fought a cultural revolution. For what? Disco?"

Annie tilted her head. "The sixties weren't all flowers and paisleys. You're forgetting Vietnam, Charlie Manson, Altamont. . . ."

"Yeah, but the sixties I remember were beautiful, full of love and possibilities. Those were magical times. The world's been goin' downhill ever since."

A Mona Lisa smile spread across Annie's lips. "I was too young to notice. You're kinda cute when you get maudlin, you know that?"

Beau blushed. The chemistry between him and Annie sizzled like tempura shrimp. Since he'd picked her up at the California bungalow in Berkeley she'd inherited from her dad, and brought her back over the bridge into the city, he'd been trying not to stare. She seemed preoccupied, though. Beau said, "I must be gettin' old. I do a lot of reminiscing these days. I'm turning into a real old fart. Must be all this death around me. These old guys goin' down. I can't stand it. It hurts. It's wrong. I want to do something, damn it."

Annie said, "Then we've got to find a way to stop him before he kills again. I don't know how, but we've somehow got to figure this out. Maybe Detective Jones can do something. I have a good feeling about him. He seems like a righteous guy." Annie's voice modulated down. She blinked as if to ward off an unwanted emotion or two. Her pretty face tightened. "I love the blues. It was my father's music. I grew up listening to Howlin' Wolf and Muddy Waters. Most people don't even know their real names."

"Chester Burnett, McKinnley Morganfield."

She shook her head. "Not you. I mean regular people. The blues means nothing to them." Beau watched Annie's eyes fill with moisture. "If my father was still alive . . . he'd want me to at least try. Try something. Anything. This can't be happening."

Beau looked away. "Maybe I could mount my own investigation."

"Are you serious?"

Beau nodded. "I could do it. I'm a reasonably intelligent guy. And I've got a friend at the medical examiner's office."

"I don't know. A murder investigation. That seems kinda heavy."

"Murder is heavy. I'm just going to sniff around a little, see what I can find. I don't intend to put myself in jeopardy or anything, but if I can help, I'm gonna. I'm a lot closer to this than George Jones. Maybe I can make a connection. Look at it this way: If I don't do it, who will?"

"You won't be in any danger, will you?"

"Not any more than I am now."

Beau slid his hand across the table and touched hers. As soon as he made contact, she responded by sliding her hand around his intimately, answering a thousand questions with her touch.

Beau said, "I remember buyin' my first blues album. The classic *King of the Delta Blues Singers* by Robert Johnson. Man, I must have played that record a million times. I knew every track by heart, even the scratches. I loved that album. It opened up a whole world to me. I tried to play the guitar riffs the way he did, but of course that's impossible. I learned pretty much all my basic licks from that guy. And not just me, all the guitarists from my generation: Eric Clapton, Jimmy Page, Jeff Beck. Robert Johnson, man. He was a god."

Annie cast a curious look at Beau. "What else do you know about Robert Johnson?"

Beau shrugged. "He died in the 1930s. That's about all I know. They say he sold his soul to the devil."

Annie looked away for a moment, debating something in her mind. Her forehead furrowed and she pressed her lightly glossed lips together. "He was poisoned at a gig, August sixteenth, 1938. According to Sonny Boy Williamson, who says he was there, Robert Johnson accepted a bottle of unmarked whiskey from a stranger. Sonny Boy knocked it out of his hand and told him it was stupid to accept mystery drinks from strangers. There was a lot of bad whiskey around in those days. Anyway, a little while later he was handed another unmarked bottle. This time Sonny Boy wasn't around to stop him, and he drank. Middle of the next set he starts feelin' dizzy and stops playin'. Next thing he's down on the floor barking like a dog. Then he just rolled over and collapsed."

"What a way to go." Beau grimaced.

"Of course, Sonny Boy Williamson is a known liar."

"How do you know that?"

Annie's eyes twinkled. "He used to come over to my house for dinner when I was a little girl. My father used to give him advice about his career."

Beau whistled. "Your father gave Sonny Boy Williamson advice?"

Annie flashed a wan smile. "Yeah. My dad was an amazing guy. Everybody loved him. Anyway, they took Robert Johnson to a house nearby. It's said he died a little while later. There were no doctors around. No way of knowing what really happened."

"Where's he buried?"

"Nobody knows." Annie's face changed. She looked around the room. She leaned forward and spoke in a conspiratorial whisper. "Beau? What if I told you Robert Johnson was still alive?"

Beau drove Annie back across the Bay Bridge through thick drizzle. Going east on the bridge, away from San Francisco, he traveled on the lower level. Every time he passed beneath a seam in the roadway above, a waterfall pounded his windshield. The rhythm of the gaps thrummed like a slow twelve-bar blues. He concentrated on negotiating the slick roadbed. The tires hummed. Beau kept a careful pace. Annie hadn't said much since dinner. She seemed deep in thought.

Her voice was soft again. "I didn't want to tell you about Robert Johnson before. I guess I sort of had to trust you first."

"You trust me now?"

"Yes, I do. It's more than that, though. I need you, Beau. I need your help."

Beau's face looked worried and prideful at the same time. The curious mix of expressions dimpled the sides of his mouth. "I'll be honest with you. I find the whole thing about Robert Johnson pretty hard to believe."

A big tractor trailer roared past, sending a blast of spray across the hood. The windshield wipers of his Dodge Dart creaked and squeaked, trying gamely to keep up. Beau squinted through the wash, driving even more intently. Annie said, "Yeah, I thought that too. Until I saw him with my own eyes. I found him playing at a barbecue place. He said a friend of his owned it and business was real bad, so he begged Robert Johnson to play to help draw a crowd. So one night he did. He hadn't played in public for thirty-nine years. And I happened to be there. The guitar style, the haunted voice, the uncanny timing, it was all there. I don't think anyone could have faked it that perfectly. He played for about an hour, and when he did 'Hell Hound on My Trail' I just knew."

"Did he claim to be Robert Johnson?"

"No, he gave me a fictitious name at first. But after I spoke with him awhile, he confessed."

Beau felt the hair on his neck rise. Something about Robert Johnson still being alive frightened him. As if the curse were still alive too. "But why has he been underground all this time?"

"Something bad happened back in '38. He thought it best to lay low." Annie shifted in her seat.

Beau said, "What proof do you have?"

She sighed. "Nothing yet. But I'm workin' on it." She turned to face Beau, her face in profile across the seat. "Will you help me?"

Beau dragged his eyes away from the road for a second and shot her a penetrating glance. "You're serious?"

"I'm dead serious. If this guy is who I think he is, a lot of people are gonna be freaked out."

"And a lot of money is gonna change hands."

Annie nodded. "Will you help me?"

"Help you what? Prove he's Robert Johnson?"

"It's vitally important to the blues, especially in light of what's been happening. Robert Johnson is the godfather. We have to set the story straight."

Beau almost smirked. "Nobody's asked for my help in a long time. It feels kinda strange." They exited the bridge, took 80 north to Berkeley. The rain began to subside. Beau ventured a look at her. The smile Annie smiled was unlike any smile he'd ever seen. It was the first truly perfect, beautiful thing he'd experienced in years. The fact that Annie needed him, and wanted his help, filled a part of his soul that had been empty for too long. She had no idea what his problems were. "You don't know anything about me," he said. "My life . . . it's all screwed up."

"You haven't killed anybody, have you?"

Beau laughed. "No."

"Well, then. Everything else we can work out."

"OK, I'll help you if you'll help me. I want to catch a killer."

Annie's hand slid across the seat and touched Beau's leg, just above the knee. "Deal."

Beau parked in front of Annie's pink stucco house on the north side of Berkeley. He was wondering whether to kiss her when she kissed him. Beau responded by kissing her back even more earnestly. Annie broke the kiss and looked into Beau's eyes. "Why are all these things happening at the same time?"

Beau didn't shrug or look away. He answered her directly, keeping his eyes on hers. "I've felt like this before, Annie. This sense of destiny, of being swept up in something momentous. Suddenly I feel like everything's linked. The blues murders, Robert Johnson's rediscovery, me and Slim, you and me . . . It's all part of something."

They sat in silence for a few moments. The rain had stopped. Annie looked away to break the spell, then looked back. "I have to go see Robert Johnson's son tomorrow. I don't know what he wants, but I'd rather not go alone."

Beau smiled. "I'd love to go with you. Where is it?"

"Robert Johnson's house in Hayward."

Beau did a Jerry Lewis double take. "Robert Johnson lives in Hayward?"

Annie didn't ask Beau to stay with her that night. She didn't have to. Once inside her place Beau took her in his arms and they kissed again. Nothing said, nothing questioned. They found their way to her bedroom and everything came together like a beautiful puzzle. They made love for the first time, perfectly, effortlessly, like two young creatures. Afterward, Beau couldn't bring himself to leave. There was no reason to. From now on he wanted to be with Annie.

* * *

A thirty-five-year-old black man with an uneven beard and one arm hurried through the kitchen and fumbled with the locks. When he saw Annie and Beau he smiled and swept his one arm, the left, through the air. He wore a faded plaid shirt and wrinkled black trousers. His teeth were brown. He smelled like alcohol.

"Come in! Come in, Miss Sweeny."

Annie and Beau stepped inside, and Leeland Dodds closed the door and relocked it against the world. The house smelled like fried fish. "This is my . . . colleague, Beau Young."

Leeland shook Beau's hand. "I'm Leeland Dodds. So glad you could come. Let's go in the front room."

They entered a living room full of overstuffed, unmatched furniture. A black-and-white TV showed a blurred vision of Lucy, and a half-eaten plate of franks and beans sat drying on the table. Leeland cleared away a pile of newspapers.

"Sit right down, Miss Sweeny, Mr. Young."

Annie eyed her host uncomfortably. She'd wondered about the son of the man who claimed to be Robert Johnson the moment she heard his voice on the phone. He struck her as being somewhat unsavory, but Annie always tried to give people the benefit of the doubt. Still, the overwhelming vibe she got was negative.

"Where's your father?" Annie said.

"Not here." Leeland slipped back into the kitchen and returned a few seconds later with three beers, two cradled under his arm and the other in his hand. He offered one to Annie, who thought about refusing it for a brief moment before finally accepting, and one to Beau, who smiled. "Dad's down at Chief's."

"Chief's?"

"The barbecue." Leeland held a can of beer against the table with his palm and pulled back the tab with a gnarled forefinger. He raised it to his lips and took a long drink. Annie watched his Adam's apple bob.

"I see. Well, what did you want to talk to me about?"

Leeland stifled a belch. "Well, it's about my father, obviously. I had to do this when he wasn't around. The old man hates for me to talk about him."

Annie shifted in her seat. She didn't know what was coming, but she had an idea it would be something to do with money. Beau cleared his throat.

Leeland said, "When you contacted my father last month, you said you would be fair and that your main interest was in the music."

"That's right. It still is."

"You said if we could prove my father's identity"—he paused and nodded for emphasis—"there'd be a whole lot of money."

"Yes," Annie replied. "I found a good law firm to sort things out. The senior partner was a friend of my father's, a blues fan, and he'll work on contingency for now. This is definitely a first. Virtually every major rock band has recorded Robert Johnson songs."

"Really? How many?"

"Well, let's see. . . . There's 'Crossroads,' 'Love in Vain,' 'Travelin' Riverside Blues,' and 'Sweet Home Chicago' just to mention a few. You're talkin' about Cream, the Stones, Led Zeppelin, and, of course, the Crawlin' Kingsnakes."

"Damn."

Annie nodded. "We have to establish what happened to the millions of dollars in publishing and songwriting royalties that were earned over the past decades, and how we go about reclaiming all future royalties. I can't think of another case like this, where a guy came back from the dead . . . in a legal sense, that is, to claim royalties."

Leeland sucked his beer. "Well, I've been looking through his things to see if there is anything we could use." Leeland handed Annie a manila envelope and told her to look inside. She opened it carefully and pulled out a yellowed piece of paper, somewhat frayed, and held it up to the light.

"What's this?" she asked.

"It's a letter," said Leeland proudly. "A letter from John Hammond inviting my father, Robert Johnson, to perform at the *From Spirituals to Swing* concert at Carnegie Hall, December twenty-third, 1938. It's dated October tenth, 1938, as you can see, but, of course, my dad was supposedly already dead by then. This arrived at my grandma's house in Greenwood a few months after he was gone."

Annie scrutinized the letter. She was no expert, but the paper seemed properly aged and bore the letterhead of John Hammond, Columbia Records, New York City. For the moment, she had no way of knowing if the signature was genuine. "This is interesting, but inconclusive. It really doesn't legally prove anything."

Leeland looked pained. "My father left Mississippi in a hurry. He was afraid for his life."

"I believe you, but we've got to convince the lawyers."

Leeland turned to Beau, addressing him as well. He had the voice of someone who'd been making excuses his entire life, a whiny, "dog ate my homework" voice. Leeland put down his beer and waved his good arm.

"Let me tell you what happened. He was afraid of a certain family down there that was out to kill him, and they nearly got him, except my father was too damn tough for their poison to work. He was a drinkin' man, you see, and his stomach was made of pure cast iron. He wouldn't die. After a couple of days laid out sick, he took off, rode the rails out west, and settled here in California. He figured they'd never find him out here.

"This here family that wanted to kill him, they were bad people. They had a vendetta against my father because they said he was messin' with the wife of the man who tried to poison him. Whether it's true or not, I don't know, but they were very powerful folks back in those days and they had eyes and ears everywhere. The woman was a witch, a mambo."

Annie looked at Beau. "A mambo?"

"Yeah. You know, a voodoo priestess."

Annie shook her head.

"Her husband wanted to kill my father, and tried to poison him, but he survived. My father had no choice but to run far and fast. He let everybody think he was dead so they would forget about him. But he never figured on his music living on for so many years. He underestimated the value of his music, but you and me know it's worth big money."

Annie kept a poker face. "But we need some more proof, Mr. Dodds. This just isn't enough."

Leeland finished his beer and produced another paper from the envelope, this one much more dog-eared and worn than the first.

From the way he handled it, Annie could sense that Leeland thought it was pretty important. He passed it to Annie with a flourish, obviously convinced that his guests would be impressed.

"Maybe this is more of what you're looking for," Leeland said.

Annie unfolded it, Beau peering over her shoulder. Their eyes played down the paper, much of it faded and barely readable. It had been folded many times, and the paper was nearly split in some places. It was some kind of official document, so faint that the handwritten parts were little more than ghosts of words.

Annie read aloud: " 'STATE OF MISSISSIPPI DEPARTMENT OF HEALTH AND VITAL RECORDS, STANDARD CERTIFICATE OF DEATH, State File number 13704, Leflore County, City of Greenwood (outside), Robert L. Johnson.' Here the page is divided in half. The left half says 'PERSONAL AND STATISTICAL PARTICULARS' and the right half says 'MEDICAL CERTIFICATE OF DEATH.' The left side has most of the writing, so I'll read that first. 'Male, black, single, twenty-six years year of age, date of death—August sixteenth, 1938.' It's signed by Jim Moore, Informant. Informant?"

"Read on."

Annie cleared her throat and continued. "Undertaker—family. Burial, cremation or removal—Zion Church, August seventeenth, 1938, filed on August eighteenth by Carnelia J. Jordan."

"Now look on the right hand side."

Annie's eyes scanned the page. The section listing the cause of death was blank except for the words "no doctor" written at an angle across the page. "No doctor," Annie read aloud.

Leeland looked pleased. "Signed by F. E. Thompson, Jr., state health officer. And it's got the great seal of the state of Mississippi right on the top."

Annie handed it to Beau. "This is Robert Johnson's death certificate."

Leeland nodded. "It says it right there in black and white. No doctor. No cause of death. No undertaker. Nobody pronounced the man officially dead. Family took him away. See? Just like I said."

✋ TEN ✋

The man claiming to be Robert Johnson sat in a leather chair in the law offices of Rosenbach, Lyman, Fong, and Ross, one of the few truly multiracial law firms in San Francisco. He was tired, his feet hurt, and he wanted some coffee. Annie Sweeny went to get him some while two senior partners, curious about their new mystery client, asked questions.

Robert Johnson answered the ones he could, and the ones he couldn't he let crash and burn without so much as a shrug. Earl Ross, a black lawyer who'd known Annie's father, led the interrogation from the glass table of the firm's conference room. Another partner, Lewis Fong, was present as well. Robert Johnson made himself as comfortable as possible, folding like a sack of old clothes into his chair.

Beau sat in the corner, watching.

"Mr. Johnson, is it true you have no Social Security number and no bank account?"

"Hell yes, it's true. I never had one in my whole life. I don't trust banks, you know."

"But where do you cash your checks?"

"The liquor store."

"The liquor store?"

"Sure, they know me there."

"But what about sums over, say, five hundred dollars—surely a liquor store wouldn't cash a check for more than five hundred dollars?"

Robert Johnson nodded. "Ain't never had no check for over five hundred dollars." Annie returned with the coffee, and Robert Johnson took it gratefully, commenting with a grunt.

Earl Ross pressed on, taking notes as he went. "And you have no birth certificate?"

"Ha! Don't you believe I was born?"

"Well, yes, we do, Mr. Johnson, but we need proof."

"I'm the proof. I'm here, ain't I?"

Earl shrugged and looked at the others. Lewis Fong picked up the questioning next. "That's all the proof I need, Mr. Johnson, but it's not that simple. We need something we can take to a court of law."

Robert drank his coffee.

"Do you know when and where you were born?"

"May eighth, 1911, in the state of Mississippi." Earl wrote that down. "Good, that's a start. Where in Mississippi?"

"I don't know, I was only a little baby at the time."

Lewis Fong cleared his throat. "Mr. Johnson, we're trying to help you—there could be hundreds of thousands of dollars coming to you if we can prove who you are. Are you aware that the Crawlin' Kingsnakes and other top rock acts have recorded some of your songs?"

Robert Johnson shook his head.

"Do you know who the Crawlin' Kingsnakes are?"

Robert Johnson shook his head. "Never heard of 'em. You got anything stronger I could put in my coffee?"

Lewis Fong looked at his partner and shook his head slightly. "I'm afraid not," he said.

"Too cheap, eh? Where I come from it's good manners to offer a man a shot of whiskey when he comes to call."

Earl Ross smiled. "I'm sorry, we have no whiskey here, but I'll tell you what, if we can get some business done this afternoon, I'll take you out and buy you that shot. And a couple others."

For the first time since he had been in the room, Robert Johnson smiled. He smiled broadly and without reserve, showing all of his aged, yellow teeth. "All right. Let's get crackin'."

Earl Ross folded his hands and gently began to probe the limits of Robert Johnson's memory. "We need to find some link, some proof that we can show to a judge that says you are who you say you are. We believe you, but we need to get others to believe you."

Robert Johnson nodded. "There ain't much. My mother's name was Julia Dodds. She had ten other children besides me to Mr. Charlie Dodds, but I was illegitimate, at least that's what I was told. We lived on a plantation, growin' cotton. My mother told me a story of how they once lived in a place called Hazlehurst before I was born, and Charlie had some trouble with a lynch mob and had to sneak out of town dressed as a woman. My mama traveled around workin' on different plantations until she had me. My daddy was a man named Noah Johnson. I never saw much of him. We were livin' in Robinsonville, but I always wanted to go to Memphis. You gettin' all this?"

Lewis Fong looked up from his notebook and nodded. Earl Ross had a cassette tape recorder going as well. "Please continue," he said.

"When I got old enough I bought me a guitar, a big old Kalamazoo model, and just started playin'. I guess you all heard the legend?"

"The legend?" asked Lewis.

Robert Johnson sipped his coffee. His long fingers wrapped like a wrinkled brown snake around the mug. "The legend about me sellin' my soul to the devil so's I could play the guitar that good."

Earl Ross sat forward, looking deep into the old man's face. A lifetime of pain was etched there, as deep and clear as the erosion on the banks of the mighty Mississippi River. He'd heard about the legend—what blues aficionado hadn't? Robert's song "Crossroads" told the story.

"What about it?"

The old man waited a few beats, his timing impeccable from a lifetime of twelve-bar blues, then said, "Well, it's true."

Annie and Beau couldn't stop talking about the lawyers' meeting. They dropped Robert Johnson at his house in Hayward and drove back to Berkeley. Beau found a rare nonmetered parking place on a side street off Telegraph Avenue. They walked a few blocks to the Cafe Mediterranean. The espresso machines gurgled and breathed, filling the air with a wonderful aroma. Beau ordered two caffè lattes, and they found a seat in the balcony, overlooking the front door.

"I'm glad Leeland wasn't there," Annie said, sipping her drink. "He could have really muddied the waters."

"What did you think?"

"I thought it went OK." Looking down through the huge windows, to the street below, Annie watched the ebb and flow of freaks along Telegraph.

Beau gave a thoughtful look. "My mind is still on the murders. I spoke with Slim today. He's been talking to that detective, George Jones."

"Any news?"

"No new news. But at least he's got Jones's ear. I'm worried because I think Slim himself might be a target. Remember, the last two murders occurred just after we were with the victims. That means he's probably seen us, heard our music, and been close enough to get to Slim."

Annie looked down to see Earl Ross enter the café. "I told Earl we'd be here," she said. She waved. Earl looked up and saw them in the balcony. He climbed the stairs and found their table.

"Don't get up. I can only stay a moment."

Annie said, "How did you rate the meeting with Robert Johnson?"

Earl's face was solemn. "Not very good, I'm afraid. We don't have much to go on at this point. The death certificate is the only document I've seen. I'm not giving up, mind you, but I think we have a long hard road before we can begin to recover any money. I just want to ask you one question before we really get into this thing with both hands."

Annie tried to sound upbeat. "Sure. What is it?"

"Are you completely convinced this guy is who he says he is?"

Annie nodded vigorously. "Absolutely."

"In your heart of hearts?"

"I'm positive."

Earl leaned back in his chair and let his gaze wander from Annie to Beau and back again. "As long as you're sure. I know your dad would have put his ass on the line if he believed in what he was doing."

Beau asked, "What can we do to help?"

Earl raised an eyebrow. "I do have one idea. It's somewhat unorthodox, but I think it might make a difference. What we need now is someone who's an expert on Robert Johnson to come out and make a public statement, someone who can rally some support for the cause."

"Who did you have in mind?"

Earl smiled. "Well, it just so happens I spoke with a colleague of mine who might be able to help. This man is the American legal representative for the English rock band known as the Crawlin' Kingsnakes. He said that one of the band members, a Mr. Heath Pritchard, is an acknowledged expert on the music of Robert Johnson. He suggested a meeting with Mr. Pritchard."

"Wow!" Beau almost shouted. "Heath? He's one of my idols. You look up rock and roll in the dictionary, and there's a picture of Heath. The Kingsnakes have been gods since the original British Invasion. They are the undisputed champs."

Earl responded with a shrug. "Apparently a lot of people feel that way. Mr. Pritchard's opinion would open a lot of doors."

"No way Heath is gonna see us," Beau said. "The Crawlin' Kingsnakes are the biggest band in the world."

"Actually, the band is in town for a few days to record some demos over in Sausalito. I was able to obtain a short appointment tomorrow afternoon. Nothing fancy, just a quick meeting to see if he's interested in helping our case."

Beau stood. "Are you kiddin' me? We get to meet the Kingsnakes?"

Earl smiled. "Well, not exactly. Just Ms. Sweeny."

"I should've known." Beau looked crestfallen.

Earl turned back to Annie. "Jake Sweeny's reputation precedes you. He sent some rare blues recordings to Mr. Pritchard several years ago, and Mr. Pritchard remembered the name."

"You're gonna meet the Crawlin' Kingsnakes," Beau almost pouted. "I'm jealous."

*   *   *

Heath Pritchard reached for a hard pack of Marlboros while he fine-tuned a guitar. The skull ring on his right hand gleamed dimly with a quick silver flash from the recessed overhead lights as he picked out notes.

He lit the Marlboro and let it dangle from his mouth while he wrestled the guitar down into an open G tuning, a Heath Pritchard trademark. The years since their first album, *Meet the Crawlin' Kingsnakes,* had lined his face many times over. The creases deepened as he squinted to keep the smoke out of his eyes. But the smile came through. Heath had an incredibly soulful smile. That was the same smile he cracked when he first heard the news from Annie Sweeny.

"It's not possible," was all he said.

"I'm just telling you what I know. The lawyers said you'd be able to tell. They said you'd be one of the few people anywhere that would know, right away, if it was a hoax," replied Annie.

Heath was a man of few words, and he didn't like repeating himself, so he just grunted and didn't bother looking up from the Conn Strobe-tuner in front of him.

"According to our research, this man's the real thing," explained the pretty blues journalist. "He's been living here in California for the last thirty-nine years, hiding out."

Heath finished tuning and plugged the vintage sunburst Fender Telecaster into a 150-watt Marshall head, turned a few knobs with practiced proficiency, and struck a chord. The sudden loud sound made Annie jump.

"Bullshit," said the Crawlin' Kingsnakes guitarist.

The conversation was over. Heath Pritchard would talk no more. The time had come to play some music. One of the secrets to the Crawlin' Kingsnakes longevity and success: when the music started, everything else stopped. Shut up and play. They got down to business like no other band in the history of rock and roll. Personal problems were left at the door; these guys came to play. While other bands fell by the wayside for one reason or another, music became the glue that held the Snakes together. And when the Beatles were busy breaking up over women, business, and egos, the Snakes crawled on oblivious. Like Heath said, if women got in the way of the band, the band got new women; if management got in the way of the band, the band got new management; if the record company got in the way of the band, the band got a new record company. The Crawlin' Kingsnakes were more than just a band, they were a way of life.

The recording studio reverberated with the chunky sounds of Heath's guitar in the open G-tuning. The Snakes were cutting demos for their next album. Annie stood there for as long as she dared, saying nothing, waiting for some kind of an answer.

Heath ignored her.

"What should I do?"

"What would old Dad do?" Heath flicked the ash from his Marlboro and cocked his head. "Lemme play with 'im. I'll tell ya if he's for real."

Annie walked back to the control room, where Rick Dagger was busy explaining something to the recording engineer. Rick looked up, didn't smile, and asked a one word question. "Well?"

None of these guys spoke too much, Annie thought, no more than three or four sentences since she'd arrived. They'd probably said all they had to say years ago, and now they just let the guitars do the talkin'. At least they'd let her in, which was more than she'd expected. Annie looked at the most famous rock singer in the world and chose her words carefully, not wanting to upset the delicate, spare balance of conversation the two Englishmen had established.

"He says if he plays with him, he'll know."

Rick nodded. "Yeah, that makes sense."

He turned his attention back to the recording console for a moment, then looked back at Annie. His face showed no emotion that she could see. She read nothing there, just the cool, impassive mask that had played to millions of people.

"You realize what a ridiculous story that is, don't you? That the legendary Robert Johnson is still alive."

The recording engineer, a swarthy little man named Reggie Fallon, looked up from the tape deck. He couldn't help but overhear. The mention of Robert Johnson grabbed his attention. Reggie had been hired by the Snakes, flown in from Chicago, because of his long association with the blues. He specialized in guitar tones. Reggie quickly went back to threading the two-inch multitrack tape.

Annie shrugged. "I didn't make it up. I've seen him with my own eyes, heard him with my own ears."

Rick's face remained vacant, his infamous lips held tightly together. He looked Annie over, letting his eyes drift up and down her slim torso. Annie knew better than to talk now. She let the situation play itself out. She wasn't used to rich international superstars and couldn't figure out how to act in their presence. She decided just to be herself, and it seemed to be working.

Rick's massive lips moved like sea anemones. "There are only two pictures of Robert Johnson that I know of, and they were taken almost forty years ago, when the man was in his twenties. People change in forty years."

Annie flashed the well-known photographs in her mind's eye—one of a handsome young black man in a pin-striped suit sitting cross-legged with a guitar in his hands, fingers stretched into an A7th chord, a curious smile beneath haunted eyes, a wide-brimmed fedora set at a jaunty angle on his head; and the other with a plain white shirt and cigarette, more of a mug shot. They were enduring images.

Someone came in with a platter of fruit and some mineral water, placing it on a small table next to the console. Rick Dagger took a banana and absently began to peel it.

Annie made sure that he wasn't going to speak again before she continued. "It all boils down to the music."

"What proof do you have?"

"Hardly any. I came up with a possible signature on a recording contract, but it's highly suspect. A man named Art Satherley conducted a recording session in a hotel room in San Antonio in 1936 for a company called ARC. Robert Johnson recorded several songs that day and signed an agreement."

Rick was listening. Annie continued. "I ran a comparison of the two signatures, the one from 1936 and one from last week, with a handwriting expert, and he said that it's possible that they could have come from the same person. Of course, that won't hold up in court, or anywhere else for that matter. So, like I said before, we've got nothing but a hunch and the word of an old man who can play the guitar like a demon."

Annie stopped talking. She got the impression that she'd already said too much, something she had promised herself she wouldn't do. Rick opened a mineral water and nodded at the studio, where the band was striking up a steady blues-style shuffle.

"Well, if anybody can tell . . . he can," he said looking at Heath through the double glass partition. The famous guitarist was bopping around the room like a teenager, playing his Tele, pushing the band. It looked like they were having a lot of fun in there. Annie could hear the music right through the wall, without the monitor speakers being turned up. Rick pointed at Heath. "The man lives and breathes Robert Johnson. He'll be able to tell from the inside out."

✋ ELEVEN ✋

The knock came to King Washington's door as he was about to close his office. He looked through the glass and saw a ghostly white figure in a black overcoat. Pink eyes stared back at him through the dusty, streaked glass. Without smiling he waved, cussing under his breath.

He unlocked the door and let Vincent Shives inside.

King Washington didn't let Vince get too close. The vibes coming off of the pale man were as thick as radio waves. Vince broadcast on the psychotic wavelength with fifty thousand hard-edged watts. He slid into the room and took a seat in front of King's battered desk. Piles of papers and stacks of records obscured the big black man's face, hiding the thinly disguised scowl, as King sat down.

They said nothing for several moments. Rainwater dripped off Vince's face. King Washington slowly leaned back and put his feet up on the big gray surface. The leather chair under him squeaked like the door to hell opening. He relaxed into his favorite pose, hands behind his head, a dead cigar clenched between his teeth.

He hadn't expected to see Vincent Shives, and he didn't particularly like the gaunt weirdo. There had always been a built-in distance. Vince cowered before King Washington.

"Mr. Shives. How pleasant to see you." King's resonant voice lied.

"Thanks, Mr. Washington. So much has happened since we last met."

I'll bet it has, you nutcase, King thought automatically. "The

Mojo Hand is strong stuff, eh? I told you, if you listen to me, I'll teach you the secrets. You got it with you?"

Vince nodded. He reached into the pocket of his capelike greatcoat and carefully removed the Mojo Hand from between the folds. He held it up proudly, smiling like a maniac. "See? See how good it is? It's a real nice one. Here, touch it."

He handed the thing to King, who took it cautiously. He sniffed it, felt its weight. He poked at it for a few moments and looked up. "This is the real thing here, Vinny-boy. You got the genuine article. No wonder it's been workin' so good. I think it's time we had a little talk."

Vincent looked away shyly. There was something else on his mind. "Did you talk to Reggie Fallon yet? Is the studio gonna be available soon? Reggie's the best engineer in town. I want him to record me. He's worked with everybody. Really knows his guitar tones, knows how to make that sucker sing."

"You got new material?"

"Oh, yeah. I got some truly great shit, I swear it. I'm touched now. I definitely got the magic. People are scared of me."

"I don't doubt that, Vincent. Not for one second." King paused, sucking a great breath through his massive lips and fixing his critical gaze on pale Vincent. "I don't think it's the right time to record you yet. You're almost ready, but not quite. I'm gonna give it a little more time. You been playin' like I told you? With the Mojo Hand out, palm up?"

"Yes, sir," Vince replied. "Everything just like you told me. And it works real good. Everything happened perfectly, just like you said."

"Good. Did you do everything Ida John told you?"

"Yeah, I followed every direction, I was real careful," Vince whined, his voice modulating upward slightly. "But . . . but . . . you said I could make a record soon, as soon as the engineer got back. You said we're gonna use the same studio where Art Spivey and Bobby Bostic worked. And we could go all night. Nights is when I'm the best."

King Washington looked unhappy. "Ah, Vincent. You're movin' too damn fast, boy. These things take time. You gotta be patient. Didn't I tell you I worked with 'em all and I know what I'm doin'?

You need a little more seasoning, you ain't quite there yet. Now, don't get me wrong, I still know you're one of the best damn guitarists in town—"

"*The* best, not one of the best, *the* best," Vince interrupted.

"Yeah, *the* best, I ain't sayin' you ain't. But you still gotta suffer some more, especially if you want to be the king. I still have every intention of making your first album soon, but you can't push me on this. I know what I'm doin'."

"When's Reggie Fallon gonna be ready?"

King played with his cigar. "Reggie's workin' with the Crawlin' Kingsnakes, man. You want him to give that up to work with you? No offense, but that's crazy. He's makin' top dollar now."

Vince squirmed. "You're the only one who has ever seen or heard me play . . . that's left alive."

King raised an eyebrow, but let that statement slide.

"You know how good I am," Vince continued, "and now I got the magic happenin' for me. You promised I could make a record soon. That's the whole point. I want to record now!"

King turned ugly. His voice became menacing and flat. "You don't talk to me like that! I give the orders around here!" The room shook with King's voice, as deep and ominous as that of the devil himself. Vince feared him when he spoke like that. "Everything you got happenin' is 'cause of me, ain't it? I rule your shitty life, and don't you forget it! There's a lot you got to learn, Vinny-boy, a whole hell of a lot. I arranged for you to get the Mojo Hand, didn't I?"

"Uh-huh."

"So shut up and listen." He took his big feet down and leaned forward. "If you want to be the king, then do what I say. This pre-production stuff is expensive. You don't think those guys at the studio work for nothin', do ya? There's gonna be expenses if you want to record. It's gonna cost you."

He knew he had Vince by the balls. He could extract money from this wimp almost without trying. He handed the Mojo Hand back to Vince.

"How much?" The albino's voice was as timid and nonthreatening as he could make it.

King Washington leaned back again and relit his cigar. Great billows of blue smoke drifted into Vince's face. Vince looked at the floor. "Six grand. Three grand to get the project started and three grand for the studio. You think you can come up with that kind of money?"

"Sure. I can get it. No problem."

"Where?" sneered King.

"Same way I got the money for the Mojo Hand," came the reply. "I'll steal it."

"You're damn right you'll steal it. You'll do anything I tell you to do."

He continued sucking on the cigar, emitting intermittent billows of smoke, making sure they hit Vince in the face. "Six big ones, Vince, and that's not counting the actual cost of making the album, you understand. That's just start-up money. The studio's gonna cost at least ten grand when we start recording . . . up front. Then there's my fee. Making records is expensive business."

"I can do it."

"I know you can, Vincent. I can see it in your soul. I can see many things. You can achieve anything you want, but you gotta do exactly as I say." His face grew dark again suddenly. "I have the power, remember that. Don't cross me, white boy."

He slid the desk drawer open and took something out. Vince looked up as the black man threw an envelope on the desktop. "Take this. Open it when you get home. When you see what it is, then use your brain and figure out what I want you to do. Don't call me and don't mess around. Figure it out and do it right away."

"What if . . ."

"No what-ifs, just do it. If you're too stupid to figure it out then you don't deserve the power."

Vince made no reply.

King Washington stood up and walked to the door. He put his hand on the knob and looked at Vince. Vince stared at him dumbly for a second, then quickly got up and started to leave. He put the Mojo Hand back in his coat pocket.

King smiled. "Good. See? I didn't have to say a thing. You just got the message. That's the way you got to be, Vincent. You gotta read people. You gotta read situations." He stopped talking and reached into his pocket. "Come over here, Vinny-boy."

Vincent came right up close to King Washington, closer than King wanted him to be. King could smell him. The weird albino had a strange, musty odor.

Vince stood directly in front of him, wondering what would happen next. He waited there obediently while the big man fished something out of his trouser pockets.

He extracted a small bottle from his pants and twisted the cap open. He moved swiftly and efficiently, his fingers suddenly becoming purposefully nimble. Vincent barely had time to see what was in the bottle when King stuck his finger in and smeared the contents onto Vince's forehead. His index finger stopped at the bridge of Vince's nose, paused there for second, then withdrew. It had drawn a line, the width of his finger, down the front of the albino's face, starting at his hairline and ending up at his nose. Vince stepped back, not knowing what had just happened.

He looked at King's finger. The tip was smeared crimson red. It looked like blood.

"Don't wash it off for seven hours."

Vince looked at him with new fear. King Washington made a sign with his hands. "Now go. And don't come back till you know."

Stunned, Vince's mouth hung open. King Washington glared at him, his eyes glistening wildly and his nostrils flaring. "Look for a sign, Vinny-boy."

Vincent hurried back out into the night wearing the bizarre war paint. The rain had stopped. The asphalt shone black and reflective. He hurried along, keeping to the shadows, not wanting to be seen. The envelope filled his pocket and the northern hemisphere of his face tingled and ached where King's finger had touched him.

King Washington closed the door and locked it. He took the cigar out of his mouth and laughed.

The phone rang behind him, and King went to his desk to answer. "Yeah?"

"This is Reggie. You better sit down. You're not gonna believe this. . . ."

* * *

Vincent didn't wipe the blood off his face—he was afraid to. It dried on the way home. No one gave him a second look. He turned the corner and darted into his apartment house.

When he opened the door to his apartment, the stench of the kitchen hit him immediately. The dehydrated remains of a pizza sat on the counter. Roaches climbed out of an old Chinese food container, ignoring his presence completely. The sink was heaped with dirty dishes, since Vince didn't have time to clean anymore.

He was too busy. Life had become too short to waste time with bullshit like housekeeping. He went to the refrigerator, opened it, and took out a budget-brand beer. He popped the beer on his way to the living room. The National Steel sat up in his easy chair, waiting for him.

"Been waitin' long?" he asked it.

He put on a B. Bobby Bostic record and chugged the beer. Vincent looked at himself in the mirror. A stranger looked back at him. His feverish pink eyes burned with manic intensity. The pale skin on his face was stretched taut, pulled across the bones of his cheeks like pallid shrink-wrap. The living skull in the mirror grinned.

He sat down and drained the beer, gently stroking the neck of the guitar. He took the envelope from his pocket and put it on the arm of the chair. He took the Mojo Hand from his pocket and put it on his lap. The more he got to know that hand, the more beautiful it became. He could stare at it for hours.

He turned his attention back to the envelope. *Be smart,* he told himself, *use your head, read the situation. Look for a sign.*

He opened the envelope. Inside were some airline tickets.

✋ TWELVE ✋

Stu Kweeder called Beau from the medical examiner's office. "You still interested in the Bobby Bostic murder? I've got some information you might find interesting."

Beau's eyes lit up. "Absolutely. Where can we meet?"

"I know a little burger place in San Rafael. I can be there in an hour."

Beau jotted down the address. One hour later he was sitting across from Stu at a tiny table in the corner of Mud Flaps. Stu munched a hamburger and spoke between bites. "The more I looked at this case, the more weird stuff I found."

Beau ordered a beer with hand signals. "Like what?"

"Take a look at this." He slid a manila folder across the table. "It's the Bostic autopsy."

Beau scanned the pages for a few moments while Stu attacked his meat patty. "What does this all mean?"

"In a nutshell, it means that B. Bobby Bostic's murder was extremely bizarre."

Beau looked confused as he scanned the pages.

"Take a look at the schedule of forensic trace evidence." Stu pointed to a page that had been stapled to the rest of the report. "There."

Beau ran his finger down the list. "What's all this? Manoaldehyde? Paraformaldehyde? Carpobol? I never heard of this stuff."

"Those are chemicals used in embalming."

"Embalming chemicals? How could that be?"

Stu shrugged. "I have no idea. I'm just showing you what they found. Which is highly illegal, by the way."

"I appreciate it, man. But I don't want you to get in trouble."

"As long as you don't tell anybody, it'll be fine."

Beau scanned the list. "How about this one—dead skin tissue? Sounds pretty ghoulish."

"Yeah, but that's what they found." Stu smiled.

Beau said, "Sounds like some dead guy committed the murder."

Stu laughed, short and unpleasant. "Yeah. Attack of the zombies."

Beau kept reading. "Murder weapon—four straight razors spaced one and a quarter inches apart? What the hell?"

"A homemade, one-of-a-kind weapon for sure. The edges made quite a distinctive cut pattern."

Beau whistled low. "Bizarre. Would you say these wounds would be easy to match on another victim?"

"Absolutely. Like a fingerprint."

"Has George Jones seen this?"

Stu nodded. "He's seen it."

Beau sipped his beer. "I didn't expect this, let me tell you."

"How could you? This is the weirdest autopsy report I've ever seen, and I've seen a lot."

"What do you make of all this?"

Stu finished his burger and wiped his mouth. "What do I think? I think there's something truly disturbing about the whole thing. I can't imagine how that stuff would show up. If I were Jones I might be thinkin' cults, devil worship, or voodoo. Something like that. Nothing normal, that's for sure."

"Autopsies are mandatory in murder cases, aren't they?" Beau asked. Stu nodded. Beau waited a few seconds to ask his next question. "Would you do me a favor?"

"Depends."

"Can you contact coroners in other cities?"

"Sure," Stu said. "I do it all the time."

"I think there've been at least two other murders like this. One in Chicago and one in St. Louis."

"Do you have the names and dates? Case numbers would really help too."

"Names and dates I can probably get," Beau said. "Case numbers . . . I don't know."

"Give me what you can and I'll see what I can do." Stu's facial expression became odd. He seemed to be suppressing a smile with a veneer of embarrassment. "But I want something in return."

"I can't pay you, if that's what you mean."

Stu waved his hand as if swatting away a fly. "Nah, that's not it. I wanna get backstage."

Beau looked bemused. "Backstage where?"

"Backstage anywhere. Just backstage. You see, for guys like you it's a common thing. You don't even think about it. But for me, hell, for most people, backstage is a mysterious, sacred place. I've never been backstage in my life. I've always wanted to go there."

It was Beau's turn to laugh. "Backstage at a blues show is nothin' special, let me tell ya."

"I don't care. I just wanna be part of that exclusive club. I want an 'all access' pass. I wanna be backstage, man."

"You help me and you'll be living backstage, man. At least any show I'm playin' at."

Stu stuck out his hand. "Shake on it."

Beau grabbed Stu's hand. "Deal."

Beau met Annie in the parking lot at Spenger's, near where he and Tom had smoked a joint. They walked inside together. Oakland Slim was already seated in the Teak Room.

"Thanks for coming," Slim said. They all took seats around a long wooden table. The remnants of a meal were still scattered there. "What did you find out?"

Beau leaned forward. "A lot. I talked to my buddy at the medical examiner's office. He said Bobby's wounds were caused by a very bizarre weapon. Something with four straight razors spaced an inch and a quarter apart. It shreds the victim. And it's homemade."

Slim gaped. "Jesus."

Beau continued. "He's working on getting the autopsy reports for Spiderman and Piano Red. If they match, it proves we're on the right track. I can go to Jones with it."

Slim shook his head. "I can't figure that Jones guy out. He acts so cagey. I can't tell if he cares or not."

"He's read the autopsy report. Maybe he's already checking out the others."

Slim snorted. "He's probably doin' nothin' and gettin' paid for it."

"You just don't like cops."

Slim rubbed his soulful eyes with the palms of his hands. He looked up, suddenly world-weary and tired. "I've been arrested a few times in my life, man. You never feel the same about cops after that. I got nothin' against Jones personally. I hope he solves the murder. I just don't expect it to happen."

Beau said, "What I want to know is why. Why would somebody do this?"

Slim's voice rumbled like a greasy truck engine. "Because whoever this guy is, he wants to kill the blues. He wants to wipe out the legacy. He's a psycho. And he only kills the greats. That makes him even more dangerous."

"You think this guy could be a blues musician himself?" Annie asked.

Slim and Beau exchanged glances. "Maybe."

"And he thinks that by killing all the masters, he'll be the king of the blues?"

"That's one possibility."

Annie slipped her hand into Beau's. He affectionately rubbed the back of her wrist with his thumb. Slim saw it. He said, "You two seem to be gettin' pretty friendly."

Beau blushed. "Well . . . Yeah, I guess we are."

Slim turned to Annie. "You actually like this guy?"

Annie nodded. "Why shouldn't I?"

"Because he's carryin' more baggage than the Chattanooga Choo Choo."

Annie recoiled in horror. "No! A musician with emotional baggage? Impossible."

Beau laughed. "I already told her everything, man."

Slim leveled his gaze at Annie. "Divorce, drugs, bankruptcy, shame, scandal, prison . . ."

"Prison?" Annie said.

"He's joking. I've never been in prison."

Slim smiled at his little joke, then changed the subject back to the murders. "I keep askin' myself what Travis McGee would do."

"He'd probably do exactly what I'm doing, start with the coroner and follow the leads."

Slim said, "Oh, I forgot to tell you, Murray the agent called. He offered us a gig this weekend. A last-minute cancellation. I took it."

"Great. I need the money. Where is it?"

"New Orleans. We're fillin' in for Ed Green at the Blues Grotto down in the French Quarter. I've played the Grotto a bunch of times. It's a great place. You'll love it. The food is excellent, too."

Annie made a sour face. "How long will you be gone?"

Slim raised an eyebrow. "Couple days. Why?"

"Beau's agreed to help me with something."

Slim shook his head. "Got your hooks in him already?"

"I do not!"

"Relax, lady. Nothin' wrong with that. It's just that whenever a band member gets involved with a woman, the next thing that happens is he quits. It happens all the time. Women don't like guys that travel, stay out late, and work in bars. It's just the way of the world. A woman needs her man to stay home. That's why more bands break up because of women than any other reason."

Annie bristled. "Oakland Slim! You old male chauvinist pig! I don't know who you're talkin' about but I have no problems with Beau traveling."

Beau raised his hand. "Hold on a second. You two are scaring me."

"If you knew what he was helping me with, you'd change your tune," Annie said.

"You gonna tell me?" Slim's tone was confrontational.

Annie looked directly into his eyes. "Robert Johnson is alive."

"What? That's crazy. Robert Johnson died years ago."

The smug smile on Annie's face replaced the look of disgust.

"That's what you think, but I happen to know he's right here in California, alive and kickin'."

Slim looked at Beau. "What's this all about?"

Beau said, "It's true. Apparently, the man is still alive. Annie discovered him playing at a Bar-B-Que place in Hayward. We're trying to prove his identity."

Slim laughed. "What are you guys smokin'? That's the most ridiculous thing I ever heard."

"If we can prove it, we'll set the blues world on its ear."

Slim shook his head. "What next? Well . . . look, you two stupid white kids, don't be messin' with things you know nothin' about. Robert Johnson made a deal with the devil. You can be sure, if Robert's really still alive like you say, that there's still a hellhound on his trail. If I were you, I'd let sleeping dogs lie."

When Beau got home there was a message from Stu Kweeder. He sounded excited. "Hey, man! You'll never believe this! Call me right away!"

Beau hastily dialed the number written on Stu's business card. The phone rang twice before Stu picked it up. "It's Beau."

"Rock on, man. I got some major news. There's been another murder."

"Holy shit."

"This one's in New Orleans."

"Don't tell me. Another bluesman?"

"Bingo. A guy named Edward Green."

Beau felt the skin of his face tighten. The dryness in the back of his throat crawled into his mouth. The odd feeling of destiny he'd carried around in his pocket since Art Spivey died had changed. Now it felt more like impending doom.

✋ THIRTEEN ✋

Ida John's handwriting was hard for Vince to read. The drawing seemed easy enough to understand though. He could see the palm lines she'd indicated, and all he had to do was match the ointment with each one.

The stuff in the bottles smelled awful. As soon as he cracked the seal on the first one and caught a whiff it made him gag. He hesitated painting it on the Mojo Hand. It would ruin the smell it already had, the one he'd grown so fond of. Vince felt reluctant to change the hand in any way. Everything had been working out so perfectly.

He sat there for half an hour, staring at the bottles and the hand, hesitant to carry out Ida's instructions. The woman scared him.

He picked up his National Steel and began to play. The bright, singular sounds of the metal guitar reverberated around his squalid apartment, bouncing off every hard, reflective surface like a ray of light off a mirror. His hands became steadier as he played, his heart calmed, and Vince relaxed. The tension that had been a part of his life, from the earliest age, subsided a little. The only time that ever happened was when Vince played.

Music was his only escape.

The more he concentrated, the more he forgot. In a world of pain, in a life of evil, playing music and being able to forget kept him going. Vince's memory burned. He sought to escape the flames whenever he could, and if it were possible to just sit in his apartment forever, the doors bristling with locks against the outside world, picking his guitar, he would.

Life had always been that way.

He worked his way along the guitar's fretboard, his fingers automatically forming the various patterns he'd learned over a lifetime of introversion. The incredible thing was that he'd managed to keep it all a secret.

Vince kept many secrets. He had been meticulously careful over the years that no one heard him play. His talent was his own, for his ears only. Besides King Washington, who had only heard tapes, only two other people had ever heard him play, and both of them were dead.

Albert DuBois and Missy Bingle, both deceased, were the only people who had ever heard the genius of Vincent Shives. Albert was the old man who had taught him, a black man who played the blues guitar and drank vanilla extract.

Albert had lived downstairs from Vince in the run-down apartment building he had lived in as a youth. To offset the time he was left alone by his mother, a cocktail waitress who seldom came home, young Vince drifted down to Albert's door. Drawn by the music, he became fascinated by the beautiful sounds that the old man could make with a slide and a National Steel. The tiny apartment reeked of vanilla. The old man wavered on his dilapidated wooden chair, rocking back and forth, slurring his speech and drooling, squinting at Vince.

The teenage Vince sat quietly watching the brown fingers make magic on the battered old slide guitar.

"You want to try, boy?"

Vince nodded.

"Then here, take it and do what I tell ya."

The weight of the guitar in his lap, still warm from Albert's body heat, thrilled him. He tentatively fingered it. Albert took Vince's young pale hands and pushed them roughly down on the strings, forming an E chord.

"Hit the chord," he commanded.

Vince pushed the pick down across the strings. The resultant sound was exquisite. Never in his wildest dreams had Vince thought he would be able to make such a sound. Beautiful and sinuous, it hung in the air, changing Vince's life forever. There was power in the sound. Vince could feel the energy tingling in his fingertips. A few seconds later the tingling turned to pain as the tightly drawn strings cut into his tender flesh, indenting his fingertips. Vince gamely kept his hands in the same position and hit another chord, willing his fingers to be like iron.

This time the chord was muted and irregular, not pure and pretty as it had been the first time. "Again!" the old man demanded.

Vince pushed the strings down with all his might now, but it seemed hopeless. Without the necessary calluses, his soft fingertips had no chance of making the magic come again. The strings seemed to sink into his flesh.

"Hold them goddamn strings down, boy! Hold 'em no matter what!"

Vince wanted to cry. The pain in his fingers was turning his hand numb, creeping up his arm and cramping his wrist and forearm. He strained to re-create the magic, giving it all the determination he had. His pink eyes darted from the strings to Albert's face and back again.

"Don't look at me! Look at the strings!"

Vince felt his hand begin to shake; a spasm twitched his palm, and even though he fought it every millimeter of the way, it began to spread up his arm.

Gritting his teeth, he tried in vain to keep the chord, but his hand lost contact and the fingers came up from the fretboard.

The back of Albert's strong, callused hand came out of the patterned wallpaper behind the rickety chair like a weighted sap. It struck Vince squarely across the face with a ferocity and measured violence far beyond anything his mother might do. Vince wheeled back but managed to hold the guitar, keeping it in the same position against all odds while his face was nearly torn off his body.

"I said look at the strings!"

Vince rubbed his cheek. The sting lingered. A spot of blood appeared at the corner of his mouth. Tears came to his eyes as he looked at the old man.

Albert twisted the cap off another tiny jar of vanilla and put the delicate brown neck to his thick, quivering lips. The pungent liquid flowed in, a drop or two dribbled down his chin, and Albert gasped. "Ahhh!"

Vince stared at him with a white, fearful face. He felt shocked, yes—the blow had been completely unexpected and he'd never been hit by anyone but his mother—but he was not repulsed by it. Coming so quickly on the heels of the ecstasy of the chord, the wonderful magic chord, the contrast made his head swim.

He realized that was the price you paid for making the beauty. He knew instinctively that this was what he wanted, what he had been waiting for all his life. The pain and the beauty were together.

"It's the only way to learn," Albert slurred in a cloud of vanilla and alcohol. "That's the way I learned and that's the way you'll learn. You can take it, can't you boy?"

Vince nodded.

"Good, I knew you could. I knew you would be different from most 'cause you're marked. You're a freak. I knew that you would be able to take the pain."

Again, Vince nodded.

"If you want to play the blues you got to suffer, and I believe by looking at you that you know about sufferin'. I hear your mama beatin' you at night. I hear the furniture gettin' pushed around. I know the bitch is drunk and out for blood, but what I don't hear is no cryin'. She beats the shit out of you but you don't cry. That means you can take pain, and pain is the name of the game."

Vince almost spoke, but the wisdom from the old man cut so deep and pure that he didn't want to break the spell. Everything Albert said was true.

"If you can take the pain, and if you stick with it, someday you'll be the king of the blues. You'll earn it. It won't come to you, you'll have to go out and take it. But it will be yours someday, I prophesize. Hear me, boy?"

Vince, still smarting from the blow, nodded yet again. His silence confirmed what Albert already knew. The boy wanted to learn, he had the temperament, and he had the capacity for suffering.

"You will learn it all. I'll teach you everything I know, then someday you'll be ready to take over the world. This guitar is a weapon, a weapon of magic. Never forget that. And if you take the beatin' and practice and play all the time, well, who knows? Maybe a white devil like you could actually do something."

Vince decided right then that he wanted the magic and he would endure the beatings until Albert beat it all into him. It was the only way to learn. He wanted it, because someday, greatness would come to him, because he had suffered.

"You gotta suffer if you want to play the blues. You want to suffer, boy?"

Vince's voice cracked as he answered, this time not with a nod, but a throaty, hurtful "Yes!"

Thus began the apprenticeship of Vincent Shives to Albert DuBois. Every day, when his mother left, he'd sneak down to Albert's apartment, where the smell of vanilla permeated the air, to suffer and learn. Sometimes Albert would tear into him with a vengeance, screaming about how he expected Vince to be better than the rest and how much Vince loved to suffer. When he hurt Vince a little too much, and the boy was unable to immediately play again, Albert explained that it had to be for his own good. And Vince believed him.

Suffering and blues came together in a marriage of pain and pleasure that transcended the beauty of the music. He used Albert's guitar. It would be a long time before he would acquire one of his own.

The years went by and Vince began to excel, but the beatings did not stop. The fact that Vince became an accomplished musician did little to alter the pattern of physical abuse. But Vince didn't want the beatings to stop—they were part of his education. They tempered his soul with the level of pain so necessary to play the blues.

Vince gave his all to the music, and his mother never knew. No one knew, and that was how it should be, according to Albert DuBois. "Never show your hand," he said. "Never let them see until you're ready."

At seventeen, Vince coveted a guitar. He wanted one in a way that he'd never wanted anything in his life. When he told Albert, the old man told him to wait. Something will happen, he said, and then you'll know that the time has come. All good things come to those who wait.

Vince waited. He even thought of getting a job, but in his heart of hearts he knew that would be impossible. His debilitating shyness and absolute terror of people he didn't know made such plans unrealistic. Vince was simply too introverted even to apply for one. Vince stayed off the streets because people ostracized him. The only place he ever went was to the used-record store, walking distance from his front door. Among the bins he found a respectable blues section. Vince spent countless hours staring at the covers, listening when the ones he liked were played in the store. King Washington came in now and then to collect money and replenish the stock, but he was mostly a shadowy figure. King's big Cadillac would be parked out front, announcing his presence. Vince recognized it, and overheard the clerk saying one day that "the blues bought him that car."

Vince walked home one day at dusk after visiting the store, and as he came into the vestibule of his apartment building he heard someone coming down the stairs. The landlord had been collecting the rents. He was an old and sickly man who smoked incessantly. His overweight bulk leaned on the banister like a sack of red potatoes. He looked down and saw Vince on the landing below. The landlord's breathing sounded strange. Vince thought the man looked sick. His face was grayish white and his hands trembled. He gasped and clutched his chest. In one hand he clenched an envelope full of money from the rents, everyone paid up except Vince's mother.

The landlord leaned over the railing and tried to say something, but Vince couldn't hear.

Vince rushed up the stairs and stood there helplessly while the landlord slid to the floor. "Help me . . . ," he croaked, and then slumped to his side.

The old man must be having a heart attack, thought Vince. Then he saw the envelope.

Vince had seen the envelope before, whenever the old man came to their apartment to collect the rent. He knew it would be stuffed with money.

The landlord died gasping and wheezing right there on the second-floor landing in front of Vince. Vince looked up and down the empty hall. He looked back at the envelope, still clutched in the landlord's hand. Without a second thought, Vince squatted down and took it. He slipped the envelope in his pocket and hurried on up the stairs, carefully stepping around the body. When he got to his mother's apartment he locked the door and examined the contents. Three hundred and twenty-five dollars. Vince hid the money, envelope and all, under the mattress of his bed.

Death had brought him the money he needed to buy a guitar. Just like Albert said, *When the time comes, you'll know.*

Now Vince knew.

Several days later he went to the pawnshop and bought an old Gibson six-string acoustic guitar. It was covered with nicks and scratches, but it sounded great. With a new set of strings it sang like the devil's jukebox.

Vince ran down to show Albert. He couldn't wait to see the old man's face when he saw it. Albert's door was unlocked, and Vince went in. It smelled like vanilla, as usual, but there was another smell too. Something bad.

He found Albert DuBois facedown on the bathroom floor, his pants at half-mast and his neck twisted into an unnatural position. Albert was dead. After never having seen a dead man his entire life, Vince had now seen two in three days.

He stood there with the new guitar in his hand and stared dumbly at the body. He couldn't believe it. His teacher, his mentor, dead. Vince backed out of the room feeling numb.

He thought all the things Albert had taught him, the most important being: *When the time comes, you'll know.*

Vince walked into the living room, picked up Albert's National Steel guitar, sat down in the chair he'd sat in a thousand times, and played. He played beautifully, his last recital, his final exam. The music had never sounded so good, so perfect. In the presence of death, Vincent Shives graduated from student to master. Now his apprenticeship was over. *When the time comes, you'll know.*

Without emotion, he finished the last song and walked out the door. He took the old man's National Steel with him. He left the

Gibson leaning against a chair, traded for another life. The landlord, the money, the Gibson. Albert, the lessons, the National Steel. Even Stephen.

Two weeks later Vince ran away from home.

The first person he ran into out in the world was Missy Bingle, a mulatto voodoo priestess. She took him in like a stray dog. Missy saw Vincent as a willing and easily controlled slave. To her, he seemed a perfect channeler of energy—a stooge, a zombie, someone completely submissive. His pink eyes and paper-white skin made him a most excellent foil for her magic. People thought Vince was something Missy had conjured up. She made him her white slave. Then she made him her lover. The superstitious folk feared her even more, the wild witch woman with her white devil lover. When they walked down the street together, people stepped away. Missy's power grew. She called it "sway."

Vince spent the next two years satisfying the aging witch, learning her craft and performing his own magic for her, his music. He liked to play for her, only her and no one else, showing off the beautiful blues licks he'd mastered from Albert. She showed him the relationship between the blues and voodoo, a tradition deep with hidden connections. Missy made Vince a man. His apprenticeship was complete.

The power of his music stoked their fire. He felt wanted—an alien emotion to the gangly albino. Missy became everything to him: mother, lover, master, teacher, employer, domineering mistress, and protector. Vince served her well, ready to die or kill for her without question. He never felt repulsed by having to satiate her. And when he kissed her sagging breasts and licked her wrinkled skin, he smelled the faint scent of dementia.

To Vince, Missy was beautiful. He loved her right up until the day she died. A bomb blew her into oblivion when she opened the door to her shop one morning. Vince never found out who did it, or why. Missy had so many enemies it would be impossible to know. Those who didn't fear her, hated her. Or both. Vince became an expert on those two emotions: fear and hatred.

* * *

Vince taught himself to play the piano and harmonica using Albert DuBois's method. He learned by self-inflicted pain.

And so it came to pass that the only two people ever to hear Vincent Shives play were dead. Until King Washington.

Used, abused, and lost in the blues. Vincent Shives reached manhood. Destiny reached out, grabbed him by the balls, and led him to the next plateau. Vince began to have visions.

He hunched over his guitar and let the world pass. He kept the memory of Albert and Missy bottled up inside. *You got to suffer if you want to play the blues,* Albert had taught him. Vince knew how to suffer. He played like a demon, faster and harder and darker and deeper. As long as the music played, Vince stayed in control.

Eventually, Vince got out the cotton swabs and set to work tracing the lines across the withered palm of the Mojo Hand. He smoothed out on the table the chart Ida had sent him, and studied it closely. Following the life lines, the lines of destiny, and the love lines, he dabbed the elixir in the deep grooves. Ida was very specific about every detail of the "awakening process." The brittle, dry skin of the palm drank up the potion, instantly absorbing every drop of the thick, hideous fluid on contact.

The hand sat motionless on the table before him, palm up. Vince waited for it to be born again.

✸ FOURTEEN ✸

King Washington ate at the same restaurant every Monday night, ordered the same thing, sat at the same table, and left the same tip. It was easy for the men he owed money to find him.

They walked up to his table and sat down without speaking, one on each side. The man on his right was Vito Guppi, the son of Salvatore Guppi, gangland boss. The one on his left was Vito's ghetto enforcer, Donnie "Diamondback" Dutton, a huge black man with a scar on his forehead and several prominent gold teeth. Built like a linebacker, Diamondback Dutton had an extremely nasty reputation. King swallowed.

Vito Guppi waited for king to put his spoon down and delicately dab his mouth with a napkin. "I don't like to come down here and deal with you people, but you leave me no other choice. Dutton says you're way behind. I wouldn't get involved except that certain people are now pissed off enough to make an example of you."

King Washington kept his exterior cool, but his stomach was suddenly awash with acid, mixing uncomfortably with the Chinese food. He forced a smile and carefully placed his napkin on the table. Hands steady, voice even, King Washington reached deep down inside and made the speech of his life. "Dutton shouldn't have to involve you, Mr. Guppi, it's unnecessary. He knows that I've been doing business in this town for a long time and I've never had a problem." He turned to Dutton and his voice became icy. "What were you thinkin' about?"

"I was thinkin' about tyin' your black ass to the whippin' post, chump."

Dutton began to stand as he said that, his voice rising above conversational tone. Vito motioned for him to sit. Several patrons stopped eating and stared. The waiter didn't know whether to edge toward the table or away from it. He decided to keep away. Vito Guppi looked around the room, making eye contact with more than one customer and causing them to turn away. People resumed eating, and Vito said softly, "Keep your voice down. You're attracting too much attention."

Dutton scowled.

"Something happened to my father a few days ago," Vito said softly, "and it really pissed him off. One of his collectors came back and said that the guy he was collectin' from couldn't pay up. So our guy starts leanin' on him, and you know what he says?"

King Washington shrugged.

"He says that he wants more time. He says, 'Hey, that King Washington, he gets more time! Why can't I have more time?' "

Vito looked into King Washington's eyes, both cold, like fish to fish. "Next thing I know, my father sends me out to have a little talk with you."

Dutton put his hands in his pockets. King watched with one eye. Vito's face remained impassive.

"Look, it's time for you to pay up, Washington. It's business. You made the bets, you lost. Your debt is becoming an embarrassment for us. People are saying we're soft, that we let people off the hook. Can't have that, can we?"

King Washington nodded. Twenty years ago he had held the Chicago record business in his clutch. Back then he'd schmoozed all the top gangsters. King had represented the black entertainment industry. He had represented glamour. All the hoods loved glamour. King could have snapped his fingers in those days and men would've died. He had provided the product for the thriving, Mob-run jukebox business in the early fifties. He had controlled the "race" records that were so popular among the teenagers. This would never have happened back then.

Not like now. King's stock had gone down considerably over

the past few years. Debts were piling up. On top of all that, King had taken to gambling to replenish the sagging bank accounts, but it had only made matters worse. His empire was crumbling at an alarming rate, and the bosses could smell a loser from a mile away. They stopped hanging out with him, and eventually began calling in their markers. Small debts became larger, larger debts then became insurmountable, insurmountable became life-threatening, and now he sat with two very unsavory characters who were giving him his last chance.

By his own estimation, King owed the Mob about a hundred thousand dollars. The debt had become a time bomb, waiting to blow his house of cards right off the table. He'd been procrastinating for years, buying time, hoping for a miracle, but guys like King Washington didn't get miracles anymore.

"I'm giving you three weeks. Pay up or make out your will," growled Dutton.

King Washington couldn't show weakness in front of Guppi. He had to make them both think he was still worth something in this town, that he could still generate money.

"You don't give me nothin'," King said to Dutton. "I been around this town a lot longer than you, and I pissed away more money than you'll ever make. Give me some respect. I've been dealin' with the Guppi family for years, and I don't need your bullshit crossin' me up."

Diamondback took his big hands out of his pockets and began to reach across the table to King's fat neck.

Vito moved as quickly as a ferret. In the time it took to imagine it, he brought the barrel of a stainless-steel .45 automatic up from under the table and, covering it partially with a napkin, pointed it in Dutton's face.

"Cool out, man," Guppi hissed. The lethal look in his eyes said he would shoot right there in front of all the people in the restaurant.

"I'll shoot you right here, don't think I won't. My old man could get me out of it, so it ain't no skin off my back. This is business, understand? Business is business. If my father finds out you did some unauthorized rough stuff, he'll show you what real rough stuff is. You wind up as pizza topping."

Dutton relaxed, his hands falling back down at his sides.

Guppi had everybody's number. A few people in the restaurant, catching a brief glimpse of the gun, quickly vacated the premises. Vito let his eyes scan the room quickly, unpleased at what he was seeing.

"You're making a scene," Guppi said softly. "Don't be such a hothead."

He slipped the gun back into the pocket of his expensive topcoat, but kept his finger on the trigger inside. He shook his head and let the faintest inclination of a smile crack his face.

"Italians and coloreds, what a mix, eh?"

Dutton fumed; Washington nearly laughed. The Italians and the blacks had been doing business a long time. Race or no race. Business would always be business.

Vito Guppi leaned forward in King's direction, dropped his voice into a confidential tone. "Dutton is a little concerned, 'cause he knows that if you don't pay up, then he's gonna be held responsible. You can understand his level of involvement, Mr. Washington. So I want you both to relax and concentrate on business, strictly business. OK? Now, here's the deal, it comes straight from the top. You got three weeks to come up with the entire amount or you get whacked."

Turning to Dutton, he said, in the same conspiratorial voice, "As for you, if he don't pay, the debt is transferred to your books, and the way I see it, your books couldn't support that kind of dough. Especially a two-bit punk like you. I don't know why I waste my time talkin' to you assholes. You're both probably gonna die, anyway. If I were you, Dutton, I'd work with this man here. I'd help him. I'd love him like a brother. Because he's your ticket to ride. And he's right, you should show him some respect. He's been dealin' with my family since before you were born."

Dutton's eyes were as wide as quarters. King could almost see the steam rising from his nostrils. The man had suddenly developed a facial tic and the side of his mouth began to twitch like a broken toy.

Vito looked down at King Washington's half-eaten chow mein. "How can you eat that crap? You should come downtown and have some nice pasta, you know?"

Vito stood up and walked out. Dutton got the message a few seconds later and pushed his chair away from the table as well. He stared at King Washington with eyes of stone. "I'll see you later," he hissed.

"Not if I see you first," replied Washington.

King Washington went home and packed his bags. He left for San Francisco that night. Things were getting too hot in Chicago. He knew the weather would be better on the Coast.

Arnett's recording studio was located in the Tenderloin neighborhood of San Francisco, behind a warehouse, on a street that could best be described as adventurous. Hookers stood on the corners harassing guys in cars, the drug dealers were out rain or shine, and the winos never went away. King Washington parked his rental car directly in front. The dented metal door to the brick warehouse building swung open.

Reggie Fallon hadn't changed much over the years—he still looked like a child molester crossed with an ax murderer. His mulatto skin was dotted with imperfections, as if he got a new pimple every time he screwed somebody. His big watery eyes looked sad all the time. Even though he'd been working with the Kingsnakes cutting demos, he still didn't have much of a career anymore. His rep carried him from gig to gig. But Reggie knew how to get killer guitar tones and work a budget, and that endeared him to King. The two men shook hands, and Reggie led him down a dark hallway into the control room.

Reggie booked Arnett's recording studio because it cost him next to nothing. Arnett's hadn't been able to keep up with the big boys and buy new state-of-the-art equipment when it came out. The place was stuck up in a time warp with an obsolete pair of four-track Ampex tape-recording machines and a control board that still had round dials on it instead of slide faders. The glory days of hit records coming out of this room were long gone. But the warm sound of the old tube-style amps and tape-delay slap reverb had been magic at one time. Reggie could still make the place sound great when he wanted to.

He sat in a squeaky chair in front of a cigarette-burned control board. A trash can overflowing with crumpled budget-brand beer cans stood against the wall. Reggie drained the one he was holding, crushed it, and flung it expertly at the pile. It landed precariously on top, teetered for a moment, and stayed.

"Nice shot," said King Washington.

Reggie let out a belch and cracked open another can.

"You don't seem too glad to see me."

Reggie spoke in labored breaths, as if every word were a big effort and he couldn't be bothered to put in the extra time. "Heard you were in deep shit, man."

King chuckled. "Good news travels fast," he said sarcastically. He lit a cigar and puffed until the end glowed angry red.

Reggie drained his next beer in three mighty swigs and heaved it onto the pile, which looked as if it couldn't take another can without disintegrating into an aluminum avalanche. "Got a business proposition for you."

King Washington smiled. "I'm listenin'."

"This Robert Johnson thing . . . it's gonna be big. I mean, really big. I did a little sniffin'."

"What's the proposition?"

"I can deliver this guy. No bullshit. I talked to his son. He says he can get the old man to sign for money. You make the deal with him, do whatever you want. I produce the records."

"What's the split?"

"I'll take points plus a percentage."

"How much?"

Reggie blinked. His beery eyes seemed to cross for a second. "How about forty?"

King Washington grinned. "I'm always open to negotiation, Reginald. You seem pretty cocksure that this old man is Robert Johnson."

"I don't care if he is or not. What matters is other people think it. But here's the punch line. Heath Pritchard and the Crawlin' Kingsnakes are gonna be involved. He works with them, we're gold."

"You're sure about this?"

"Sure as shit, man. I heard Heath Pritchard say he wanted to play music with the guy."

"Let's go see him right now."

Reggie looked at his watch. "Heath?"

King Washington reached out and rapped his knuckles against Reggie's forehead. "No. Robert Johnson, you peckerhead."

King Washington filled Robert Johnson's door like a black oak tree. He commanded a strong presence in his three-piece suit with a fresh red boutonniere. Reggie Fallon stood behind him. Leeland Dodds bared them welcome.

"Come on in, gentlemen. Make yourselves at home." Something about Leeland's left-handed handshake suggested desperation to King, who could predatorily sniff out the weak and diseased. Leeland seemed too eager, too accommodating. King said nothing about the missing arm.

King smiled broadly as he stepped into the tiny house. Beyond the entrance, Robert Johnson waited in the living room, folded into a La-Z-Boy recliner in the full recline position. Robert appeared to be asleep. He had a white cotton bib around his neck, so at King's first glimpse, the legendary bluesman resembled a customer at the barbershop, awaiting a shave.

"I'll wake him up," Leeland said. He shook Robert gently. "Hey, Pop, the men are here."

Robert opened his eyes. "The men?"

"Yeah, Pop. Remember?"

"The white men?" Robert raised the bib and wiped at some drool on the side of his mouth.

"No, Pop. The black men from the record company. The ones I told you about. They want to talk to you."

Leeland reached down and pulled on the chair's handle. Robert Johnson raised to a sitting position. "This chair keeps his feet up."

King Washington stepped forward and stuck out his hand. "Pleased to meet you, Mr. Johnson. I'm King Washington, president of Royal Records and Management. This is my associate, Mr. Fallon."

Robert looked at the offered hand and hesitated. "You sure?"

King laughed. He kept his hand out. "Yes, I'm sure. You want to see some ID?"

Robert reached out and shook King's hand tentatively. Leeland came around the side of the chair and spoke into Robert's ear like an interpreter. "These are the men I told you about. They might want to make a record with you."

Robert frowned. "What for?"

King Washington towered over them. His voice boomed. "What for? To make money! That's what for! Hell, I'm talkin' about a lot of money. Could you use a lot of money, Mr. Johnson?"

Leeland answered instead of his father. "We sure could. How much are you talkin' about?"

King raised an eyebrow. "Well, let's roll up our sleeves and have us a drink and talk this over." He reached into his pocket and withdrew a brown half-pint bottle of Old Grand-Dad.

Leeland acted as if he'd never seen booze before. "Whiskey? Well, I'll be damned. How do you like that? The man brought whiskey. You want a drink, Pop?"

Robert eyed the bottle suspiciously. "OK, let's hear what the man's got to say."

✋ FIFTEEN ✋

Beau stared at the ASCAP check in his hand. It represented his quarterly distribution of the writer's share for domestic airplay for his 1.5 hit records. Though he hadn't been on the *Billboard* charts since 1967, his two compositions still garnered occasional airplay and had been included on several compilation albums. Beau chuckled every time he saw a *Hits of the Sixties* package with a Beau and the Savages song. Eleven hundred dollars. He thought, *If I get eleven hundred for these two tunes, imagine what Robert Johnson would get for a song like "Crossroads," which has been covered by most bands in the Western Hemisphere.* The math staggered him. Beau tucked the check in his pocket and grabbed his keys.

The 1967 white Dodge Dart rattled and coughed but started right away. The car seemed unusually dependable, considering that Beau had never changed the oil. He put in a quart every week or so, most of which would wind up in the driveway, in inky spots. Beau had nicknamed the car "the Refrigerator." Beau pushed the R button on the dashboard transmission selector and the Frig rumbled backward into the street. He quickly pressed D and lurched forward. The car's distinctive sound and aroma filled the air.

The sky overhead glinted partial sun through a light San Francisco fog. He knew it would be sunnier across the bay in Oakland, where the temperature was usually around ten degrees warmer.

Beau felt strange. On the one hand, his spirits were buoyed by his relationship with Annie, his victory over the coke Tom had given him, and his newfound resolve to somehow do the right thing. But the crushing weight of the blues murders seemed to reduce all his little personal triumphs to roadkill. Beau reflected on the insignificance of the individual in the cosmos.

We are all just visitors here, sharing space. Each of us has a destiny to fulfill.

What is mine?

And what if he, for some reason, could not fulfill his destiny? What then?

The Dodge rattled over the Bay Bridge and into Oakland. Beau rolled down the window and enjoyed the California sun. He stopped for gas, relieved to see no long lines. A few years ago the street would have been jammed, but today there were only a few cars ahead of him. He cursed the oil companies as he pumped ten gallons into his rusty tank and paid in cash at the window. He scanned the AM radio dial for a station that wasn't playing the Bee Gees and drove down Telegraph Avenue.

He parked in front of the house he had once owned and stared at the front door. He could hear Woody laughing inside. His heart swelled at the sound. He climbed out of the car and ran up the steps.

"Hey, Woody!" he shouted.

"It's Daddy!" Woody screamed from inside. The door opened and Woody rushed to embrace his dad. Beau suddenly felt his eyes moisten. His love for Woody overwhelmed him. Beau hugged tighter and nuzzled the boy's shaggy blond hair. Gayle watched silently.

"What are we gonna do today, Daddy?"

Woody looked into Beau's face. Beau felt a lump in his throat as he spoke. "I don't know. Anything you want."

"Pinball! Sleazy adults!"

Behind him, Gayle suddenly laughed. Beau turned around quickly, pleasantly surprised. Gayle's hostility had temporarily evaporated, it seemed.

"I swear. You two," she said. Her voice sounded relaxed, like it used to be. It had been a long time since they had talked.

Beau pinched a rueful smile. "Sorry about that."

"Well, this is a surprise. What brings you east of Alcatraz? We thought your visit was tomorrow."

Beau put Woody down. "I was just in the neighborhood."

Gayle slipped her hands into her back pockets, Bette Davis style, as Dylan would say. She stood there and looked at him curiously. "You're never in this neighborhood, and you know it. You came all the way over here for a reason. So spit it out."

Beau checked the oil on Gayle's emotional crankcase before answering. She did seem nicer today. "I know Woody wants to see that new sci-fi movie, *Close Encounters of the Third Kind*. I thought maybe . . . Well, I . . . Actually I wanted to talk to you."

Gayle made eye contact and held it. She studied his face, a face she thought she knew very well. "Oh," she said, as if nothing mattered.

"I want to say . . . I wanted to say I'm sorry. I acted like a jerk. I didn't mean to suddenly turn into the bad guy. That's not me. I don't want to be the bad guy. I want to be friends."

"Beau?"

"I know, I know. You think I'm playing a game or something, but it's true. The fact is I love Woody and I still care for you. I don't like what's going on. We've become adversaries. It's not good for Woody."

"Beau?"

"I'm the father. I want to do a better job at it, if you'll let me. We're in this together. Woody's too precious to let it go."

"Beau?"

"Bein' a musician is hard on your family. I'm sorry, but that's my career. It's all I really know how to do. I've never had a real job, never had to be responsible. I play music. That's what I do. Sometimes it's a sacred quest and sometimes it sucks. It's a job that chews you up spits you out. I can't think of one musician I know who hasn't been divorced at least once. It's the number one occupational hazard in my line of work. I'm tired of being a gypsy. But I want to make up for the times I wasn't here for Woody's birthday, or the first day of school, or when his tooth fell out."

Gayle closed her eyes for a second. "I believe you. I don't know why, but I do. I hope you're not just saying that, because me and

Woody have been waiting for you to have that revelation. This is still a family, even though it's pretty screwed up."

Beau hugged Gayle. It was the first time they'd touched in years. She put her head on his shoulders and began to cry. "Oh, Beau. You don't know how hard it's been. I can't do it alone. You just left us hanging with no security, no future, no nothing. Woody needs you, I need you, we both need you."

Beau smiled. "I've been doin' a lot of thinkin' lately. There's some real weird shit happening in my life right now and it's makin' me think about the other parts of my life, the good parts."

"What do you mean?"

Beau told Gayle everything. He told her about Art Spivey and Bobby, and Robert Johnson. He told her about running into Tom and the bindle he'd slipped into his pocket, and how he'd turned the corner on his coke problem at last by letting it blow away in the wind. He told her about Slim and the gun and George Jones and Stu Kweeder. He even told her about Annie.

"Are you serious about this woman?"

Beau looked down. "Yeah, kinda."

"Are you in love with her?"

"I feel weird talkin' about it with you."

Gayle smiled. "It's OK. I just hope she can put up with you. I'm not seeing anybody . . . yet. At least one of us can be happy for now. You think you'll ever marry again?"

"No," Beau said automatically. "That's not in the cards for me. At least not for a long time. Marriage is too much like war."

Gayle's eyes were sad. "It's the only war where you sleep with the enemy every night."

Beau wrote a check to Gayle for eleven hundred dollars and told her to tell the DA she'd received it directly so he'd get credit. He took Woody to see *Close Encounters of the Third Kind* at the neighborhood theater.

Slim's favorite used-book store had an excellent mystery section. Beau met him there, and they decided to get some food. Slim had a pile of John D. MacDonald paperbacks.

"How'd it go?" Slim asked.

"It went pretty good."

"They believe all that crap about you wantin' to be a better father?"

Beau smiled. "It's not crap, man. I'm committed."

"I know you. You just feel guilty because of Annie. You feel like you don't deserve her, so it's makin' you compensate in other areas. Like your ex."

"Guilty?"

Slim looked at the covers of the Travis McGee series paperbacks he'd selected. "Yeah, you feel guilty about everything. Guilty about your kid, guilty about drugs, guilty about bein' white. You're a mess, you know that? But I like you. I think you got potential."

"Well, thanks . . . I guess. Let's go get some food. I'm starving."

"You tell her about Annie?"

Beau nodded.

"You're braver than I thought. Or dumber."

"She said that marriage is the only war where you sleep with the enemy every night."

Slim looked up, eyebrow raised. "She must've read it somewhere."

Beau met Annie later that night. They played records and talked until the sun came up. Then they made love. As they lay in the warm afterglow, Annie said, "I got something for you."

She slipped out of bed and picked up a small bag from the dresser.

"What is it?"

She climbed back into bed carrying a tiny black felt jewelry box. Her eyes twinkled behind a mischievous smile. She thrust the box at him. "Go ahead. Open it."

He raised the lid with his thumb and looked inside.

"It's a mood ring," she said.

"Looks like something Count Dracula would wear."

"No. It really works. Read the card."

Beau squinted at the instruction card in the faint early-morning light. "Adjustable."

Annie snatched the box away from him. "Not that part. The other part. See? It changes color with your mood."

"Yeah, right."

"The stone actually changes color. Here, try it on."

"This is goofy."

Annie took Beau's finger and slipped the ring over his knuckle. "Now just relax. I want to see what color you are."

Beau eyed the ring. "I don't know about this."

"Give it some time. I'll tell you what the colors mean while we wait, OK?"

Beau nodded. "I'm game."

"Black means anxious or excited. Amber is nervous or tense. Amber-green is troubled or uneasy. Green is sensitive. Blue-green is relaxed. Dark blue means love. Isn't that neat? I found it at a little head shop on Telegraph."

Beau held the ring up. "Take a look."

The color had turned to dark blue.

✋ SIXTEEN ✋

The awful slaughterhouse smell hung in the unmoving air. It didn't bother Ida John. She dealt with it as well as any human being could deal with the stench of death. Inconvenient but necessary to her goal.

The cauldron bubbled on her woodstove, a thick layer of white slime breathing and muttering on the surface. Ida stirred it gently, careful not to break the skin, just delicately enough to agitate the foul things that cooked beneath. She withdrew the wooden spoon, discolored and slick, and placed it on the small table next to her.

She picked up a plastic Ziploc bag and used her long fingernails to pry it open. She turned it over and dropped the contents into the foul boiling broth. Two eyes plopped like grapes into the liquid, bobbed on the surface for a moment, then sank slowly into the dark heart of the seething elixir.

Ida consulted a tattered notebook, read a passage, then closed her eyes. She went through a series of whispered incantations of evil words in ancient languages. She drew another bizarre offering from her tabletop.

She pulled some congealed muscle apart, stringy like catgut, and dropped it into the mix.

Muscle for movement, eyes for sight, bone for strength—she had two more key ingredients yet to go, the two most important. Ida's contacts at the university medical school were reliable, and though the specimens they provided her with were fouled with embalming chemicals, they were still reasonably fresh and undeniably authentic. She couldn't fill her entire shopping list with those people, and a few things had to be acquired through the old grave-robbing voodoo black market.

For her most important items, she insisted on fresh cadavers. These she readied now, holding them in her wrinkled hands, dried blood sticky on her fingers. Ida could have been the picture of depravity: an old crone holding human organs aloft with her bony arms, eyes closed, as the macabre steam swirled around her.

A brain and a heart fell heavily into the steaming cauldron, splashing putrid droplets back onto her dress. Ida did not move. She stared into the iron pot with unblinking bloodshot eyes.

She shook some dark brown powder, her secret ingredient, into the mix. Something she used to ensure the success of all her potions. Something nobody else had. A powerful and secret concoction she'd distilled from items her mother had showed her—the Most High Gris-Gris.

She voiced the final incantations just above a whisper into the flickering candles. The words squirmed out of her into the flame. As they burned, the temperature in her swamp house rose.

"Mojo," she chanted. "Mojo Hand . . ."

The Combat Shop in San Leandro stayed open seven days a week and featured the largest inventory of precision firearms in the San Francisco Bay Area. Oakland Slim knew the place well. The owner, Lance Rigney, was one of the biggest Raiders fans in the known world. Slim shared a passion for the silver and black.

When Lance suggested that Slim pick up a bit of insurance, he wasn't talking about State Farm or Allstate. Lanced referred to the kind of policy issued by Smith & Wesson.

Lance was surprised to see Slim enter the shop with a young white man. He pulled Slim aside and squeezed his arm.

"Who's the white kid?" Lance asked incredulously.

Slim smiled. "Oh, that's one of my fans," he answered.

"One of your fans? Don't bullshit me, Jerome. I know what your fans look like. They look like you."

"Actually, that's my new guitar player. Beau Young. He's pretty good." Slim turned to Beau. "Beau, meet Lance Rigney, a close personal friend of mine."

Beau stuck out a hand and Lance shook it. "Well, I'll be damned," Lance muttered. "You play guitar with this old coot?"

"Yes, sir."

"What's the world comin' to? So you're here to witness the arming of Oakland Slim," Lance said.

"Something like that," Beau replied. "He's my friend."

"Why on earth would you waste your time?"

"Like I said—"

"I know, he's your friend. Well, I gotta tell you. I don't trust white people. Never did. Nothin' against you personally, but that's just the way it is. You're not a cop, are you?"

Slim laughed. "Hey, Lance, I just told you, he's my new guitar player. The kid plays great. Don't go givin' him the third degree."

Lance eyed Beau suspiciously. "He looks like a cop to me."

"You're not doin' anything illegal, are you, Lance?" Slim asked with mock gravity.

Lance flashed a banker's smile. "This conversation's goin' nowhere. You want to buy some guns?"

"Lead on," Slim said.

Lance took them to a spot in the back of the store, to an examination area consisting of a solid wooden counter covered with green felt and a strong overhead light. A mirror hung on the wall behind. "Most people want guns for protection. Nine out of ten people who come in here got bad problems. I don't ask 'em about it, they don't tell me. But one thing's always the same— they're afraid of somethin'. Somethin' bad happened to 'em and they feel like their life's in danger. That's where I come in. I'm the equalizer. I've known you for a long time, Slim. I ain't gonna ask you why."

"Fair enough, Lance."

Lance cracked his knuckles. "OK. Well, I've got a few things I'd like you to look at," he said as he pulled a mean-looking black shotgun with a pistol grip from beneath the counter. "This is the best personal protection money can buy. It's a Mossberg 500, sturdy, reliable, and some hellacious firepower. It's a friggin' cannon."

Lance handed it to Slim, who weighed it in his hands.

"This gun aims itself," Lance continued. "It spreads out, clears a wide path, depending on what kind of shells you use. What I do is put in birdshot for the first five rounds and then magnums for the last four. In case you don't get the job done with the first five shots, the next four can take the wall out."

Slim was impressed. "What do you call this thing?"

"A Bullpup twelve-gauge. It's a whole lot of gun, ain't it?"

Slim handed it back to Lance and said, "I need something I can travel with, man, something small but powerful. I need a handgun, Lance, not this kind of heavy artillery."

Beau had never held a gun in his life and was reluctant to touch it when Lance tried to hand the Mossberg to him.

"Show me something in a small piece," Slim said. "Something James Bond would use."

"I thought you'd say that. I've got one all picked out for you. Take a look at this." He pulled a beautiful blue steel automatic pistol from below and placed it on the felt.

Slim picked it up and whistled one long, low note. "That's a nice-looking hunk of metal."

"It's a Beretta Model 92F," Lance replied. "It's accurate, holds fifteen rounds, weighs two point fifty-two pounds loaded, has a muzzle velocity of about one thousand two hundred eighty feet per second, and generally kicks ass. A real nice firearm, topnotch."

Beau asked to look at it, and Slim handed it to him. "It looks pretty lethal." He handed the gun back to Slim.

Lance snorted. "It is lethal." He turned to Slim. "This is a very popular piece, and I can let you have it at cost. 'Cause I like you. I'll even let you use my firing range. What do you think?"

Slim passed it from hand to hand, feeling the deadly force of the thing and hoping he'd never have to use it. "I think I'll take it."

Lance made the sale, wrapped up the Beretta, threw in twenty rounds of ammunition, and told Slim he'd made the correct choice. Beau asked about the waiting period that all handgun buyers had to go through. Lance said he'd already taken the liberty of having Slim checked out. "I did it last week, after he told me he might be comin' in. I wanted to make it convenient for the old lizard."

Slim laughed. "What service. Lance, you're the best."

As Beau and Slim walked out the door and back into the streets, Slim asked if he'd made the right decision.

"Yeah," Beau said after thinking about it. "Considering what happened to Bobby, I think you made a wise move. But be careful with that thing."

King Washington said, "It's a whole lot of money, Mr. Johnson, more than I would normally give, but seeing who you are . . ."

"Who I am? Jesus, after all the goings-on, I rightly don't know anymore!" the man who claimed to be Robert Johnson said. The whiskey made him feel warm and easy. Leeland Dodds and King Washington laughed. Reggie Fallon said nothing.

Leeland held the check in his hand and beamed. "This is the most money I ever seen! Damn!" His shirt was pinned with a safety pin where his right arm should have been; the empty sleeve flapped when he moved.

King Washington poured another shot of whiskey for all four of them and knocked his back with a vengeance. "Ahhhhhh!" He smacked his lips. "That tastes mighty good!" He rocked forward on the chair and put his hand on Leeland's father's knee. "Well, all you have to do now is sign the contract and we can settle this thing. Ten thousand dollars advance to you for the publishing rights to all your songs and three record albums to be recorded for my label, with an option for five more. It's a damn good deal, if you ask me."

Leeland handed his father a cheap ballpoint pen and said, "Go on, Dad, sign this thing and let's celebrate."

Robert Johnson looked doubtful. "I don't know. . . ."

King Washington smiled like an alligator and tried not to show his teeth. "I've worked with 'em all, everybody who ever meant anything in the blues, and they'll all vouch for me. I made a lot of money for a lot of musicians. You can look it up. I know how to market this kind of stuff, I've made it my life's work. I've survived over the years because I know what I'm doing. In a business run primarily by white men, I stand alone." he turned to Reggie Fallon.

"Ain't that right, Reggie?"

Reggie nodded.

"Go ahead, Pop," Leeland urged. "Sign it before he changes his mind. How many chances are you gonna get?"

The old man hesitated, wondering what Pandora's box he might be about to open. Something deep inside was telling him, screaming at him, to not do it. But a man did things for his family. They needed the money, and this man was willing to give it to them. Still, the same voice that years ago had said, "Run, hide," now said, "Wait." Robert looked into King Washington's face, searching for the spark of honesty. He found nothing.

King eyed the old man. He knew the score. He'd talked people just like this into all kinds of pacts with the devil. King thought it was ironic that the old man sitting before him in a pair of threadbare brown pants actually had made a pact with the real devil many years ago, according to legend. King sipped his whiskey and spun his web. "I know why your dad's hesitatin', son. He's a hard businessman, a deal maker. He's holding out for something, I can see that, and I think I know what it is."

King Washington's baritone voice held authority, persuasiveness, and seduction. It compelled you to listen, to agree with him. He'd used it successfully many times over the years, rubbing it on like butter while he dangled the money. This was one deal he wasn't about to let slip through his fingers.

Leeland looked dumbly at him across the whiskey glass. "Huh?"

"Your father, he's a smart man. He's dealt with worse than me." King raised an eyebrow. The implications of that were not lost on Leeland. "He sees this check and he says, 'How do I know it's good?' Am I right, Mr. Johnson? I think we understand each other. A check is trash, so give me the cash. Eh?"

Robert Johnson said nothing.

"I'll cash this check," King Washington crooned.

Leeland stood up, nearly spilling his whiskey. "Shit!" He looked at his father imploringly.

"I'll cash it right now."

King Washington planned on this grandstand play putting them over the top. He'd done it before and knew its effectiveness. There ain't nothin' like good old American currency. He pulled an envelope from his pocket as easily as if he were handling a pack of Luckies and counted out ten thousand dollars in one-hundred-dollar bills. When he was finished, and the shock value of that pile of money on the sagging Formica table stood at its peak, Leeland poured himself another hasty shot and threw it back like iced tea.

"Jesus Christ! Would you look at that? Come on, Pop, what are you waitin' for? There it is, sitting right there in front of you."

King Washington rocked back in his chair and smiled like a snake.

"Why are you so all-fired up to get me to sign that thing? Last time I signed a record contract I wound up almost dead. I ain't gonna jump into anything. I think I might wanna talk to Miss Sweeny first. She's been helpin' me."

King reacted to the name instantly. "Miss Sweeny? You got to ask that little white bitch for permission to sign my contract? She ain't nothin' but a little whore. I tell you what. She's got no money, she's got no connections, she ain't got shit. Besides, she's white! I'm black! That right there ought to tell you. When's the last time white folks cut you some slack? I don't want to bust your balls, but come on, don't insult me. Miss Sweeny? God damn, Mr. Johnson. Let's be men about this."

Robert sighed and looked down at the contract.

King said, "How much money is she offerin'?"

Robert shook his head slowly.

"Nothin'. I knew it. And she's probably been talkin' a lot of trash too, makin' a bunch of promises, fillin' your head with crap. I know how she operates."

Robert leaned back. "She's been straight with me."

King fingered the cash. "Money talks. Bullshit walks. Ain't I right, Reggie?"

Reggie Fallon nodded.

Leeland looked imploringly at his father. "Come on, Pop. Sign it."

King Washington stood. "OK, I know when I'm licked. I guess I'll have to withdraw the offer." He reached for the money.

"Wait a minute!" Leeland shouted. "Give him time. Give him time. He'll sign. I know he will."

"He appears to have made up his mind."

Leeland grabbed his father's shoulder and shook. The old man's head wobbled like a Kewpie doll's. "Sign it! Sign it, you old turd! Sign it or I'll wring your neck!"

King Washington put his hand out as if to stop Leeland, but let it hang in space. It dropped back to his side as Leeland nearly pulled Robert Johnson out of the chair.

Leeland's voice cracked. "We need that money, damn it!" He let go, and Robert slumped back in his chair, his eyes wide.

King said, "Don't hurt him. You can't make him sign if he don't want to. I just hope he knows what he's givin' up. This money is just the beginning. If he sells like I think he'll sell, you could be lookin' at two or three times that. Ain't that right, Reggie?"

Reggie Fallon nodded.

Robert Johnson said, "I'm afraid."

Leeland and King looked suddenly in his direction. "Afraid of what?"

"The devil."

King knelt by Robert's knee. "You don't have to be afraid. I'll protect you. I know all about the devil."

"You do?"

King nodded. "I know the devil well. I've made a few deals in my lifetime too. Let me handle it for you."

Robert Johnson looked gravely at King Washington. "Each man has to face his own destiny."

"That's true, but there's nothin' says he can't have a little help." King put the pen in Robert's hand. "But first you have to choose. Ten thousand dollars, Mr. Johnson. Take it or leave it."

Leeland's lip quivered as if he were about to cry. "Please . . . the money, Pop. The money."

Without speaking, the old man lifted the pen, looked one last time into the eyes of the men seated around the faded yellow kitchen table, and slowly, laboriously, signed the paper.

King Washington sat back down, poured himself another shot, and raised his glass. "I propose a toast."

Leeland lifted his glass. Robert stared.

"To Robert Johnson! King of the Delta blues singers!"

☙ SEVENTEEN ☙

Annie held the phone away from her face, as if it smelled of methane. "You did what?"

Robert Johnson's voice sounded slow and thick over the line. "I said, I just signed a record contract for ten thousand dollars."

Beau watched Annie stutter. "What is it?" he asked.

Annie cupped the receiver. "Robert Johnson just signed a recording contract."

Beau frowned. "With who?"

Annie spoke into the mouthpiece. "Who did you sign the contract with?"

Robert said, "With a real nice man named King Washington."

Annie's face twisted downward. Beau stood behind her, listening to the phone. "King Washington? He's a crook!"

"That's what he said about you," Robert said.

"For ten thousand dollars?"

Beau strained to hear what Robert said. "Yep," the voice on the phone said. "Ten thousand. That's a whole lotta money."

"But Robert . . . That's not enough."

"Not enough? That's more than I ever had in my life."

Beau touched Annie's shoulder. "Let me talk to him." Annie handed Beau the phone. "Mr. Johnson? Beau Young here, Annie's friend. I heard you signed for ten grand, is that right?"

"That's right."

Beau cleared his throat. "That's just for making the records, right?"

"I don't remember. I think it's for a lotta things."

Beau stood close to Annie so she could hear. Her scent swirled around him. "Does the contract mention publishing?"

"Yeah, I think that's in there."

"How about management?"

"That too. Mr. Washington said it was a package deal."

Beau took a deep breath. "I think you may have been burned. You see, when you cut up the music pie, publishing royalties for writing your own songs account for the most money. Every time they play your songs on the radio, or someone else records them, or uses them in a movie or for TV, the writer and the publisher get money."

The tone of Robert's voice changed. "Yeah? Who keeps track of all that?"

Beau said, "There's two organizations that collect royalties, ASCAP and BMI. They keep track of who plays what, and each time your song is played you get a few cents. That adds up. They figure out how much the song made, and then they give half to the publisher and half to the writer."

"Well, I'll be damned. You mean the writer only gets half?"

"That's right. The publisher gets the other half. So for every dollar that comes in, fifty cents goes to the writer and fifty cents goes to the publisher. These days, a lot of musicians form their own publishing companies so they can keep it all. If you signed over your publishing, the best you can get is fifty cents on the dollar. Checks are sent out four times a year, and twice for foreign royalties. That can add up to a lot of money. You should copyright all your songs immediately and register with either ASCAP or BMI. It's for your own protection."

Robert didn't respond.

Beau said, "I can help you, Mr. Johnson. I can do the lead sheets and fill out the forms."

"Lead sheets?"

"Yeah. The basic melody written down in musical form with the lyrics. It doesn't have to be fancy. You send it to the Library of Congress. I can do it for you if you want."

"What about that other stuff?"

"The lawyers can help you. All we want is for you to get a fair deal."

"That's what King Washington said."

When Beau read the contract he was appalled. Annie waited until he was finished to ask questions.

"Does King Washington own the publishing?"

Beau nodded. "And the masters. And the merchandising. Plus he's the manager and the record company president. He even retains the rights to the use of the name Robert Johnson."

"What?"

Beau read from the contract. "And he's registered the trademark names: Robert Johnson, King of the Blues, King of the Delta Blues, King of All Blues, Father of the Blues, Godfather of the Blues, and the Crossroads Man."

"What about management?"

"He gets forty percent for being the manager. Plus he's the president of the record company. This contract is a real freak show."

Annie Sweeny's apartment was dark. Beau's body was only a shadow next to her. Their lovemaking had been glorious, but Annie could tell something was wrong.

"What is it?"

Beau stared at the ceiling, hands behind his head. "I don't know."

Annie rolled onto her side and propped her head up with her hand. "You can tell me, Beau. I won't judge."

"It's a lot of things. The murders, the fleecing of Robert Johnson . . . And I got this nagging feeling of destiny, too. I don't know where it comes from. I felt it once before, ten years ago."

"You told me that before. What happened?"

Beau sighed in the dark. "A lot of really bad shit. I don't want to go into it. But the feeling's the same. It's like an old familiar taste in my mouth. I feel exactly the way I did right before something big happened. I felt like I was swept up in destiny, and there was nothing I could do about it. It scared me then. It scares me now."

They lay together in silence.

Suddenly Beau sat up. "That's it!"

Annie sat up next to him. "What?"

Beau climbed out of bed. "I gotta go somewhere." He began to climb into his pants. Annie wrapped a robe around her and switched on the light.

"In the middle of the night?"

Beau looked at her strangely. "Yeah . . . I need to go get something."

Annie put her hands on her hips. "Just what do you need so much at this hour?"

Beau pulled on his shirt. "I can't explain it. I'll just have to show you. It's a weapon, a weapon against evil. I'd forgotten all about it until just now."

"But why now? Can't it wait till morning?"

"It can, but I can't. You want to come along?"

The garage Beau rented for storage was in Rockridge, down College Avenue from Berkeley. Beau drove through the empty streets. It was nearly 3:00 A.M. The radio played Bruce Springsteen. Annie sat next to him in the front seat of the Dodge.

"Aren't you gonna tell me where we're going?"

"To a garage."

The garage was on a side street, tucked between two buildings. Beau parked in front and searched the glove compartment for his keys. He clutched them in his hand and grinned. "The sacred keys."

Annie rolled her eyes. "OK, let's see what's so important."

Beau got out of the car and squatted at the garage door, unlocking the locks. He pulled the door open and stared into a dark mass of boxes. He flicked on a flashlight and shined the light into the corner. An old guitar case covered with half-rubbed-off decals stood against the wall.

"There it is." Beau walked over and hoisted the case onto some boxes. He opened it reverently. A curious odor wafted up from the case—cigarette smoke, pot, sweat, beer, all gig smells, and something else he couldn't identify.

Beau handed Annie the flashlight and lifted an electric guitar out of the case. "This is it. This is my baby. An original 1958 Gibson Flying V. This guitar and me go back a long time. We lived through some amazing shit together. I used to play it all the time. It's been retired for the last couple years."

Annie shined the light over the guitar. "Radical design. It looks like an arrow."

"Yeah . . ." Beau sighed. He held the guitar against his body and strummed an E chord. The cold, rusted strings twanged like rubber bands. "Jeez, it's still in tune."

"And that's your weapon against evil?"

Beau waited a few beats before answering. The guitar felt cold in his hands. He hadn't touched it in years. "It might be hard to understand, but this guitar has magic. It can defeat the power of evil. I know because it saved my life once."

✋ EIGHTEEN ✋

The swamp teemed with energy. Like the primordial soup from which all life sprang, it hadn't changed since the dawn of creation. Mosquitoes buzzed around Ida John's head as she walked on the soft earth, her footsteps sinking in a few inches with each pace, then filling back up again, spongelike, when she withdrew her feet. Her rubber boots made a wet smacking sound like a cartoon kiss as she pulled them from the soggy loam.

Spanish moss hung from the trees, reaching for her hair as she brushed by. She walked hunched over, staring at the ground, hunting for herbs.

There were herbs which grew near her shack in the swamp that grew nowhere else. Ida kept her residence there, on the edge of that steamy, godforsaken bog, because of those rare plants.

Ida's mother had taught her daughter well. She had showed her what to look for and how to use it. Three special herbs that grew here made her magic work. Only a handful of witches down through the generations knew. Without the powerful extracts from these three herbs, their magic would be as ordinary as regular black magic or run-of-the-mill island voodoo. But using the three ingredients, Ida could tap into the great force and summon forth powers light-years past what anyone else could conjure.

As Ida stooped, scanning the ground for the obscure and nearly extinct plants she needed, she thought about the mechanics of her magic. She comprehended very little on a scientific level of what she actually did, but she knew enough to know that all of it could be explained one way or another. What was magic but nature that science had yet to understand? She knew the basic concept of what she did. *Magic is transferring power.* Power, or energy, could not be created; it merely changed form, and that's what Ida did.

She summoned power, in the form of unseen forces, and directed those forces to do her bidding, as long as the bidding was something that the forces would already be disposed to do. She didn't create energy; she changed its form, directed it, and in this way controlled its ultimate destiny. *Magic.*

Magic is, essentially, forces summoned. Pure and simple. Her mother, the great Madame Louise, had taught her that.

Directing the force was the hard part. For that she used representational magic. Without the real object or person present to direct the forces against, Ida used something that represented that person, like hair or fingernails. These shavings of a person's worldly body contained his or her essence, and DNA. Science had just discovered that the slightest bit of organic matter from our bodies contains a unique genetic blueprint, something the world of magic had known for centuries. To direct the forces summoned to affect only the person designated, she used his or her DNA for identification. More or less.

Ida knew the great secret of accessing the forces directly. That required certain elixirs only she could concoct from certain plants only she could find, processed in a way only she could process them. And this all began with foraging for the elusive leaves and roots and spores of the three key plants. Her trained eye scanned the watery banks.

Ida searched for John the Conqueror Root, a common ingredient in many New Orleans magic potions. She also looked for the datura plant, or concombre zombie. The local zombie cucumber yielded a powerful poison and psychoactive drug. Used in the creation of zombies, datura's mysterious effects were little understood by science but were used in black magic circles from the Caribbean to the mountains of Asia. Ida knew a secret way to process the datura plant that made it different from all others. Ida raised a certain species of huge, iridescent African silver beetle. She fed it the datura plant, then used its excrement in her potion instead of the plant itself. Something in the beetle's digestive track processed the poison in a unique way, making its magic even stronger.

Ida pulled back the bushes to hunt for fungus. The albino death's-head mushroom was easy to spot if you knew what to look for. A strong hallucinogen, the tiny ivory-fleshed mushroom packed a major psychedelic punch.

She boiled these three ingredients down to their essences, then mixed them with three other magic potions to make the Most High Gris-Gris. "Breakwings" gave it strength, "Respect the Crossroads" gave it darkness, and "Cut Water" gave it stability. When combined with the gris-gris, their magic became a generator of supernatural energy. She had learned all this from her mother.

The final ingredient that made Ida's magic real came from her own blood: a powerful psychic ability to jump-start the herbs and potions from within her own mind. Ida had the second sight.

After a few hours of hunting, she found everything she needed and began to walk slowly back to her shack. She thought about the big house she owned in Gretna, the servants and the finery, and reflected on how much money she had made using her knowledge.

The only mistake she had made was to fall in love as a young girl. She had met and married a man in her nineteenth year. He was a musician, just like her father. He was a handsome man who never could decide whether to smile or frown, so he did neither. His blank, impassive face showed the scars of a thousand indecisive turning points that he had sidestepped with the agility and charm of a born liar. They were never happy.

She smiled at the recollection now, decades later. It remained safely buried in her subconscious. Willy Benoit had been a handsome man indeed, and she had been so foolish. She was a child and he was a grown man. Their marriage had been the worst part of Ida's life. The child he'd left her with never knew him, and barely knew her. He was sent off to live with relatives at the age of three.

Ida never thought of the boy. As far as she was concerned, he was Willy Benoit's son, the hateful progeny she couldn't love.

*   *   *

Robert Johnson tuned his guitar. The old Kalamazoo model Gibson was scarred from years of life without a proper hard-shell case, yet with new strings it could still sing with a golden throat that newer guitars couldn't imagine. He tuned slowly, painfully, without the use of a tuning machine. He did it the old-fashioned way, using his own excellent pitch. When at last he was ready, he signaled to King Washington.

Through the double glass of the control-room window, he could see the two men clearly. Reggie Fallon, unshaven and bleary-eyed, leaned over the console letting cigarette ashes fall onto the dials and switches. King Washington hitched his hands on his suspenders and sat back chewing his cigar thoughtfully.

"OK, let's get some levels. Why don't you get in a little closer to those microphones?" It startled Robert when Reggie spoke through the talk-back mike. He looked around.

"Been a long time since you been in a recording studio, huh?"

"I ain't never been in a real studio, boys. In my day they did it in a hotel room on a big old portable machine. They would cut that sumbitch direct to lacquer disc. One take, two takes maybe."

"You had to be a man," King Washington said. "Ain't that right?"

"A man amongst men."

Robert sat in a folding chair in front of a bank of three microphones, one for his voice and two on the guitar. Reggie, a big believer in ambient "room" sound, had placed an additional two overhead mikes on tall boom stands. They hovered above the old man like slim steel giraffes.

Robert Johnson began to strum tentatively, smoothing out a few chords to see what would happen.

"Hey, Robert!" King Washington said through the talk-back. "We ain't got all day! Hit that thing the way you're gonna play when we got the tape runnin'!"

"What's that?"

"Play somethin'."

The old man began to play. Complex, delicate riffs filled the air and absorbed all thought.

Inside the control room, Reggie nodded. "Didn't I tell ya? Christ, this guy's great. Even if he wasn't Robert Johnson, he can still play like a son of a bitch!"

King leaned forward and pressed the talk-back button and cut the old man off in midnote. "That's enough. Let's hear the voice."

Robert Johnson looked up; he wasn't used to being stopped in midsong. "Sure. You want to hear my voice?"

"Well, whose voice do you want to use?"

"Shit, I only got the one!"

Reggie shrugged. "All right, let's try the one you got. There ain't nobody else out there, so I guess we're stuck with it. Just do me a favor, OK? Don't eat the mike."

Robert Johnson looked at the microphone. "Eat that?"

"What I mean is, don't get too close to the diaphragm of the microphone. Stay about six inches back from it when you sing. It sounds better that way."

"Oh."

"All right, hit it!" King shouted.

Robert Johnson began to sing. His high jagged voice cut like a rusty sword through the room. A voice that made you cry to hear. A voice of pain so visible, so real. It hadn't changed much since 1934, except that it had dropped a few keys. But it still had that airy, sinful quality that made it one of the most expressive voices in the blues. It was instantly recognizable to anyone who had ever heard it. The guitar plunked along between the phrases.

> *"When I die please bury me*
> *In any graveyard that you please*
> *I won't mind 'cause I'll be gone*
> *From now on hell gonna be my home*
> *Gonna be my home, gonna be my home*
> *From now on hell gonna be my home."*

Reggie Fallon looked at King Washington. Neither man said anything for a few seconds. Robert's voice sounded insane. It split the plane between singer and song like the plane wasn't there. Even to hardened, cynical studio dogs like themselves, it was apparent that this man's voice was the most soulful instrument in the world. It chilled them. To watch it coming out of the old man was riveting.

Reggie didn't want to interrupt Robert with the talk-back mike to say that they had already adjusted the level and were now ready to record. He sat frozen with his hands across the board, eyes locked on the old man sitting amid the small forest of boom stands. They looked like stainless-steel arms bent at the elbows, all pointing to the source.

Robert finished his song. He let the last chord ring out and smiled, sure that he had done well.

"Ahhh . . . that was great Robert, just great. Now could you do it for the tape?"

Robert looked confused. "The tape?"

"You gotta do it again. We weren't recording yet."

Robert sighed. "If that's what you want."

He started the song again immediately and Reggie had to stop him. "Whoa, hold on there, Roberto, I gotta start the tape. What's the name of this one?"

Robert cleared his throat. "It's called 'Any Graveyard Blues.' "

King Washington interrupted. "You write this?"

"Uh-huh. Wrote 'em all."

King lifted his finger off the talk-back button and turned to Reggie. "All new Robert Johnson material. That's money in the bank."

Reggie rolled the tape and slated the song. "Robert Johnson, 'Any Graveyard Blues,' take one. OK, let it happen, Roberto!"

"Roberto?" inquired Robert. "Who's that?"

Reggie answered with the tape still rolling. "Roberto, that's your new nickname. You see, I give everyone a nickname when I record 'em, it helps me remember who they are."

Robert nodded, although it looked as if he really didn't understand. "What's yours?" he asked.

"Ain't got one yet," he replied.

Robert smiled. "How about 'Shithead'?"

King Washington broke down laughing, but Reggie didn't react. "Tape's still rollin'. Roberto Johnson, 'Any Graveyard Blues,' take one!"

Robert Johnson performed the song again, even better than the first time. He went on to record twenty songs, most of them in one take, during the next four hours. He never seemed to get tired or lose his concentration. Every single take of every single song was perfect. He did it all without a lyric sheet or any musical notation of any kind. Robert Johnson did not read music. He had everything stored in his head, and he didn't miss a beat.

Robert Johnson proved to be every inch a legend. In the studio, when it counted, he delivered. Twenty new original compositions.

The playbacks were stunning. Reggie shaded the vocal with a little echo and created a haunting, spooky effect. Robert's vocals were so convincing and soulful that they were almost supernatural.

Around midnight, King Washington let Robert have a glass of whiskey. "God knows he's earned it," he said.

As they drank together, the door buzzer sounded. "Now who the hell could that be?"

It rang again. Then someone began pounding. King walked down the short hallway to the metal door. "I'm coming! I'm coming! Keep your damn pants on!"

King Washington fumbled with the line of locks. The pounding did not diminish.

"Jesus, give me a chance!" he shouted as he unlocked the last dead bolt.

At last the door swung open, and there stood the guitar player for the world's greatest rock and roll band, Heath Pritchard. King recognized him immediately and stepped back. A long black limo gleamed in the alley behind him, the driver standing by the door.

"Pardon me," asked Heath, his English accent thick and hip. "Is this where Robert Johnson is recording?"

King stuttered. "Y-yeah. Uh-huh."

"Mind if I come in?"

King pulled the door open wide. "Be my guest," he managed to say.

Heath stepped into the battered hallway, his expensive snakeskin boots crunching over some garbage. "Is he in there?" he asked, pointing down the hall.

"Yes, he most certainly is," King said, regaining his cool.

"Is it OK if I go in?"

"Absolutely." King hustled down the hall and opened the door to the studio.

Heath strode into the dimly lit room the same way he entered every studio, like he owned it. Robert Johnson looked up. He had a glass of whiskey in one hand and a guitar in the other.

"This person would like to meet you, Robert," said King. "He's a very famous man."

"That's nice," answered Robert, taking the last sip of amber liquid and putting down his glass.

"Nice to meet you," Heath said without hesitation. "I've always been an admirer of yours."

Robert Johnson mumbled something and shook his head.

"He's with the Crawlin' Kingsnakes," said King.

"Don't mean shit to me," said Robert. "How about another drink?"

Heath dug it. The fact that the old man with the guitar sitting in front of him couldn't care less who he was appealed to him. Heath knew there was only one language spoken here—music. He had his chauffeur bring in a Martin D28 acoustic guitar and a bottle of Fighting Cock Kentucky straight bourbon whiskey from the limo. He opened the bottle, then the case, took the guitar out, and tuned it up without saying a word.

"Try this stuff, I think you'll like it," he said to Robert, nodding at the bottle. "One hundred three proof. Aged six years."

"Sounds good to me," Robert replied. Heath filled two glasses and they drank.

Reggie Fallon waved to Heath through the control-room window. He spoke into the talk-back. "Hey, man. I see you got my message."

Heath flashed a thumbs-up sign. "Yeah, Reg. I wouldn't miss it for the world."

The old man eyed Heath's guitar, a real beauty. Some guys had an eye for women, and in his younger days Robert was like that, but now his eye strayed only to fine wooden instruments, and Heath's

Martin was a knockout. Mother-of-pearl inlay in an intricate pattern covered the fretboard, the grain of the wood was perfectly aligned, and the tuning pegs appeared to be gold-plated.

When Heath struck a G chord and let it ring, the warmth of the tone filled the room with a special glow that spread through them like Kentucky whiskey.

"Nice guitar," Robert Johnson grunted, the height of understatement.

Heath started playing an old Robert Johnson composition called "Hell Hound on My Trail," a song his group had recorded. Heath's no-nonsense approach to his guitar playing was crisp and spare. Heath was a groove man, part rhythm guitar, part lead. His honest, direct interpretation of Robert's song brought a smile to the old man's face.

The old man tapped his foot and nodded his head. He began to play along.

The two guitars sounded like one instrument.

King Washington slid into the control room, where Reggie Fallon was busy listening to the music as it came over the still-open microphones. "Roll tape," King barked.

Reggie looked up. "Roll tape? Without them knowing?"

King Washington almost laughed. "No. Let's stop them and ask permission. Just get some fuckin' tape going! Now!"

Reggie shook his head. "You ain't gonna believe this, but I'm out of fresh tape!"

"Then tape over something, man, just get this shit on tape! It's worth more than your entire life!"

"I can't!"

King Washington walked over to some shelves and pulled down a roll of two-inch master tape and handed it to him.

"Here," he said boldly.

"That's Rock-A-Day Johnny's new album. I haven't even mixed it yet!"

"Hey, listen, numbnuts," hissed Washington. "Screw Rock-A-Day Johnny! Tape over it. This is Heath Pritchard jamming with Robert Johnson! Jesus Christ, show some brains!"

As quickly as he could, Reggie threaded up the wide black

recording tape and hit the record button. The mikes were still placed from earlier in the evening, and while they weren't in the optimum position, they could still pick up everything that happened. Luckily, Reggie's overhead ambient room mikes were getting a nice blend of both players.

"Roll, you son of a bitch! Roll!" King shouted. "Roll and make me rich!"

After two hours, Heath stopped playing. "I don't know who this guy is," he told Reggie, "but he's the best damn guitarist I've ever seen. Whether he's Robert Johnson or not is totally irrelevant, man. He's *better than Robert Johnson.*"

✋ NINETEEN ✋

Beau squeezed through the narrow aisles of Annie's father's blues record collection. It filled the entire first floor of the converted warehouse *Bluesworthy* magazine called home.

"He must have every blues album ever made," Beau said. The metal racks extended from floor to ceiling.

"Pretty much," Annie said from behind. "One hundred thousand LPs and almost as many forty-fives. There's even a section for old-time seventy-eights. And that's just his personal collection. The mail-order items are kept separately. I know the layout, so just tell me what you want and I'll pull it for you."

"Let's start with all the Art Spivey stuff."

Annie cocked her head. Today she wore a baggy pair of khakis, an oversized men's shirt, and a tie, the Annie Hall look. The truth was Annie looked good in anything, and even shapeless clothes couldn't hide her natural beauty. "I've already pulled all the murder victim's albums, silly. They're on my desk. Spivey, Red Tunney, B. Bobby Bostic, and Ed Green. My dad had all the original issues."

"You're way ahead of me."

"What are you looking for?"

"I want to double-check all the credits. I don't know exactly what I'm looking for, but I'll know it when I see it. I've been in the music business my whole life, and I've been screwed by experts. I know every possible way a musician can get burned, because it's all happened to me. I'm looking for a link."

Annie touched Beau's cheek. "Blues musicians have always gotten screwed. My father called it the shame of the entertainment business." She lead him through the stacks back to her office. Mail orders cluttered the floor. Brown cardboard boxes of records were everywhere. "Pardon the mess, but I'm pretty much alone in this. I only have one part-time helper."

"Looks like a lot of work." He automatically slipped his arms around her and pulled her close.

They hugged for a moment until Annie broke away and took a step back. She waved her arm at the jumble of boxes. "The mail-order business is very work-intensive. Somebody's got to process all these orders. And then there's the magazine."

Beau peered into one of the open boxes. It was an order for several B. Bobby Bostic records. Beau noticed the name and thought it odd. Vincent Shives. "How do you find the time?"

She led him to a chair and sat him down with the precious weight of her hands. "I don't. I'm way behind. And now with this Robert Johnson business and the murder investigation . . ." She let her voice fade out, like the end of slow blues.

Beau picked up the first record on the pile. He read the title. "Art Spivey. *Spiderman Blues.* Royal Records. A lot of these guys were on Royal."

"That doesn't mean much. Just about every major bluesman recorded for Royal at one time or another. They had a huge catalog. Besides, Ed Green wasn't on Royal."

Beau sifted through the album covers and pulled an Ed Green album from the stack. "Ed Green. *Wailin' the Night Away.* Segwick Records, Chicago, 1952." He pulled the record out of the sleeve.

"Careful with that. Don't get any fingerprints on it."

Beau smiled. "I've handled records before."

"It's just that—"

"I know. It's your father's. I'll be careful." He delicately slid the shiny black vinyl disc from its paper inner sleeve. He held the record by the edges and squinted at the credits. "Ed Green wrote all his own music, but it's all on different publishers. I count three. Regional Music, ASCAP; Mambo Music, ASCAP; Standard Music, BMI. That's weird. If he was an ASCAP artist, why would he jump to BMI?"

Annie shrugged. "Let's make a list of all the music publishers."

The paper inner sleeve was yellowed and torn, and Beau had to be extra careful putting the delicate record back in its cover.

"I love records," Annie said. "The smell of vinyl, the shrink-wrap, the way you have to treat them like gold. They're so fragile. They warp and get scratched. Unless someone watches over them, they'll disappear."

Beau opened another Ed Green record. "This one's on Vance Records, out of Cleveland, with yet another music publisher under the song titles. Browntown Music, BMI. Ed Green bounced around quite a bit."

"Old blues guys took what they could get."

Beau returned the record to its cover and inspected several more albums. Of the nineteen LPs Ed Green cut in his life, only four were on the same label, Vance. The rest were a hodgepodge of industry standards. The music publishing also seemed scattered across the board. "Let's look at Bostic. He's the one who made the most money."

One hour later, Beau had a list of all Bobby's credits. "He spent the first part of his career bouncing around, then he stuck with Royal for a while. Then he signed with a major. The music publishing settles down around that time. He must have wised up and started his own company. But before that, he signed with some of the same publishers that Ed Green used. Little fly-by-night companies I've never heard of. Interesting."

They spent the rest of the afternoon listing all the credits on the victims' albums and comparing notes. The end result was a prodigious chunk of data that did little to prove Beau's theory that somehow the credits were linked. A few were, but not consistently. "Well, so much for that."

Someone banged on the warehouse door, and Annie went to open it. Standing silhouetted in the bright sunlight was Robert Johnson.

Annie was taken aback. She knew Robert rarely left the house. "Mr. Johnson! Please come in."

Robert shuffled inside. Behind him came Leeland. "Well, I made myself a record."

Beau hurried to Annie's side. "A record? That fast?"

Leeland frowned. "What's wrong with that? The man says make a record, Pop makes a record."

Beau looked at Leeland. "Nothing's wrong with that. I'm glad he went into the studio. The world's been waiting a long time for new recordings from Robert Johnson."

"Damn right. And now they got 'em," said Leeland. "Look, I don't want to waste your time, but Pop has something he wants to ask you."

Beau and Annie looked at Robert. "What is it?"

Robert Johnson made a shuffling step forward. "Can I sit down somewhere?"

Annie guided him to a chair, and he sat down with a groan. "My old bones are achin'."

"You want anything?"

"No. I just want to talk. Seems to me like you told me you played with that harmonica player, Oakland Slim. Well, I might be needin' some backup players."

Leeland nodded. "Seems like Pop might be workin' live jobs again real soon. Some big gigs. I mean, really big. Heath Pritchard told him he needs a band."

"But you never worked with a band before. Why now?"

Robert's rubber face stretched into a smile. "Gonna need one. Besides, ain't no different with a bass and drum. Same chords. Same beat."

"Did you meet with Heath?"

Robert said, "Yep, last night. He came down to the studio. We played some music together. Real nice English boy."

Annie looked concerned. "How did that happen? We were supposed to know when he was coming over so we could be there. He was going to sign an affidavit stating that he thought you were the real Robert Johnson. We're trying to recover lost royalties, remember?"

Although Annie directed her questions to Robert, it was Leeland who answered. "It was a last-minute deal. The recording engineer called him. Guy named Reggie."

Annie knew about Reggie Fallon, and the fact that he was
involved made her even more suspicious. "What did Heath say?"

Leeland answered again. "He said he thought Pop was the best
guitar player he ever saw."

"But did he say he thought your father was Robert Johnson?"

"He said it didn't matter."

Annie blinked; her mouth hung open. "But that was the whole
point!"

Leeland cleared his throat. "We got money comin' in, Ms.
Sweeny. We ain't so concerned about chasin' some pie in the
sky."

"But . . ."

"Heath said we should talk to you about puttin' together a
band. He said you knew everybody. Said you were fair. King
Washington didn't like it, though. He was all against it. You
shoulda heard him. He said he could get a band with one phone
call."

Robert said, "Yeah, but Heath liked you, Miss Sweeny. He
thought your daddy was a righteous man. He overruled Mr. Washington. Much as he hated it, Mr. Washington had to agree. So here
we are."

Beau studied Robert's face. "A band does help fill out the
sound in big arenas. What size hall you gonna play?"

"I can't say right now."

"OK, that's cool. Well, if it's a band you need, me and Slim can
help you out."

"I need bass and drums, maybe a little harp."

Beau looked crestfallen. "No guitar?"

Robert shook his head. "Nope, that's what I play."

"How about a rhythm guitar?"

Robert shook his head again. "Don't need no rhythm. I play
both rhythm and lead at the same time."

Beau nodded. "I can play bass."

"You're hired," Robert said.

"We can start just as soon as we get back from New Orleans."

Vincent Shives had passed out, drunk. When he opened his eyes again, he found that he was still sitting in a chair, head down, face mashed into the table.

He lifted his aching head and squinted around the room. He felt an overwhelming urge to urinate, and staggered to his feet. His legs felt like they were encased in concrete, and he moved them laboriously, one in front of the other. He made his way slowly across the linoleum floor toward the bathroom.

When he opened the door to the toilet he was shocked to see the dead body of Albert DuBois laying on the floor, exactly as he had found it years before.

Vince yelped and stepped back. *Is this real?* For Vince, it was getting harder and harder to tell the difference between reality and fantasy. *How could this be?* The possibility that he might be dreaming occurred to him, and he cleaved to the idea like a drowning man to a life preserver. But the stimuli were too real, the cold air, the fullness in his bladder, the feel of the floor through his socks; he dreaded that he might be wide-awake.

Then he heard the voices. Vince had heard voices before and counted it as a dangerous sign, a sign that something was about to happen. Sometimes they were indistinct, snatches of conversation, but one thing remained the same: they were talking about him. He strained to hear what they were saying. They seemed to be coming from beyond his door.

He's a coward, I know that much. . . .

He wants to be the king but he hasn't suffered enough. . . .

Vince pressed his ear against the door and tried to pick up every sound.

What about the others, have they suffered?

He hasn't got the guts. . . .

He tried to recognize the voices, which sounded vaguely familiar. Could it be the people next door? He'd seen them through the curtains. *Buncha assholes, near as I can tell.* Now they must be spying on him! He pressed his ear harder against the door. More snatches of conversation drifted in.

. . . kill them . . .

The hand does all the work. He does nothing.

. . . a coward . . .

. . . kill them . . .

Vince fumbled with the locks, frantically pulling back the bolts and turning the keys. At last the door swung open, and he thrust his face into the hall.

There was no one there.

He stayed for a few more minutes, until he was satisfied that whoever it had been was gone or hiding. Behind, inside, he heard the blues. *Who's in there?*

He could hear music clearly, coming from his living room. Someone had gotten in and was playing his guitar, Albert's old guitar! *Jesus Christ! They must have come through the window when I was out in the hall!*

He rushed in, and as he rounded the corner, his eyes panned the room. They came to rest on something that made him gasp.

Oh! My God!

The Mojo Hand danced on the guitar, plucking out notes, pulling the strings and letting them snap back. It walked across the frets, arched and deliberate, snapping down hard on the strings, the technique known as hammering-on. It played one of the blues progressions that Vince had learned from Albert. The yellowed bone stuck out, wagging back and forth as the fingers contorted into freakish augmented chords. The tortured, haunted sound paralyzed Vince.

It's alive!

His brain and eyes refused to believe. The Hand of Glory crouched on his guitar, playing perfectly. It snapped down a jagged melody, pinching and pulling the strings.

The hand was incredible. It could do anything. Vince could feel its power.

Then, in a flash of dry, dark skin, it jumped away and landed on the floor. Vince took a step toward it, and it crawled under the couch. He could hear it moving like a rat beneath the heavy piece of furniture.

He ran to the bathroom and vomited. Bent over the toilet, his eyes watering and his stomach heaving uncontrollably, he hardly noticed that the body of Albert DuBois was gone.

✹ TWENTY ✹

Annie hugged Beau in front of the United Airlines curbside check-in stand at San Francisco International Airport. She held him tightly, as if she didn't want to give him up.

"It's OK, babe. I'll be back in a couple of days."

"I'm worried," she said. "I don't want you to go."

Beau cupped her face in his hands like a flower. He could see the worry tightening the skin across her brow. "Hey, who said they didn't have a problem with me traveling?"

Annie nodded. "I lied. Everything's happening so fast."

Beau smiled. "Don't worry. Nothing's going to happen in the next few days."

"Promise me you'll be careful," she said emotionally.

"I promise," he replied.

"Promise me you're not going to get into any trouble."

"I promise."

"Promise me you'll come right back after it's over."

"I promise."

"I'm scared."

Annie blinked, fighting back the gathering tears. "The killer's down there, honey. It's not safe."

Beau pulled her close. "No place is safe. Look, I know it's freaky that Ed Green died there, but the owner, Turk Hemond, still had a booking to fulfill. He's an old friend of Slim's. Turk's guaranteed our safety."

"How can he guarantee anything? Ed Green was murdered right under his nose!"

Beau shook his head. "Turk asked Slim personally to come down and do the show. He doesn't want to close his doors. Can't you see? We're just trying to make a positive situation out of a negative one."

"I don't care about Turk Hemond!" she snapped. "I don't care about his nightclub, or New Orleans, or anything! I just care about you!" Her voice started to crack. "And Slim," she added. "The killer is down there. You're going right down into the thick of things."

"I'll be careful, I promise," he said calmly.

Slim finished dealing with the baggage handler, pressing a wad of dollar bills in his hand. "Take care of my babies," he said, nodding at the guitars and road cases. Beau had packed an extra Anvil guitar case.

Beau whispered into Annie's ear. "You better not let Slim see you like this. He'll think you're putting a head trip on me. Pull yourself together."

Suddenly Annie kissed Beau, deeply and soulfully. Their mouths opened and tongues touched. Beau hadn't felt Annie kiss like this outside the bedroom. His surprise melted like sugar over the heat of her passion. "Just be careful," she said. "I love you."

Beau's breath caught in his throat. "You do?"

Annie nodded vigorously, a tear forming in the corner of her eye.

"Are you sure?"

"Yes. I'm sure."

Slim interrupted before Beau could respond. "Hey, you two finished making a scene? Christ, this is the airport. Let's show a little dignity."

"We're just saying good-bye."

"Really? You could've fooled me."

"Why don't you go on ahead and I'll meet you at the gate?"

Slim handed Beau his ticket. "Youth is wasted on young people. Gate fourteen. Be there in ten minutes."

The plane took off without incident. Slim pulled out a John Mac-Donald mystery and started to read.

Beau stared out the window. Down below, thousands of cars crawled the highways, millions of people moved along the ground.

Beau thought about all those people, all with their own lives, all moving in their own directions. They knew where they were going. He realized for the first time that he knew where he was going too. He'd gained a direction but hadn't recognized it. For the first time in a long time, Beau understood who he was and what he was going to do. He was going to save the blues.

The beverage cart went past and Beau ordered. "Two whiskeys for my friend and a beer for me," he told the stewardess. Slim raised an eyebrow.

"You tryin' to get me drunk?" he asked.

"Yeah," Beau replied truthfully. "You gotta shake this melancholy off. We got a gig to play. Frankly, I'm glad to get you out of town and do some work. I mean, Annie's great and everything, but we're musicians and we need to play. It's the best thing for us."

The stewardess handed Slim two miniature bottles and a plastic cup with ice. Slim emptied both bottles into the cup and raised it. "Here's to New Orleans!"

Beau tapped his cup against Slim's, plastic to plastic. There was no sound. They downed their drinks and ordered another brace. An hour later, Beau's lips were numb and he smiled for no reason.

Slim held his liquor like he held everything else, by the balls. He began to talk about the great city of New Orleans and how many times he'd been there. Beau had been there once in the sixties, with the Stone Savages. He smiled remembering the gig. "We played outside at a big fair on Lake Pontchartrain. It was midsummer and the humidity almost knocked me out. The stage lights attracted a swarm of huge flying insects. I don't know what they were but they were fierce. One flew in my mouth when I was singin' and I barfed behind the amps."

Slim laughed. "How'd it taste?"

"Like dirt."

"None of that at the Blues Grotto. Just cockroaches. It's a great club, man. You're gonna love it. There's more musicians per square inch down there than anywhere, and they're all good. I'm gonna take care of you, so don't you worry about a thing. I can't wait to show you the French Quarter."

Beau nodded. Slim had slipped out of his grief for the moment. "Did you know much about Alligator Ed Green?"

Beau shrugged. "Not really. I've heard of him, that's about it."

"I can't believe he's dead. The sumbitch must've been older than God," Slim said. "He was old when I first went there back in 1952, he could barely walk then. He must be ancient by now." Slim paused, realized his error. "Oh . . . I forgot. Ed Green is dead, like Red Tunney, Art Spivey, and Bobby Bostic." Beau could see the clouds gathering in his friend's eye but said nothing. "He was into that Professor Longhair thing. He did a kind of barrelhouse boogie-woogie, and the amazing thing was that he could still play right up to the end. He had to be close to ninety. Of course, down there they don't care; they like old men. Have you ever heard of the Preservation Hall Jazz Band? Shit, there ain't a guy under eighty-seven in the whole group. People down there love it. They sell out every night. I hope that we're as lucky."

Oakland Slim and Beau Young booked rooms in the Marie Antoinette Hotel, one block from Bourbon Street, in the heart of the French Quarter. The hotel was everything that Beau had hoped it would be, an old building in the French style, with iron balconies overlooking the street. The rooms were decorated with fake French provincial furniture.

The air was dense and humid. It swirled with exotic smells and marvelous sounds. Spicy Cajun food simmered in a hundred pots. Dixieland jazz and blues spilled out of the clubs. People walked down the street with drinks in their hands, perfectly legal, compliments of the many bars along the block. Even though it was not the season, an aura of Mardi Gras hung in the atmosphere. Music played everywhere.

The hotel bar, the Zydeco Room, was tiny and atmospheric. It had an ancient jukebox full of blues and jazz records. The ornate 1950s Rockola was bass-heavy and wonderful, aglow with lights and chrome. It dominated a corner of the room like a miniature Taj Mahal, a shrine to better times. As soon as Beau saw it, he began pumping it full of warm, questing quarters.

Ironically, it had several B. Bobby Bostic records in its circular record carousel. Beau and Slim immediately had a couple of beers and listened to the throbbing sound of those classic fifteen-inch speakers.

"Those suckers can really push some air," Slim said. "Ain't nothin' like 'em anymore."

"There's magic in that thing," Beau replied, pointing to the neon-lit, dome-topped music cabinet. It flashed like a pinball time machine.

The sound of B. Bobby Bostic filled the room. Beau and Slim sat in appreciative, holy silence. As long as the music played, Bobby was still alive. At least in their hearts. Beau stood in front of the juke and watched the records spin. He noticed that the labels on the Bobby Bostic records were different. They were reissues. The music publisher was different too. He couldn't make out the name as the records spun. He played an Art Spivey record and saw the same thing.

Beau walked over to the bar and asked the bartender if he had the keys to the jukebox. The bartender seemed surprised. "You mean you want me to open it up?"

"Yeah. I want to check the publishers on a couple of records in there."

"You're not from ASCAP, are ya?"

Beau laughed, slightly buzzed from the beer. "No. I'm a musician. See that guy over there?" He pointed at Slim. "That's Oakland Slim."

"The blues guy?"

"Yeah. He wants to see the reissue labels on some of this old stuff you got. Maybe he can get a deal."

"A record deal?"

"Yeah. He's playing at the Blues Grotto tonight. I can put you on the guest list if you like."

The bartender grinned. "Sure, man." He pulled a large key ring off his belt and sorted through some odd-sized keys. "Here it is. This is the first time a customer ever asked me to open the jukebox. We gotta wait until this record plays and then unplug it."

After the song ended, Beau and the bartender unlocked the jukebox. With Slim looking on, Beau checked the Bobby Bostic and

Art Spivey records. He scribbled the credits down on a napkin. *Knave Records, Mambo Music.*

An hour later they walked a few blocks to the Blues Grotto to do their sound check. Tonight they would be performing without a band, as a duo. Under the circumstances, they both preferred to perform that way this time around. Just the two of them allowed for an intimacy they needed right now.

Beau enjoyed the walk; the exotic atmosphere of the Old World European-style town captured his imagination. In his mind's eye, Beau visualized the pirate Jean Lafitte strolling down these narrow streets. Jazz lived on every corner, the blues in every alley.

When they entered the dark club, they could hear Turk Hemond onstage, getting his sound system ready. His incredibly raspy voice sounded like ten thousand sleepless nights. "Check! Check one! Two! Two! Git that damn high-end buzz out! Sheeit! Check! Check one! Two! Two!"

It took over a minute for their eyes to adjust to the lack of light. The nightclub smell of stale beer and cigarette smoke assailed their nostrils, the smell of the blues. *Ahh, yes. It does smell good.* Here in New Orleans, with the moist gulf breezes, it seemed to hang a little thicker, a little stronger.

"Hey! Who's that? Is that that harmonica man, Oakland Slim?"

Slim squinted up at the stage. He could see the diminutive figure of Turk Hemond hunched over his console, silhouetted by the blue backlights. Stage right.

"Yes sir, that's exactly who it is. That you, Turk?"

"Well come on out here in the light so I can get a look at you, Jerome. My eyes ain't as good as they once were. I remember when you were first startin' out, you couldn't play worth a shit then. Course you did improve with time."

"I'm still tryin'."

"You know, son, the Bible tells us that God helps those that help themselves. Have you been helpin' yourself, Jerome?"

Oakland Slim couldn't let a straight line like that go unanswered. "Yeah. Helpin' myself to a free drink!"

Turk Hemond laughed like a wild jackal, hoarse, phlegmy, and unrestrained. "Wait right there," he shouted, and stepped back into the shadows.

A moment later he was busy pumping Slim's hand. "Thanks for doin' this, man. I can't tell you how this thing has shook me up. I almost closed my doors for the weekend, and I ain't been dark on a Saturday night in twenty years. I can't afford to lose the money."

"Well, I'm glad we could help you out. How was Ed?"

Turk smiled. "He was beautiful, may he rest in peace. The guy could have gone on forever. It was a privilege having him here at the club. I hope they catch the fucker that did it."

Slim nodded. "The cops know anything?"

"Nah, they're just pissin' in the dark like the rest of us. All I know is that it happened back at the hotel after the first night."

"Anybody unusual hang out the night of Ed's last gig?"

Turk snorted. "Shit, ain't nothin' but unusual people around here. This is the Big Easy, remember? For Ed, it was even worse. He drew people out of the woodwork I ain't seen in years."

Slim nodded. "Yeah, I hear ya."

"Say, you're not worried, are ya?"

"About what?"

"About that killer showing back up," Turk said, lighting a cigarette.

"Not us," Slim lied. "We ain't scared of nothin'." He turned to Beau. "Are we?"

Beau shook his head.

"Well, let's get to work," said Slim, pointing to the stage.

They sound-checked their equipment, such as it was: one guitar, one microphone, and two attitudes. Turk Hemond stood nearby and listened, his bony old frame leaning up against the scuffed bar, a smile cracking his ebony face into a myriad of deep creases.

"That sounds real good! Y'all might have some potential."

They went through several songs that they were planning to do that night, including "Key to the Highway," "Little Red Rooster," and "Bright Lights, Big City." To the delight of the bartender, a guy sweeping the floor, and one tired cocktail waitress, Slim and Beau grooved.

After the sound check, Slim took Beau to an authentic Cajun

restaurant. "This is Da Kine, can you dig it? The only Cajun food you ever had was that Hollywood Chi-Chi stuff on Sunset Boulevard, right? Well, this here's the truth. The blackened soft-shell crabs are out of this world, and the catfish . . . oh my Lord! Believe me, you won't get anything like this out in California. There's only one place in the world where you can get food like this, right here. My man Antoine has got a table in the back for us. He's a true fan."

They entered the tiny storefront restaurant and were immediately taken under Antoine's lavender wing. He was a huge man with a full beard and a permanent smile. The food was incredible. Beau's mouth burned for hours.

The Blues Grotto was filled with hard-core blues fans. Smoke curled from their cigarettes into the already dense atmosphere. Turk Hemond, the owner and master of ceremonies, stood before the microphone. The crowd quieted. Cocktail glasses clinked like crickets.

"Welcome to the Blues Grotto. It grieves me to have to stand up here and announce this show, because it's a memorial, and the man we're eulogizing, Ed Green, was a friend of mine. I first booked Ed in 1957. Today, twenty years later, Ed Green has gone home to Jesus. This is something that, I think, Ed would have wanted. He knew this guy, and when Ed passed away, I could only think of one man to call. He came all the way out here from California to be here tonight and play for you, and, hopefully, do something to show how we all feel about the blues. And the memory of Ed Green. I personally want to thank these guys for coming down, and thank all of you for showing up. Ladies and gentlemen, please welcome the legendary Oakland Slim!"

Slim walked out to the center of the stage and cupped the microphone to his harp. He blew a long lonesome riff. The sound system amplified it and sent it swirling around the room.

Beau plugged in his Gibson Flying V guitar. A murmur went up among the crowd when they saw the flashy V-shaped guitar body. Slim was as surprised as anyone else. Beau had kept the Flying V a secret until now.

Without a second look, Slim launched into the first song,

snarling the lyrics. The slow groove percolated like espresso with a shot of Jack.

Slim growled into the mike. "I am . . . a backdoor man."

The place locked into the groove of Slim's harp and the snake-like guitar line. Beautiful syncopation took place.

Slim's vocals melted between the lines. "When everybody's tryin' to sleep . . . I'm somewhere makin' my midnight creep."

People were sucked into the dark imagery. The lyrics cut through the respectable night like a machete. Slim knew the effect on people of this particular song, a voodoo homage to Howlin' Wolf. The lights were hot, and Beau was sweating before the first solo.

"I am . . . a backdoor man."

The song's pauses worked like black holes.

When the music ended, and the magic lifted, there was a brief moment of absolute silence. Everyone seemed to collectively take a breath. A second or two later the crowd erupted with loud approval. Slim didn't say a word. He knew it was good. Before the clapping died out he counted off the next song.

The show built to a crescendo. Slim could do no wrong. After the last song, Slim thanked everyone and said a few words about Ed Green. There was a moment of prayer in his honor. Turk Hemond joined them onstage, bowed his head, and led them in a short prayer. Slim played "Amazing Grace" on his harmonica.

Backstage, Turk hugged Slim and said, "That was beautiful, man, really beautiful. You're the best." Slim nodded, accepting the praise graciously. When Turk cried, Slim comforted him.

"It's all right, man. The blues goes on. Life goes on."

A voice from behind Beau broke the sanctity of the moment. Beau turned as he recognized the sound.

"How are you guys?" George Jones smiled. "Am I in the right place?"

Beau said, "Right place, wrong time. We just finished."

"Damn! That taxi driver said I'd make the last show."

Oakland Slim regarded George with a critical eye. "Why are you here? A little out of your jurisdiction, ain't it?"

George lit a Tiparillo. "Actually, I came down here to check a few things. The Edward Green homicide, for one. I talked to the cops, took a look at the body. You'll never guess."

"The wounds matched Bobby Bostic's," Beau said.

"Bingo. An exact match."

Slim pointed. "What did I tell you?"

George said, "I guess I owe you an apology. I thought your conspiracy theory was full of crap, but I was wrong. This proves that the same weapon killed both Green and Bostic."

"What about the others?"

George's face and flattop haircut were unreadable. "Funny you should mention that. I stopped off in Chicago and St. Louis on my way here. Checked up on Tunney and Spivey. Matches all the way around."

"I told you!" Slim crowed. "What are you gonna do now?"

George puffed his Tipperillo. "I'm gonna catch the son of a bitch that did it."

⊛ TWENTY-ONE ⊛

Robert Johnson had never had so many things to do in his life. His son, Leeland, wrote down the next day's itinerary on a small spiral notebook while King Washington dictated. His wrist held the notebook against his knee as he wrote, a practiced gesture for the one-armed man. Leeland had been born right-handed, and had had to learn to write with his left. His scrawl was barely legible.

They sat in King Washington's hotel room, the sun filtering in through the smoky air, and waited to hear what King had to say. So far, he'd said a lot.

Robert wondered when he was going to find the time to do all the things that they were expecting of him, and still play music. The more Robert rejected all the activity, the more Leeland embraced it. Suddenly, Robert was a celebrity. Suddenly Leeland had money in his pocket.

"Tomorrow morning, at ten o'clock, there's going to be a news conference. I got a TV crew comin'. I wrote a press release about your father's rediscovery. It should be front-page news. Two hours later he meets with the press. I've got several major newspapers coming, plus the wire services."

Leeland rolled his eyes, "Your face is gonna be in every check-out stand in America, Pop! Can you believe it? You're gonna scare a lot of shoppers."

Robert shook his head, his brow creased even more than usual. The skin on his forehead resembled the Grand Canyon. After a lifetime of suffering, Robert Johnson's television face folded into itself. It became hard to read for all the lines.

Robert was disgusted. These two yahoos, one of whom was his own flesh and blood, had gone completely crazy on him. All he really wanted to do was be left alone to make his music. He didn't give a rat's ass for publicity.

King Washington had a different idea. A publicity campaign to rival a Beatles reunion was being orchestrated while the old man sipped a glass of iced tea and scratched his balls.

King said, "The limo picks you up at nine o'clock, so be ready. It'll bring you to the hotel. You'll be checked in already. Look for Reggie in the lobby. He'll have your key. Let Reggie take you up to the room. Sit there until I show up. Now, I was thinkin' that maybe I should make the formal announcement, because I know the ropes, and I've done this before. I'll meet you at the hotel and bring you down to the conference room, OK? Don't go anywhere without me. Just stay in your room and wait until you see me. And don't talk to anybody."

Leeland took one of King's cigars from a box on the table and smelled it. King noticed and smiled. "It's a Macanudo, want to light up?"

He flicked his expensive lighter under Leeland's nose and encouraged him to puff the big stogie into a major four-alarm fire.

The smoke danced around Leeland's face and ran up his nostrils as he inhaled the cigar like a cigarette. He coughed violently, sending flecks of spittle flying in a wide pattern across the room, one of which hit Robert on the eyebrow and awoke him out of his trance.

"What the hell?!" he sputtered as he wiped it away and glared at his son.

King interceded. "Don't chastise the boy, Mr. Johnson, he's just delighted to share in your success. It's the excitability and inexperience of youth."

Robert frowned. "He spit on me."

"Just an accident, I assure you. We got a lot of hard work to do before tomorrow, so let's not let anything spoil it, OK? First off, the man needs a new suit and a haircut. He's gotta look good for all those photographers. Leeland, can you handle that?"

"Sure enough."

Robert snapped his fingers. "I don't care about no magazines, that ain't got nothin' to do with the blues!" he said. "It's bullshit."

Leeland said, "Don't be jumping down Mr. Washington's throat, Dad. He's just trying to help."

King Washington smiled. "Do I detect a note of discontent, Mr. Johnson?"

"You're gonna be on TV, Pop," Leeland said with a patronizing tone.

Robert Johnson shifted in his seat. "I don't watch no TV," he grumbled.

"Maybe you don't, but everybody else does," King said with a wave of his unlit cigar. "Now, I realize it's been a long time since you were involved in the record business, but let me explain something to you. Nowadays you have to get out and promote your record. Maybe you don't much feel like talkin' to a bunch of white folks, I can understand that, but you owe it to me, so I can make some money on this thing. And to your son, so he can have something more than a beat-up old guitar when you die. There's a whole lot more to this than just how you feel. It's for your family too. The boy's handicapped. I'd consider all that before you make up your mind, Mr. Johnson. How old are you?"

Robert Johnson started to answer but King Washington cut him off.

"Don't matter. You ain't no spring chicken, I know that much. How many years do you think you got left? Don't you think you owe it to your family to make some money before you kick the bucket?"

He paused now, waiting for the old man to answer.

"I guess so," Robert said barely above a whisper. "I never much thought about that."

"Well, think about it now. I got half the damn world waitin' on this story and you don't want to play ball."

Leeland was agreeing profusely. "Yeah, don't you care about me?"

King Washington stared intently at Robert's face. The moment of truth had arrived. The old bluesman put his hand on Leeland's arm. "Of course I care, son. Don't say that. You were just fine before all this happened. Didn't I take care of you then?"

Leeland blinked, his thickness unpierced.

"Didn't I always take care of you? You never missed that other arm, did you? Everything I did, I did for you, so don't go saying that stuff. If you want more money, all right, just say so, but don't wrap that greed in a cloak of guilt. It pisses me off."

King Washington was impressed. The old man knew how to put words together. A natural-born poet. "Hey, all I want is a press conference and a couple of gigs out of you. How hard could that be?"

Robert sighed. "Yeah, yeah . . ."

"There's one other thing you should know. In case you haven't heard, the blues is dying. There ain't much left, and these young kids today don't know shit from Shinola. I make my living from the blues, and so do a whole bunch of other people. When the story of Robert Johnson hits the streets, I should say the *miracle of Robert Johnson,* every kid with a guitar is gonna start playing the blues. You're gonna breathe life back into it, you're gonna resurrect it, and that's gonna help us all. You're gonna single-handedly do what nobody else could. You're gonna save the blues."

Robert Johnson looked up. "Me?"

"Yeah, you."

"You're crazy." Robert Johnson didn't know what else to say. "Save the blues? Save my ass."

"Don't let us down," King finished, with prayerlike conviction.

Robert Johnson looked right into his eyes and said, "What're you smokin'?"

King Washington laughed. "I don't get it, old man. I'm tryin' to make you rich."

Robert said, "For forty years I've been in hiding, living the life of a fugitive. The whole thing goes up in smoke the minute I walk out in front of those cameras. I didn't go into hiding for nothing. The family I ran from might still be around, just as pissed off and mean as ever, and as soon as they realize I'm not laying in a grave in Greenwood, they gonna come after me all over again. I got that feelin' again. The old nightmare is comin' back."

Robert looked at his hands. They were wrinkled and old now,

but once they had been slender and beautiful, like a piano player's hands. He'd sold his soul to the devil for the talent in those hands. Now, decades later, the payoff must be due.

Robert's throat was suddenly dry, and he sipped his iced tea again.

The operator answered on the third ring. "Hello? Marie Antoinette Hotel, how may I help y'all?" To Annie Sweeny, the southern accent sounded like a put-on. She realized it was real and smiled.

"Yes, I would like to talk to Beau Young."

"I'll ring his room for you, ma'am," the operator said thickly.

Beau picked up on the first ring. "Hello?"

"Hi, it's me," Annie said.

"Hi, babe. I miss you."

"I miss you too. How was the gig?"

"The gig was great. No problems. Nobody got killed."

Annie sighed. "Don't be sarcastic."

"Sorry, I just woke up. Guess what? George Jones showed up at the gig. He said he checked the other murders, and the wounds match. Looks like he's got a real case now."

"That's great. Maybe he'll pay more attention to us now."

"I think he's convinced. I discovered something myself. I didn't think of this before, but could you check something for me? Most of this stuff has been reissued and I'd like to know who bought the publishing. That wouldn't show up on your father's original discs. People buy publishing companies all the time. I noticed Mambo Music again. Could you check with ASCAP and see who owns that?"

"Sure. I made a list of all the publishing companies plus the authors of the songs. Somebody named M. Leveau wrote songs with all four murder victims."

"How many dealt with Mambo Music?"

"Two. Spivey and Bostic."

"That's interesting."

"There's something else. I got an invitation to a press conference at the Fairmount Hotel in San Francisco. King Washington is making a major announcement to the press. Must be about Robert."

"Oh, man. I hope he doesn't get screwed."

"I guess it's starting. I get the feeling nothing can stop it now. Oh, Beau, I hope I did the right thing."

"You mean about rediscovering Robert Johnson?"

"Maybe I should have left him alone."

Beau felt numb at the gig that night. Later, back at the hotel, he pumped quarters into the jukebox and thought about Annie.

✋ TWENTY-TWO ✋

Robert Johnson and Leeland Dodds checked into their room at the Fairmount Hotel and couldn't believe the opulence. It felt like a dream. Nothing that had happened to them in the last week seemed real.

Leeland was beside himself thinking that his own father was a star. All his life, Leeland had been a second-class citizen, a one-armed black man with no education, no job, and no future. Now, however, the future seemed brighter than he could ever have imagined.

But Robert Johnson felt uneasy.

After decades in hiding, careful to not let anyone know who he was, he was about to tell the whole world. A feeling in the pit of his stomach had been gnawing at him since the studio. Something was not right.

He looked out the window at San Francisco below, wondering what would happen to him next. For four decades he'd managed to stay alive, to beat the odds, to cheat the devil. Now, in 1977, for the sake of money, he would tempt death once again.

"What's wrong, Pop? You look like your dog just died."

"I'm scared, son."

Leeland plopped down on the bed. "Scared of what?"

Robert turned. "Let me tell you a little story. I remember the night just like it was last week. The crickets and frogs were singin' a furious gospel tune. The full moon rose in a clear sky, so close you could almost touch it. The cotton fields shimmered like the great

Mississippi River. I went to the crossroads outside Clarksdale. Just two little ole dirt roads, one headin' north to south, the other runnin' east to west. Four directions to go, but I didn't go anywhere. I had a bottle of wine in one hand and a guitar in the other. I was miles from the closest building, a long way to walk, the middle of nowhere. I stood in the cross of the roads just where the old woman had told me to stand, and I waited.

"I drank from the bottle of wine and strummed the guitar I didn't know how to play too good . . . yet.

"There was no way of knowing when it was midnight, except that I knew that *he* would come at midnight. I played the one chord I knew over and over again, making up a song to go with it.

"I looked up into the stars and prayed to God. I dropped to my knees in the muddy road and I threw my head back and pleaded to the heavens.

"I said, 'If you give me this one prayer, if you grant me this one wish, Lord, I'll never ask another. But I've got to learn to play this thing, can you hear me? I'm burnin' to learn and I know I got the talent. Please get me out of this place, Lord. It's something I gotta do. There's music inside me and it's got to come out. You gotta give me the gift, I can't wait anymore. . . . Because if you refuse me, Lord, if you turn your back on this poor country boy, well, then I'm gonna have to ask *him*. So please don't let me make a deal with the devil, Lord, please. I'll be a good Christian and never do wrong if you just grant me this one wish. Please!' "

Leeland's eyes were as big as quarters. "What happened next?"

"That's when I heard some branches crack behind me. Damn! Like to scare me half to death. I smelled something sulfury, like tar burning. There was a man standing in the darkness. I couldn't make out who it was."

Robert paused. "You know who it was, Leeland?"

Leeland shook his head.

" 'What you doin'?' the man asked. I didn't know what to say. So I just stood there like a dummy. I was scared. 'Answer me, boy!' he says.

" 'I was praying,' I said. Then he laughs. He asks me if I ever get any answers to my prayers. I said, 'No.' "

Robert swallowed. Telling the story now dried his throat. "So I looked at the stranger, and I said, 'Not yet.' "

Robert's voice had dropped to a hushed whisper. "He says, 'Well, none's coming from up there.' His finger went up, pointin' to the sky. I felt a cold wind blowin' in my heart. The stranger says, 'What you got there, boy? Is that a guitar?' I say, 'Yes.' He says, 'Can you play it?' and I say, 'No.' He says, 'Do you want to?' And I say, 'Yes.' 'How much?' he asks me. I say, 'More than anything.' Then he smiled. 'Anything?' 'Yeah, anything,' I said."

Leeland felt the hair on the back of his neck stand up.

"The man stepped closer. His eyes were glowing like charcoal embers. He asked me if I knew who he was and I said I thought I did. So then he says, 'Give me that guitar.' I knew when I handed over my guitar to that man, I was handin' my soul to the devil."

Leeland looked at Robert's old guitar. He knew it was the same instrument his father had owned for years.

Robert continued. " 'That's right,' the man said. 'You give me that guitar, and your life will change. You won't be a poor negro cotton picker anymore. You're gonna have talent, ungodly talent. It's gonna make people sit up and take notice. Money, women, drink, good food, everything! Even respect. It's all yours . . . and all I want in return is . . . your soul.' "

"Oh, shit," Leeland said.

"The man said, 'I know you ain't drunk, and you enter into this contract fair and square, and you understand what I'm telling you. Unlike *Him*.' He pointed to the sky. 'I deliver on my promises. As long as you keep your part of the bargain, I'll keep mine.' "

Robert paused again. He wiped some sweat from his face and took a deep breath. "So I handed him my guitar. And he says to watch his fingers. And he starts playin'. Oh, God, how he played. So fast and smooth. He played the blues. Best I ever heard. After a long while he hands me the guitar back and I don't say anything. He just smiled and took three steps into the darkness and he was gone. Later that night I walked back to town, back to a honky-tonk bar I knew, and from then on I could play like the devil."

Leeland's mouth hung open. "Damn!"

Robert nodded slowly. "That's why I'm afraid. You see, I cheated him once. I don't know if I can cheat him again."

"What about King Washington?"

The cruel smile on Robert's face chilled Leeland. "King Washington can't beat the devil, son. Nobody can."

The Fairmount Hotel conference room smelled like a crowd of reporters. Music journalists and mainstream sat knee to knee in the folding chairs and enjoyed the free lunch. Somehow the story had gotten out that a major lost blues musician had been found and was making a comeback. "Hey, Sweeny, what's gonna happen? What do you know?"

"No comment," she said.

"Aw, come on, everybody's gonna know at the same time, nobody can file first here. Why don't you have a heart?"

Annie turned a cold shoulder. "Forget it. I don't know any more than you do. I'm a member of the press too."

Annie had her cassette recorder and her notepad ready as King Washington approached the podium. Sweat beaded on the big man's ebony face and he seemed nervous.

He stood at the rostrum and pulled out a packet of note cards. "Good morning. Thank you all for coming out today. My name is King Washington, and as many of you know, I am president and founder of Royal Records and Management in Chicago. Recently, it came to my attention that a very famous blues guitarist, vocalist, and composer, believed to have been dead for many years, is not dead at all, but living under another name in the city of Hayward, California. This individual is perhaps the most legendary and mysterious of all the blues originals, and his influence is felt throughout the world of music to this very day. Up until last week, he had not recorded since 1936, yet his original records are still in print and continue to sell steadily. I take great pride in announcing the release of a new album of original songs on Royal Records. And now, the man who came back from the dead, the legendary Robert Johnson, King of the Delta Blues Singers!"

There was a gasp from the knowledgeable music journalists, the ones who knew, the ones who cared about such things. *Robert John-*

son! It was unthinkable! People began to turn to each other and talk in hushed tones about how it must be a hoax. As the murmur spread across the room, Annie craned her neck to see what was happening down in front.

A frail old black man was being led to the microphone by a one-armed younger man who resembled him more than superficially. The one-armed man said, "My name is Leeland Dodds, and this is my father, Robert Johnson."

Robert stepped up to the microphone as flashbulbs went off. There was a crush of questions, and the old man peered out at the crowd, bewildered. The flood of questions, all asked at the same time, confused the old man, and he stammered for a moment before Leeland took over.

"Please, one question at a time. And speak slowly, my father has trouble hearing," he said.

"Why did you drop out of sight?"

"I was hidin' out," answered the old man.

"How long?"

"Almost forty years."

"Why?"

"Somebody wanted to kill me. They tried, and they almost got away with it, but I survived. Then, instead of going back and maybe gettin' killed for real, I took off and stayed out of sight all this time."

"Why did they want to kill you?"

"Because I was con-new-vue-latin' with another man's wife."

"Con-new-vue-latin'? What's that?"

"Humpin'," Robert said. "I was humpin' another man's wife."

There were snickers. King Washington looked embarrassed. He leaned into the mike and diplomatically said, "He was having an affair with a woman and her husband tried to kill him. It's an unfortunate incident that Mr. Johnson would like to forget."

"It wasn't that bad," Robert Johnson quipped, his eyes sparkling. There were more snickers. King Washington frowned. "Course, I ain't proud of it, neither."

"Next question, please," King said.

"How did they try to kill you?"

"They put poison in my whiskey."

"How did you survive?"

"My stomach's made of lead."

The questions came fast and furious, with the old man doing his best to keep up. Robert resented the invasion of his sacred privacy. Why did all these white crackers want to know about him? What the hell good would it do to tell them?

King Washington handed Robert a guitar. "I would like to invite everyone present to witness a historic first: Robert Johnson performing live after forty years."

Robert took the guitar in his ancient hands and played two songs, one old, one new. The performance convinced and moved. Annie was impressed.

As soon as the music started, you could actually feel the pressure drop in the room. The high, lonesome voice and the nimble, expressive guitar work were a most persuasive argument. Robert hunched over his instrument, squeezing the notes out passionately, losing himself in the music. As awkward and uncomfortable for him as the press conference had been, that's how natural and effortless the music felt. Robert Johnson said more in ten minutes with the guitar than in hours of trying to answer questions.

After the performance, the media interrogation began in earnest. The room seemed to be divided between those who were convinced and the disbelievers.

Somebody brought up the legend.

"Is it true you sold your soul to the devil?" someone from the back of the room asked.

That question stopped the flow for a few seconds. Conversation ceased, pens were at the ready, all eyes were on Robert. It was the question every blues aficionado wanted to ask.

The reporter repeated the question, louder this time, and the words bounced off the walls like a handclap in a tomb. "Is it true you sold your soul to the devil in exchange for your ability to play the guitar?"

The room fell deathly silent. Somebody coughed. A pencil dropped. Somewhere far away a phone rang.

Robert leveled his gaze at the young white man, took a deep

breath, exhaled thoughtfully, and said, "Yes. Yes, it's true. Lord have mercy on me."

The press conference lasted one hour and had a surprise ending. As most of the members of the press packed away their notebooks and cassette recorders, Heath Pritchard walked in. He strode directly to the podium and addressed the crowd without a moment's hesitation.

"You all know me, right?"

There were a few laughs and murmurs, and everyone nodded their heads.

Heath's English accent was thick. "Well, you know that I don't need the money, the fame, or the bullshit. I am not here to tell you that this man is, indeed, the legendary Robert Johnson, although I am personally convinced that he is, but I am here to say that it doesn't matter." He looked out into the sea of faces. "It doesn't matter at all. Because whoever this man is and wherever he comes from are irrelevant. He is the best blues guitarist and singer I have ever heard."

Someone in the back, a nonbeliever, shouted him down.

"Come on, Heath, this is the biggest load of crap I've ever heard. Why should you dirty your hands with it? How could this guy possibly be the real thing?"

Heath smiled. "Well, if he ain't the real thing, he does the best Robert Johnson I've ever heard!"

There were titters of laughter.

"Seriously, I don't care who he is, I think he's great!" Heath said, ignoring more questions being shouted from every part of the room. "Whoever this man is, he's opening for the Crawlin' Kingsnakes on August sixteenth, 1977, at the Day on the Green concert at the Oakland Coliseum!"

All the TV cameras, radio microphones, and print media reporters caught Heath's words. The story hit the news wires hard, and within an hour, it was front-page news around the world. King Washington repeated the mail-order address for advance copies of the new album. Several times.

And the world knew. Robert Johnson was back.

* * *

Beau and Slim landed at San Francisco International Airport in the early evening. The Robert Johnson story had already made the TV news. Annie hugged Beau tightly when she saw him. "I'm so glad you're back."

Beau smiled. "So Robert's opening for the Snakes? I guess that's the gig he mentioned. We'd better set up a rehearsal right away."

Annie said nothing, but Beau could feel a tremble across her shoulders.

✋ TWENTY-THREE ✋

King Washington walked up the path to Ida John's house in Gretna, Louisiana, with a stutter in his step. It was a universe away from her shack in the swamp, where the "other" Ida did business. Kudzu vines smothered the vegetation. Cicadas sang in the trees. The air felt oppressively humid and King sweated profusely. He hadn't seen the old woman in years, and she always made him nervous.

Not that King believed in voodoo. He didn't. He considered it the superstitious ravings of ignorant people. Ida John was nothing more than a manipulator of people, a shrewd businesswoman with a persuasive personality. Nothing supernatural about that. She was a witch mainly in the sense that she preyed on the stupidity of others. In that context, King was no different.

Ida waited inside, aware of his presence. His footsteps echoed in her mind.

He rang the bell and a butler answered the door. King stepped inside. The house was huge, like a museum, only more quiet, almost tomblike. The butler led King through several rooms, all of them exquisitely furnished and absolutely still. Through a set of double French doors he entered the parlor and came face-to-face with Ida John.

She sat on a thronelike antique chair, high backed and thickly cushioned, a tiny troll atop a boulder. Her white hair was gathered in a bun, held in place with a golden comb. Cosmetics hid the true Ida John, the real Ida. Here, in this house, she was civilized. All voodoo stayed in her shack by the swamp. Ida seemed to look directly through King as he approached her. He took her outstretched hand and kissed it.

"Welcome to my house," she said. All trace of accent was gone.

"Thank you, Ida John. It's been a long time."

She nodded. Her Creole features were hard, as if set in stone. King could see the remnants of a beauty that had once been robust. He knew that at one time, men had found her irresistible. The ghost of that beauty now haunted her face like a lost memory. She stared. And King felt uncomfortable.

"The pink-eyed man you sent to me is perfect," she said. "Where did you find him?"

"I've known him for years."

"He's a pure fool. A wonderful puppet."

"He manages to do what needs to be done."

She parted her lips and took a sip of tea from a cup at her side. "He has the Mojo Hand, but he doesn't know how to use it," she said.

"Well, he thinks he does, and that's all I need."

"He can learn the ways of voodoo."

"You know I don't believe in that stuff."

Ida put down her tea. "Maybe you should."

"Why? So I could let some old woman convince me that I'm going to drop dead tomorrow night? Fat chance. I'm a businessman."

Ida studied his face. She could see the tension there; she knew he kept too much inside. "Let's not kid ourselves. I know why you're here." Her voice got tougher with each word.

"Oh, you do, do you?"

"Yes. You came here to beg me not to kill him."

King Washington glared. "Beg you?" he asked.

"That's right, beg me."

"But why?"

"Because Robert Johnson escaped me once." She began to shout. "But never again! His blood is on my hands!" The last sentence shook the china on the table next to her.

"Bullshit," he said calmly.

"You talk to me like that?"

"I'm not afraid of you."

Ida's eyes glazed over. "People have died for less than that," she spat.

"So? You think you can bully me around like one of your idiot customers? That crap don't work where I come from," he declared.

"Where do you come from, Mr. Washington?" she asked contemptuously.

"The modern world, Ida John. You know, the one with the TVs and the jet planes?"

The old lady shifted in her seat, straightening her dress and smoothing her legs. Her voice dropped to a pleasant level. "Robert Johnson dishonored me. He lay with me and bragged about it. He brought shame to my family. My husband did what he thought he had to do to save face."

"Your husband was a damn fool who couldn't control his woman. You were nothin' but a brazen hussy when you were young. How old were you? Sixteen? God, it's been nearly forty years. Give it up. This is madness, old woman."

Ida felt the insult. It slapped her across the face like a wet leather glove. She looked at King with disgust. "I know how that man survived. The poison was too weak. I didn't use enough gris-gris.

"When my husband gave it to Robert Johnson, he thought it was real poison. I told him it was, and he believed me. He believed everything I told him. I told him Robert raped me. Oh, you should've seen his face. My whole family was furious. My husband poured that poison into Robert Johnson's whiskey with murder in his heart. Everyone thought he was dead. I went back and found his body. He was lyin' in a shed with an old rucksack over his head. I brought him back with the antidote. It was the zombie poison, of course. Datura."

King Washington snorted. "What are you sayin'? Are you tellin' me that you killed him and then brought him back to life?"

Ida nodded. "That's exactly what I'm sayin'. I killed Robert Johnson and brought him back from the dead. My husband and my family never knew.

"False death from the zombie poison is very convincing, you

know. There're no signs of life. No heartbeat, no pulse, no breathin'. Even the doctors think it's death . . . but it's not. It's like sleep, real deep sleep. In Robert's case there was no doctor around anyway. The whole damn town thought the man was dead. But I brought him back to life. I wanted to control him. Most people who've been brought back from the false grave are just as gentle and obedient as you please. Zombies. And he was at first. But in time, as the datura wore off, he regained his senses, and ran away. I didn't use strong enough gris-gris."

"Trash. Utter nonsense," King muttered.

Ida ignored him and rambled on. "I won't make the same mistake again. This grudge will never die. No matter how far he runs and how deep he hides, I'll find him. And this time, when I kill him, he'll stay dead."

King Washington raised his palm. She could see the lines etched on it like the grooves of an old 78 rpm record. "I will block it," he said. "I want him alive. He represents a lot of money to me."

"You will do no such thing!" she shouted. "Robert Johnson must die! Can't you see? No amount of money can change that."

"I'll pay you."

"No!"

"There's a million dollars at stake, old woman."

"No! On my mother's grave, he must die!"

King Washington had known this would happen; the old bitch lived in another world, a world where money took a backseat to revenge. King wanted to drag her kicking and screaming into the twentieth century. "Just because he screwed you forty years ago doesn't mean he has to die—that's ridiculous. How do you know it's even the same guy? Your husband thought he'd killed him! That's what everybody thought, right? Nobody lost face. So why should you care?"

"I lost face with myself. He bragged about how he had me for breakfast, lunch, and dinner."

"Come on! You had the satisfaction of driving him underground for the better part of his life, kept him from collecting a fortune in royalties, ain't that enough? Christ, he's just a little shriveled-up old man. What harm can he do? You're takin' this revenge thing too far. Nobody cares. Nobody remembers. You're livin' in the past, old woman. This is business."

Ida John started to shake. "My mama left me with that curse on her grave. She knew what happened. You couldn't hide anything from mama. She told me to find him and kill him or my magic would never work the same way again. I have the right to vengeance."

"You're a mean, twisted old woman, and you don't know when to leave well enough alone," King said. He began the monologue that he'd practiced at home, delivering it with force and eloquence, making sure she heard every word, just as he'd planned it. "I was ready for this. I knew you'd find out he was alive and start brewing up your hate campaign, so I came here to block it. I don't want anything to happen to him, do you understand me? If anything happens to him, you won't last long enough to enjoy your victory. I don't use no bullshit voodoo, I use the real hing."

The old woman spat and hissed like an alley cat. Her face contorted like a gargoyle's. "You dare to threaten me?"

King smiled callously. "Yep, and I don't think you want to mess with me. Don't you know? Don't you remember? I have some of your hair."

"What?"

"And your old false teeth."

"You—" She remembered, years ago, the brush she'd carelessly left at her sister's house, the old teeth she'd thought she'd destroyed in the incinerator. Somehow he'd stolen them! Her ancient black heart began to pound angrily. The cardinal rule of witchcraft had been broken. Never let any part of you fall into the wrong hands. It will be used against you. "You can't—"

King chuckled under his breath. "Oh, yes I can. I knew this day would come sooner or later, and I knew you'd try to use your voodoo bullshit on me, so I took the liberty of swiping a few items for protection. Now, anything you try to do to me will come right back on you."

Ida's voice scraped the back of King's brain. "You will never defeat me."

King sighed. "If I were you I'd just let this whole thing go. Ain't worth the trouble it's gonna bring."

"Get out of my house!" she screamed, jumping like a badger from her chair. "Get out now!"

She pushed him toward the door.

Real venom began to flow from her, the kind of thing King kept telling himself he didn't believe in. Voodoo. Witchcraft. Black magic. Devil worship. Conjuring. Demonology. He denied it all.

There would be no rehearsal. Robert Johnson told Slim and Beau to learn the songs on the new record, plus his old stuff, and just show up ready to play.

Slim suggested that they play a club date a few days before the coliseum show, to work the kinks out. Robert turned him down. "I don't see why I have to rehearse," he explained. "I been playin' these songs my whole life."

Slim couldn't argue with logic like that. He booked the date anyway so Beau could work with the rhythm section. His friends at the infamous Keystone Berkeley nightclub were only too happy to provide a venue. Everyone knew the Keystone rocked. It was a perfect place to test the new material.

The hollow plywood door to Vince's New Orleans motel room shook. The sound jolted him back to reality from the trancelike state he'd been in for what seemed like days. The door boomed again, the cheap composition-wood construction resonating as if it were being hit by a sledgehammer.

He hurried to the peephole, squinted through it, and saw Ida John's face in the lens, as foul as an angry demon's.

She pounded impatiently. He fumbled with the locks. She heard the bolts withdraw and the chain rattle while she stared defiantly at the battered motel-room door. The paint seemed to peel under her steely gaze. "Hurry up!" she hissed. "I have a job for you!"

When he swung it open, she was in his room like a bat, swooping into his world like a thirsty vampire. He stepped back, out of the way.

"Look at me, pink eye," she hissed.

Fear flashed in Vince's eyes when he saw her face, which seemed to shimmer with intensity. "I have a job for you," she repeated. "Close the door."

He did.

"Can you drive?"

Vince didn't have a license and wasn't a skilled driver, but he could point a car in the right direction, and of course he would try anything. He nodded.

"I want you to drive my car up to Mississippi tonight. I have an urgent mission for you. Write this down so you don't forget. I'll give you explicit directions. Follow them perfectly."

She told him every road, every turn, and every landmark that he would encounter. Lastly, she told him where to dig.

"Is it a grave?" he wanted to know.

She looked at him strangely, as if his question didn't deserve an answer. "Yes, it's my husband's grave," she said. "Willy Benoit."

Vince was stunned. Her voice sounded as if it came from inside a dream. "I want you to retrieve something from the coffin."

Vince stared at her dumbly, unable to fathom what she'd just told him.

"You want me to dig him up?"

Ida's eyes burned into him. "Yes," she said firmly. "And you'll do it, you'll do everything I say. The Mojo Hand will protect you."

Her husband's grave! The thought of it excited and frightened him at the same time. Vince began to squirm, the push-pull of his emotions boiling over into an unstable mixture. He wanted to hide, he wanted to cry.

She reached out, and Vince flinched like a child who has been beaten once too often. Instead of hitting him, she gently touched his head. He trembled as her hand brushed him.

Ida John put her hands on Vince's temples, and at once he felt the burning influence of her contact spread through his body. A sublime emptiness filled him. Time became distorted. He forgot who and where he was. But he remembered what he had to do.

"Rise," she whispered.

He rose.

"Look there, in the mirror."

Vince looked.

"Tell me what you see."

Vince swallowed. "I see a beautiful young girl standing next to me."

Ida smiled. "Is it me?"

Vince whispered, "Yes."

"Look at me. Look at my smooth chocolate skin, my full breasts, my long legs. Look at the fire in my eyes. Do you want me?"

Vince's throat became dry. The mirror image of Ida burned into his mind. "Yes . . ."

"Then go."

Vincent Shives could follow directions. He found the cemetery, opened the unlocked entrance gate, located the grave, and read the marking stone. Willy Benoit's grave, neglected and unvisited for decades, was exactly where she had said it would be. The tombstone had begun to lean to the south.

He waited until he was sure no one was around, then began to dig. The moist earth yielded to his shovel without protest, and within three hard hours he was tapping the dirty blade against the coffin lid. Vince felt the Mojo Hand squirm in his pocket.

Clearing the dirt away from the casket, he felt around for the handle to open it. It was locked, just as Ida had said it would be. Using a crowbar, he snapped the restraining clasp and prepared to open the coffin. There wasn't much room in the grave: Vince had dug a hole only as big as the coffin. He had to dig out a small step a few inches above the level of the coffin to have enough footing to open it. He tensed at the terrible moment before him. Vince waited for his chest to stop pounding. His hands trembled as they touched the coldness of the handle.

He took a deep breath and pulled up with all his strength. The seal broke and a hiss of foul air escaped like a dead sigh. The dreadful odor of the grave assailed him. He felt the lid move, give way an inch, stick, then give another. As soon as he had enough of an angle on it, he bent and put his back into the task. The lid came up. More appalling odors issued forth. Dirt clods fell into the coffin.

Vince shined his flashlight into the dark rectangle and shrank back. The earthly remains of Ida's long-dead husband, Willy Benoit, were in terrible condition, little more than organized compost after all the years.

He could not bring himself to look at the face; the hands were bad enough. Not at all noble like his beloved Mojo, this man's hands were skeletal decayed sticks, a few bits of hideous pulp strung between the hollows. He'd never dreamed of such a revolting end to living tissue.

Cradled in the dead man's hands was a metal box the size of a deck of cards. It was the kind of box that might once have held jewelry.

Without touching the corpse, he carefully tried to remove the box. The hands and box had fused in places, and as he lifted it, the fingertips tugged back. It was almost as if the thing in the grave did not want to relinquish its eternal prize. He gently shook it free, the fingers settling back into their final resting position. As soon as he'd liberated the box from its bed, he began to climb out of the grave.

Gripped with a sudden chill, Vince began to shake uncontrollably. He could barely move his limbs to escape that terrible hole in the ground. He shook so violently that the box slipped from his hands and fell back into the open casket.

"Shit!" he whispered sharply. Shining his flashlight into the coffin, he saw the dead man grinning up at him.

Vince screamed and scrambled upward. He clawed at the loose soil frantically. He half expected the corpse to reach up and grab his foot. He imagined cold, carrion fingers snaking up from the coffin and attaching themselves to his ankle. He could almost feel the pull of the dead thing, its unnatural strength as unyielding as a machine.

Dirt fell in great chunks. Muddy clods thumped behind him, covering the dead face and obscuring the grin.

The Mojo Hand tugged restlessly at his inner pocket. And he realized he had to go back down. The Mojo Hand would protect him.

The metal box had fallen on the chest of the thing, cracking the fragile surface and lodging itself inside. Only a tiny bit of its corner protruded. Vince had to reach inside the putrid corpse, letting his own warm fingers come in contact with the dead tissue, and retrieve the box.

Why does Ida John want this?

"Care for another shot?"

"Yeah, let it happen, man. I ain't got nothin' else to look forward to. Might as well get good and drunk."

Oakland Slim poured Robert Johnson his third shot of whiskey in a row. While on the TV screen in front of them, Jethro Bodine tried in vain to be a "double-naught spy," they drank from plastic cups. "I still can't believe you signed with that crook, King Washington. He owes me money."

"You weren't around."

"Yeah, but Annie and Beau coulda told you that."

"Washington came over to the house. He talked a silver streak. Flashed his money around. Leeland went for it hook, line, and sinker. The boy's a fool. I got nothin' to be thankful for."

"You shouldn't say that Robert," Slim said. "You've got a hell of a lot to be thankful for. Do you realize that I got to work damn near every night of the year to make the kind of money you're gonna make in one day? Man, you're making me feel like my life don't mean a thing."

Robert nodded, and put his hand on Slim's shoulder. His touch seemed unusually heavy, as if the weight of the world were in his flesh. "I'm sorry, Jerome. You're a good man. I don't mean to be disrespectful, but the circus that's goin' on out there"—he waved his hand at the door—"just ain't right. I don't want no press conferences. I'm a musician."

Slim laughed. "Hey man, bein' a musician in this day and age has as much to do with press conferences as it has to do with tuning your guitar. Things have changed. Just playin' music don't cut it anymore."

Robert shook his head. "It might be good for everybody else, but not for me. I don't take shit. Not offa Washington, not offa Leeland, not offa nobody. They can all kiss my ass. I don't think I'll be doin' any more press conferences."

"Good for you."

"I don't cotton to all the crap," Robert continued. "I play the blues, period. That's it, man. If you don't like it, you don't have to buy the record." Robert drained his plastic cup and coughed.

Slim said, "You go ahead and do things the way you want, Robert. You got the right idea. Me and Beau got a crackerjack band put together for you. Guy's I've worked with before. They know the ropes. All you gotta do is make me out a set list and we'll rehearse without you. Piece of cake."

Robert Johnson seemed distant. He wrung his hands. Slim said, "What's botherin' you, Robert? You seem as skittish as a colt."

"I wish I hadn't made that damn deal with the devil," Robert said gravely. "I'm afraid somethin' bad's gonna happen."

Outside, a siren wailed as an ambulance tore off into the night, passing directly in front of the house. The undulating shriek faded into the distance. Slim said, "Can't you undo it?"

"What do you mean?"

"Can't you get the devil to take it back? It's been done before, in literature. Remember Daniel Webster?"

Robert laughed. It sounded like a crackling fire. "Forget it, man. That ain't possible. Go back to Greenwood?"

"You know the place."

Robert nodded. "There's a little old roadhouse about a two miles down called the 49 Club where I played my guitar that first night." Robert paused, smiling wistfully at the memory. "Oh how I played. It was the first time I ever saw the power of music, and felt it in my fingers. The ladies were all lookin' me over, people were buyin' me drinks, and I thought to myself, this is almost worth it. Course, it wasn't."

"There's no way out?"

Robert shook his head. "Just one. Death," he whispered. "That's the only way out."

Slim took another drink. "Ain't you a happy-go-lucky sumbitch! You should hear yourself."

"Maybe I should go back to that crossroads and see if he'll show up and talk to me. I doubt if he was fooled by that thirty-nine-year vacation."

Slim nodded. "At least you won't be doin' any press conferences."

Robert laughed. "Yeah. Amen to that."

Slim wagged his finger. "Beau could take you back to the crossroads. If anyone could find that place, he could. The kid's got an American Express card."

"Maybe after the gig."

Vince took the metal box directly to Ida. He delivered it as the sun came up. Ida seized it and shouted. "At last! Robert Johnson is mine!"

She looked into Vince's shining face, their eyes locked, and she said, "Go, pink eye. It's time."

✸ TWENTY-FOUR ✸

The Keystone Berkeley had begun its existence as a supermarket before being converted into a nightclub. It stood at the corner of University and Shattuck Avenues just a few blocks from the University of California campus in the heart of Berkeley. Run by people who cared about music, the Keystone offered a full menu of rock and blues cuisine. On Saturday nights it featured local headliners like Earth Quake and the Greg Kihn Band, who a few months earlier had set a record for playing three separate gigs on the same night. A loyal following returned year after year. Good blues bands became a featured staple. For Oakland Slim it felt like coming home. He walked from the dressing room at the back of the club, through the audience, and up to the stage as people spontaneously cheered. At the Keystone, the audience got to touch the musicians as they passed.

Beau was already on stage, in front of his amp, warmed up and ready. The Flying V guitar gleamed like a rocket to Mars. The drummer went around his kit to check the heads, the bass player boomed a few riffs. People filled in the spaces at the front of the stage.

Slim almost collided with the pole in the middle of the stage, a Keystone landmark, but managed to dance around it at the last moment. Beau watched for Slim's signal, and when it came he counted off the opening song. His guitar riff rang out, bright and clean.

"Crossroads" started. The Robert Johnson story had run in the *San Francisco Chronicle,* the *Oakland Tribune,* and the *San Jose*

Mercury News, as well as *BAM* magazine and other music publications. The audience seemed to know the gig was a dry run for the band, and they expected to hear renditions of new material from the master. Interest in Robert Johnson ran high. The place rocked. Some people expected Heath and the Kingsnakes to be there, or maybe even Robert Johnson himself, but they stayed away. This night belonged to Slim.

The band rolled through the set without a problem. New numbers written by Robert Johnson were introduced as "somethin' by a friend of ours." The classic Johnson compositions never sounded better. Beau and Slim's arrangements were sparse and simple. They wanted Robert to have a nice wide canvas to paint come gig time. Beau played guitar tonight, but understood that he'd be on bass come coliseum time. He watched and memorized what the bass player did tonight.

George Jones and Annie Sweeny watched from the balcony. "These guys sound great!" George shouted above the music.

"Yeah," Annie shouted back. "The coliseum show should be unbelievable!"

"Can you get me backstage?"

Annie smiled. "I'm with the band, you know."

A voice behind them shouted over their heads. "Backstage? You'll need one of these." Stu Kweeder held up his laminated "All Access" pass. "I'm with the band too."

Slim led the group through a scorching set and several encores. He left the stage with the audience screaming for more. As Beau walked through the sea of excited, satisfied faces he wondered, *What will it be like for Robert Johnson?* He could feel the strange combination of vibes in the room. He passed the pool table and Foosball machines. The main dressing room was already crowded with people.

George and Annie made their way backstage, following Stu Kweeder, who kept flashing his pass at anyone who'd look. As soon as Beau saw Annie, he ran to embrace her.

George shook Slim's hand. "I believe I've been converted, sir. Your blues is downright inspirational."

"It's just like country music, George, it's got the same three chords. What do you think old Hank Williams was singin' all those years?"

George shrugged.

Vince put the Mojo Hand in his pocket. It didn't look too notice-able. He started singing to himself as he looked at his image in the dusty mirror. "I got my mojo workin', but it just don't work on you."

It had become Vince's favorite song of late, except it was wrong. It *did* work on you. It worked on everybody. The mojo was as strong as uncut heroin.

He left his motel room and walked ten blocks up University Avenue to the Keystone. He stood in line and bought a ticket, then slipped into the room and found a place to sit in the back. The nice thing about bars and nightclubs, he thought, was that they were always poorly lit places where a man could hide.

Vince was always hiding from something.

He watched Slim's set and marveled at the old man's energy. He kept one eye on the backstage door. *There's a room back there,* he thought, *a stinkin' little room full of graffiti and empty whiskey bottles. That's where I'll find him.*

When the set ended, he put out his cigarette and waited. He counted the people going in and coming out. He saw Beau and Annie leave and stroll out to the bar, shaking hands with well-wishers. Vince didn't want Beau to see him, because he knew that Beau had gotten a good look at him at the San Francisco Blues Festival. If he saw him here he might make the connection and become suspicious. Vince stayed as far away from them as possible, trying to keep to the opposite side of the room.

George Jones wandered out to join Beau and Annie. A few stragglers departed. And then Vince knew Oakland Slim was alone.

Slim left the backstage area and stepped through the back door for a smoke and a few moments alone.

The Keystone Berkeley had a back door that led to an alley behind the club. There was a small parking area and some Dumpsters. Slim stepped out and smoked a cigarette in the quiet privacy of the alley.

Vince checked the bar again. Slim's friends were busy drinking and laughing. Slim was alone back there.

Vince left the club and went around the block to the alley behind the club. He slithered through the darkness and hid behind some garbage cans. He could see Slim's silhouette in the security light, the smoke curling from his cigarette.

Vince took a deep breath and began to move forward through the gloom. He crouched behind a can, inching closer, then slid behind a stinking metal Dumpster.

Something crunched under his feet.

"What was that?" Slim said to the dark.

Slim flicked his cigarette at the Dumpster. It rolled to Vince's feet. He looked down and saw it smoldering at his shoe, an unfiltered Lucky Strike burning down to almost nothing the way only unfiltereds did when you tossed them.

"Somebody there?" Slim asked.

Vince silently felt in the pocket of his overcoat and slipped his fingers around the Mojo Hand. His hand tingled as if a low-grade electric charge were running through it. He fitted the kill brace over the Mojo. It locked in place. The razors gleamed.

His stomach flushed full of acid, growling in the dark. A feeling of pure evil, as black and unsettling as the night around him, wrapped an icy hand around his heart. He could taste it like bitter grit in his mouth.

Vince's right hand became numb. The Mojo felt like ice. He eased it from his pocket and held it up to his face. The Mojo Hand began to twitch. The brace shifted like diabolical knuckle-dusters. *Alive.*

Vince stepped from the shadows quietly, hoping for every last second of invisibility. He raised the hand to strike, took a deep breath, and sprang.

Vince came at Slim as he turned to open the door. Slim looked up when he sensed a movement from the shadows. Suddenly a body came hurtling toward him, an upraised claw shining something metallic in the night. "What?!"

Slim was too stunned to react. The Mojo Hand came up. Vince lunged.

Slim's heart skipped a beat when he saw Vince, his pink eyes wild, his white hair flying, with the death claw in his hand.

Adrenaline exploded in Slim's nervous system, his ears rung, an acid taste came up in his mouth. He pivoted away from the freakish albino, moving for his life.

Vince shouted, "Mojo!" as the claw came down. The razors whistled through the air just inches from Slim's face. Vince lost his footing, took an instant to regain it, and lunged again. This time the claw flailed diagonally through the air. It caught Slim's shirt and a button went flying, a two-inch rip appeared in the fabric, a dot of red appeared.

Slim dodged, trying to work his way back to the open door and call for help. The music and light coming from inside were reassuring. Slim skipped sideways, staying a step ahead of death.

Vince was clumsy and overanxious, succumbing to an unbelievable intensity rush. He lashed out wildly, desperate to spill blood. The Mojo Hand twitched and flexed. In a frantic attempt to keep Slim from making it to the door, Vince stumbled.

Surprised and angry, he jumped back up to his feet with the agility of a pissed-off alley cat. One of the razors bent on impact with the alley. Vince let out a war whoop.

Slim used the time to scramble back toward the door.

He hurtled through the open door and fell across the dressing room in an effort to reach his harmonica case. He pulled it open, then flipped the secret compartment lid up.

The 9mm Beretta was there. *Salvation.* Slim had been carrying the gun in his harmonica case since he bought it. He kept it loaded and ready. As he reached for it, he felt a searing pain on the side of his neck. Two of the razors bit deeply into his flesh. Blood began to flow.

Slim pivoted away, his natural reaction being to get as far from the attacker as possible. The gun stayed in its case, tantalizingly out of reach. He tried to scream but his rough old voice could barely dent the noise from the club.

Vince moved closer. Slim's only defensive move was back out the door. He dove for it, knocking over some trash cans. Vince followed, a step behind.

Beau and Annie were engaged in conversation with some fans. Beau looked around the room and wondered aloud, "Where's Slim?"

"He was still in the back room, last I saw of him," Annie said.

"I thought he came out here with us," Beau replied. "I'll go get him."

He walked to the back room and put his hand on the doorknob. A loud clanging sound erupted from the other side. *What the hell was that?* It sounded to him like trash cans going over. Beau twisted the handle and began to open the door.

"Slim, what are you doin' back there?"

Beau swung the door open and saw Vince rushing at Slim's back as the old man fled.

Vince didn't see Beau. He had tunnel vision now, focused only on the half-finished job in front of him. *Oakland Slim must die,* he thought. *Nothing can stop the Mojo Hand.* He clutched the Hand of Glory while the hand of fate gripped his heart. A few more seconds and he'd jerk Slim's life away as easy as snatching money from a dead man's palm.

Beau stepped into the room, unsure what to do. Vince disappeared outside, chasing Slim into the alley. Beau looked down and saw the open harmonica case. Big droplets of blood were everywhere. The burnished metal finish of the gun attracted his eye. He grabbed it without thinking. The Beretta, compact and powerful in his palm, waited faithfully for its call to service. Beau raised it, flicked off the safety, and leapt into the alley.

Slim managed to dance away from Vince for one step. Blood flowed from his neck, staining his shirt and jacket. He moved in a panicked burst, diving behind the Dumpster. Vince came down on him like a hungry predator. The Mojo Hand poised to strike again.

Slim looked up into the eyes of Vincent Shives, and for one terrifying moment saw the razors dripping his own crimson gore. He steeled himself for the blow. *This is it,* he thought. The claw descended. Slim tried to shout. He raised his arm to block the final blow.

Beau fired once.

Vince felt a powerful shock to the side of his head. The sound of the gunshot cracked through the alley, ricocheting through the humid night. *That's not how it's supposed to be! The Mojo should protect me! Nobody can hurt me!*

The report was loud and short, not at all like the gunshots on TV or in the movies. It sounded more like a pop than a bang. The gun jumped in Beau's hand, and he was unaware that he'd already fired it when the bullet struck Vince in the head.

Beau's teeth were clenched and his breathing was rapid. When the gun jerked in his hand, he felt rather than saw the result and sensed the terrible power of the Beretta.

The bullet knocked Vince down. His head twisted violently as if he'd been kicked. He fell forward against the Dumpster, the Mojo Hand gouging the wall as he grabbed for support.

Beau braced to fire again but it was not necessary. Vince fell down, bleeding from the head.

Vince felt the impact as dramatically as if someone had slammed his head with a baseball bat.

He didn't feel the concrete rise up and smash the back of his skull any more than he felt the Mojo Hand slip when it hit the ground.

George Jones was laughing at one of his own jokes when he heard the unmistakable sound of gunfire. His hand jerked inside his coat where his own weapon was ready, but he resisted drawing it out in the crowded bar. Everyone heard the shot, and people were looking around in confusion. George bolted for the back room.

The door was closed. George pulled his gun and kicked the door open in one fluid motion.

He came in low, just as he'd done so many times before, expecting the worst. The room was empty. The door to the alley stood open. He could see Beau standing just beyond the light, the Beretta smoking in his hand, his eyes fixed on something on the ground.

George rushed through the door, his gun ahead of him, ready to shoot. He looked up and down the alley, and when he saw that there was no one fleeing he turned his attention to Beau.

"I shot him," Beau croaked.

Someone with white hair had been shot in the head and was lying on the ground in front of him. A few yards away, Slim was curled up in a fetal position, gasping for breath. George, seeing the pool of blood around the two figures, shouted, "Call an ambulance! Call the cops!" without looking up. "Hurry!"

Annie, who'd followed George, ran to find a phone.

George checked Slim. A pulse, as weak as pond water, throbbed delicately in his wrist. His breathing was terribly shallow, his face ashen. "Jesus," Slim rasped. "He got me in the neck. How bad is it?"

"I can't tell," George replied.

Beau rushed to Slim's side, saw the rip in the old man's flesh and gasped. "An ambulance is on the way. You're gonna make it, man."

George's trained eye went over the scene. Two bodies, both seriously bleeding, one man shot, the other cut badly. The body closest to the door was albino, longhaired, strange.

Then he saw it. The Mojo Hand. A droplet of Slim's blood glistened on the tip of one of the steel blades. *Razors?*

The murder weapon.

George Jones knew it as surely and absolutely as he knew his old badge number. He knew it as soon as he saw it. The demon hand, razor-tipped and blood-primed, was halfway out of Vince's grasp.

George looked at Vince's face and saw a look of confusion. A pool of blood was collecting on the ground under his ear. The dark red contrasted with his pale skin and white hair. Madness hovered over him like the soul of a dying man, caught between two worlds.

As George looked, wondering what this man could tell him if he didn't die, Vince opened his eyes. A shallow breath issued from his naked mouth. He was trying to speak. Something important.

George leaned closer, put his ear near the strange man's face. Sirens wailed in the distance, drawing closer as the night closed in around them. George strained to hear everything Vince was struggling to say.

He wasn't aware that a small crowd had gathered around them. Beau was there, the Beretta still in his hand, still in shock, and Annie, nervously watching the mouth of the alley for the cops or the ambulance, whichever showed first.

George leaned closer.

"What is it?"

"I . . ." Vince wheezed, coughed, tried to swallow.

"Say it, man."

Vince coughed again. His eyes tried to focus on George. "I want to say something," he whispered.

"Yes?"

Vince lapsed again, fighting to stay conscious.

"I'm a police officer," George said softly. "Is there something you want to say to me?"

When Vince heard the word "police" he seemed to draw what little force he had left and rally another effort at communication. His eyes fluttered. Bubbles formed on his lips. He sucked in air.

"It was the hand," Vince murmured. His voice was otherworldly now, as if he were talking in his sleep.

"Did you kill Bobby Bostic?" George asked.

In the back of his mind George wanted to obtain a dying confession from this man, and he psychically willed him to speak, to draw another breath. The murder weapon was still partially in his hand. He had just attempted to kill Oakland Slim. "Did you kill the bluesmen?"

Vince looked into George's eyes. George saw confusion, fear, desperation, and a spark of truth. "The bluesmen!" he yelled into Vince's ear. "Did you kill them?"

Vince looked beyond George, at the night sky above his head, as if looking into heaven. His eyes glazed over. George waited for an answer.

"Don't die, you asshole," he said.

Suddenly, Vince pulled another breath. The sirens were less than a block away. "It was the hand," he whispered.

"What?"

"The hand killed them. Not me."

"The hand?"

"The Mojo Hand. It's alive. It . . . killed . . . them . . . all. . . ."

The breath went out of him. George waited for more. After an interminable amount of time, Vince inhaled again, pushing what George believed to be the last breath he would ever take between his teeth. He repeated, "It was . . . the hand."

The first Berkeley police car entered the alley. Spotlights hit the crowd and bathed it in guilty white candlepower like a lynch mob. The doors swung open, and George saw the muzzles of the cops' guns. Vince's head slumped to one side. George saw the chest stop rising and falling.

Vince stopped breathing; his eyes fluttered shut. George reached into his jacket, pulled out his badge, and shoved it toward the advancing cops. "Marin Sheriff's Department!" he shouted. "We need medical assistance here."

George knelt over Vince, putting his ear next to Vince's bloody lips. Vince's eyes popped open. "The king is dead," Vince said suddenly, drawing a sharp, unexpected breath. "Long live the king."

George looked into Vince's face. The truth shone like a signal fire there. Vince seemed to be smiling as he passed out.

☙ TWENTY-FIVE ☙

The paramedics did what they could for Oakland Slim. The first ambulance that responded was equipped for emergency surgical procedures and the technicians knew exactly what to do. They took a quick look at Vince and administered first aid. Knowing that the next team was only a few minutes behind, they decided to work on Slim.

George knew that every second counted when a person was losing as much blood as Slim. The speed and proficiency of the emergency team was reassuring. Slim remained conscious as they wheeled him out in less than three minutes and loaded him into the ambulance. A moment later, they were gone in a squeal and a shriek. It all happened so fast that most of the people standing around in the alley didn't know what to do.

The second emergency team arrived as the first pulled out. Beau and Annie decided to go with Slim in the ambulance. The ride to Alta Bates Hospital was a short one.

George stayed with Vince. A Berkeley homicide detective talked to George and made it clear that the city of Berkeley had precedence in its own charges against the as yet unidentified assailant. George wanted the Berkeley police crime lab to examine the dead hand. It was now a key piece of evidence in both cases.

George said, "This guy is a suspect in a homicide in Marin County, and possibly three other, out-of-state murders. I could use the cooperation of your lab on that weapon."

"He's facing one count of attempted murder and aggravated assault right here. We'll let the DAs sort it out. In the meantime, the Berkeley Police Department will render all reasonable cooperation to you, Detective Jones."

George kept a tight-lipped, stoic expression on his face. "Why don't we try to get a make on this guy?"

The albino looked to be in delicate condition to George. But he had been lucid enough to talk to him before he passed out, so George had reason to believe he'd be able to talk again.

The bullet had grazed his skull, lodging just beneath the skin, the paramedics said.

George couldn't help wondering what was going on inside this man's mind that he would use a severed human hand as a murder weapon. There had to be an explanation. George considered cultists or voodoo.

The Berkeley forensics team made the first breakthrough: a key to room 13 at the Tiki Lodge Motel in the assailant's coat pocket. "The Tiki's right down the street," the cop said.

"Let's go."

George and the Berkeley cops rushed to the motel, opened the room, and found the assailant's belongings, including a National Steel Dobro and an Illinois driver's license under the name Vincent Shives.

The Berkeley cops made good on their promise to expedite the lab report on the weapon. The report said everything George needed it to say. Traces of blood were found, as well as dead skin tissue and the embalming chemicals; and the wounds matched the pattern of the razors. Everything.

Vincent Shives had to be the blues killer.

George waited outside Vince's room at the hospital to speak with the doctor, a sad-faced man with weary eyes. The doctor clutched a clipboard against his chest like a cheap particleboard shield.

He nodded at the detective.

"I'm the police officer who found him, Doctor," George said, presenting his badge. "Will he live?"

The doctor glanced at George's credentials carefully, not only his badge but the picture police ID as well. "Marin County Sheriff's Department?"

"This man is a suspect in a homicide over there. We'll want to bring charges as soon as possible."

"I see. Well, the patient is in a coma. The bullet struck his head at an angle and ricocheted off his skull, lodging between the skin and the cranium. He's lucky to be alive. If the bullet would have come in at a different angle, his brain would have been damaged beyond repair. He's a very lucky person."

"Will he recover?" George asked.

"Head injuries are impossible to project. He received one hell of a concussion, and the extent of subdural hemorrhage and hematoma are unknown at this time."

George's look showed his ignorance of things medical.

"Blood on the brain."

"Oh," said George.

The doctor cleared his throat. "It can cause permanent damage. You see, blood collects beneath the membranes that cover the brain itself. It causes pressure. In a severe head injury like this, it's anybody's guess what will happen. Right now, the man is in a coma. As to when he may come out of it, well, it's impossible to say. A day, a week, a year, ten years, nobody knows. And even when he comes out of it, if he ever does, he may have received such acute damage to the brain that he could suffer paralysis, loss of memory, speech problems . . . who knows? It's completely unpredictable. Will he ever be able to stand trial? Can't say. Maybe never. That's my professional opinion."

George nodded his head. "I understand. Thank you for the information."

In the same hospital, on another floor, Beau Young tried to get an irate coffee machine to function. He cursed it and it cursed him back, spitting bitter coffee grounds into his cup. He looked at the mudlike goop and made a face.

"Dump it, babe, it's disgusting," Annie said diplomatically.

"Hey, I need some coffee, OK?"

"I'll get you some from a take-out place. Anything's better than that sludge."

"You will?"

Annie came up behind Beau and smiled. "Sure, you stay here and I'll go find something open," she said. "You're pretty stressed out right now. . . . Look at your mood ring."

Beau glanced at his finger. He'd forgotten that he still wore the mood ring. He'd put it on as a joke before going onstage. It was black as night.

Annie said, "You should stay here with Slim anyway, don't you think? I'll be back in a few minutes."

"You're the best." The night's events were just now starting to sink in. Beau savored his first chance to think. Everything up to this point, since he'd walked through the backstage door at the Keystone, was a frantic blur. Beau's hands shook and his mouth was dry.

The police had questioned him for hours. The night had been hell.

Beau's nightmare had just begun. In a matter of hours he would become a hero the likes of which the blues had never seen. In the morning paper, the media painted him as a knight in shining armor, the savior to thousands of grateful fans out there who had no idea what really happened in that alley. Beau knew it was bullshit. He hated everything about it.

In fact, since the incident in the alley, nothing felt right.

Annie returned from her expedition with doughnuts and reasonable coffee. Slim's condition stabilized. At five o'clock in the morning, a doctor came out and said Jerome Butts was going to recover. The surgery to repair the wounds on his back had been successful, and now he just needed time to heal.

George Jones arrived and told them that Vince was in a coma.

"Is he the one?" asked Annie.

"It looks like we got our man," George replied. "The lab tests are positive, they match the weapon with the Bostic murder. The only problem is he may never come out of the coma."

Beau looked pensive. "What did he say to you before he went out?"

George raised an eyebrow. "He said the hand did it."

Ida John seethed. Hearing about Vince being shot only made her more angry. King Washington blocked her vendetta against Robert Johnson. *We'll just see about that.*

Ida John was a resourceful and determined woman, as powerful a Houngan as her mother had been, and smarter. She wasn't blinded by lust or greed. Her vengeance was pure.

She walked through her big house cursing and recursing the names of her tormentors, Robert Johnson, Vincent Shives, and King Washington.

As she read the newspaper account of Vince's unfortunate incident in the alley behind the Keystone Berkeley, a feeling of rage welled up inside with volcanic potency.

She crushed the paper up in her hands. It made a sound like crackling fire, and she knew she had to go to back to the swamp. Back to her roots, to the cauldron.

The answer was waiting there, in the swamp. This part of her life, the respectable part, was only the thin facade she used to fool the world. The real Ida John was back in the shack, hunched over her cauldron, dispensing the black arts. The way to deal with Robert Johnson would be there, among the Spanish moss and mosquitoes.

She threw the crumpled newspaper on the floor and stormed out of the room, more determined than ever to bring death to the man who had violated her.

She went to her library, unlocked the great oak desk, and took out the metal box that Vince had brought her.

She had buried Willy Benoit with the bits of Robert Johnson that she had gleaned from him while he was her zombie.

The complex world of hatred and revenge that the handsome young Robert Johnson had stumbled into would come back to haunt him. The whiskey, the voodoo, and the dense Mississippi nights all began to swirl out of control.

She'd sucked a little piece of his soul out and kept it in a bottle, along with the hair and some fingernail clippings.

It seemed so simple. She'd watched her mother make false-death zombies before, and knew the procedure. The zombie poison was the key. The right blend slowed the heartbeat, lowered the body temperature, and sent the mind into a state of somnolence. The datura elixir had to be perfect: too much of any one ingredient and the victim never woke up; too little and he never slept.

Datura gave the appearance of clinical death. Haitian voodoo practitioners knew this. They knew the antidote and knew the secrets for controlling the disoriented victim when he was revived.

The psychoactive properties of the zombie poison left the victim in a completely vulnerable condition, perfect for the mind control of the Houngan. Sometimes the victims never awoke. But Ida's mother had known the craft well. Two days after Robert was pronounced dead, Ida skillfully brought him back into the world again. As a zombie.

Ida wondered how Robert Johnson had escaped. She'd heard the legend that he had made a deal with the devil. Maybe it had kept him from being called to the gates of hell too early. The devil, apparently, had his own plans for Robert Johnson.

Well, the devil can go back to hell where he belongs!

Now it was Ida's turn. This time, Robert Johnson would be dead to stay. Ida opened the box that had been closed for forty years. The hair and some fingernail clippings were still there, and so was the little bottle. She held it up to the light and looked through it. Inside, something like smoke moved. It undulated like a restless fog. A piece of his soul was there, eternal and lonely. *It's still alive.*

Ida smiled. According to legend, Robert's soul was the real property of the devil. She held it up to the light and marveled at it. She, Ida John, had outwitted the devil himself.

She had read in the papers that Robert Johnson's comeback gig was set for August 16. August 16, 1938, was the date she had killed him the first time. *The same day. Perfect. The hands of fate are tightening around his neck.*

The box she'd sent Vince to retrieve was the key to unlock Robert Johnson. Later that night she left for the swamp.

King Washington should have been a happy man. Robert Johnson was ready to play the Crawlin' Kingsnakes' date at the Oakland Coliseum. But King was unhappy about Robert's choice of backup musicians. Oakland Slim and Beau Young had been recommended by Annie Sweeny and Heath Pritchard, people Robert trusted. Slim appeared to be recovering and would be able to perform by the day of the show. His wounds, though dramatic, were more or less superficial. The fact that he had survived the attack of the blues killer only made Robert respect him more. And the fact that Beau had actually fired the shot that felled the killer made him a hero in Robert's eyes. "These two men are blessed. They are the chosen ones," the old man said.

But Oakland Slim had been a thorn in King's side for years. He'd been claiming massive fraud on the part of Royal Records and had been demanding an audit to set the record straight.

King Washington had a reputation for being the most tight-fisted record company owner in the Western world. He claimed that the records weren't selling or that they'd been returned unsold or defective. He routinely held mechanical royalties against artists' recoupable expenses. In other words, every time money came in, King found a way to not pay. Every artist he'd ever been successful with now threatened litigation as a result of Oakland Slim's lawsuit. King worried that if Slim was successful, all the others would be on him like flies on fecal matter.

You had to put a gun to his head to collect. Literally. King frowned when he remembered the time, years ago, that B. Bobby Bostic stormed into his office demanding money. King feigned ignorance. Bobby pulled a gun. "Now surely you got some cash around here someplace."

King kept his cool. "Nope. I'm broke, man. I swear."

Bobby pointed the gun at King's head. "Think again."

King began to sweat. "Actually, I keep a little money in the safe for emergencies."

"I'd consider this an emergency," Bobby snarled.

That was the only time King could remember actually paying an artist beyond the advance.

King Washington estimated a gross of thirty-five thousand dollars from the gig, a figure he kept confidential between himself and the booking agent. He'd promised Robert Johnson five thousand. King intended to pocket the rest. He was already counting the money.

Lately, King had adopted the habit of keeping a gris-gris charm around his neck, a small pouch with the only thing that could deflect Ida John's magic away from him, a piece of herself.

King Washington hated to do it. Only fools believed in voodoo, he thought. He put it out of his mind. King lived in the twentieth century. He did not believe.

But he still wore the charm.

Ida John finished her preparations and packed her bags for California.

August 16 would be a day when the forces of evil would walk the earth.

On the morning of the gig, Beau and Slim got up early and went over to the venue to sound-check their instruments. Neither Slim nor Beau had played a place so huge, and the thought of something going wrong concerned them.

They walked through the stadium looking up at the seats and marveled at the size. There was a strange feel to the place that disoriented them slightly. On the vast stage, dwarfed by the speakers and the unbelievable scale of it all, Slim blew his harp. He felt incredibly small, one lone man blowing a tiny set of reeds, trying to fill the air.

Their equipment seemed Lilliputian. The drums had been set up directly on the stage, without a riser. The guitar and bass amps were on either side. They seemed puny in front of the monolithic Kingsnake setup.

When Slim saw the frail, bent frame of Robert Johnson hobble out onto the enormous expanse of the Snakes' custom-designed stage, complete with ramps, video screens, and lasers, he began to feel different. The courage and resolve of this amazing man transcended the gig.

Beau, on the other hand, seemed anxious. After a few notes, Slim knew Beau was playing way too hard. And he could see an ember of fear in his eye.

And it made Slim think. Self-doubt is the performer's nightmare. Slim motioned for Beau to come close to him, and the two men had a quiet talk on the stage.

"How you gonna play this one tonight?" Slim asked his nervous young colleague.

"I'm gonna try to do my best," Beau said unevenly. "I'm gonna try to fill this stage."

Slim shook his head. "Uh-uh. That ain't gonna work, man."

Beau was puzzled. "What do you mean?"

"The tendency in a place this size is to overplay. Especially because it's outdoors. If you do that and try to play up to the crowd like you're the Crawlin' Kingsnakes, you're gonna fall flat on your face."

"I am?"

Slim smiled. "Yep. It'll happen so fast you won't even be aware of it. I've seen it before, in places one-fifth this size. You blow too hard, move too much, and wind up doin' a goddamn song and dance. That's when you start overdoing everything. Then the spectacle takes over. The first thing that suffers is the music. When the music goes, it all goes."

Beau's face sagged. He looked doubtfully out at the ocean of space in front of him. The pristine green tarps that covered the outfield grass ran in patterns away from the stage. "What should I do?"

Slim spat on the stage, marking his turf. "Just go out and play this gig like it was a little nightclub."

"What? In a place this size?"

"Play as if you were playing to about two hundred people, in a smoky little room somewhere in Georgia."

Beau rolled his eyes. "There's gonna be eighty thousand people out there."

"So? What're you gonna do, try to please 'em all?"

Beau sputtered. "Well, I . . ."

"You'll never do it. These people came to see the Crawlin' Kingsnakes. They don't care about us, we're just the hors d'oeuvre. Snake is the main course here, man."

Beau listened. Slim kept talking. "Your job is to be the best damn hors d'oeuvre you can be, and not try to compete with the main course, 'cause that's impossible. See?"

Beau saw. Overhead, a huge lighting truss was being dollied into position. Hundreds of workmen were swarming, bringing the multimillion-dollar stage into focus. The magnitude of the staging staggered the individual man.

Slim looked up at the scaffolding and sighed. "We're a blues act, for Christ's sake. Let's go out and act like one. We're gonna play the same way whether there's eighty people or eighty thousand, right?"

"Right."

"Just stay within yourself."

Robert Johnson walked toward them. Slim winked. "This ought to be good."

Some stagehands set up a chair in front of a bank of microphones. The mike stands fanned out like silver spider legs.

A stagehand said, "Have a seat, Mr. Johnson. Let's get you wired for sound."

Robert eased into the chair like a sack of sleeping pythons. When he was set, someone handed him his guitar. He looked up at Slim and grinned. "Don't this beat all?"

"Sure does."

"These white folks are all crazy."

Slim laughed soulfully. "I heard that."

A voice boomed over the monitor speakers so loudly it made them jump. "Go ahead and strum a bit for us."

"Who said that?" Robert shouted. His own voice came back through those same speakers at a decibel level he'd never dreamed of. He held his ears.

"A little less volume onstage!" Beau shouted.

The speakers hummed and sizzled, then quieted to half their original volume. "I said it. I'm over here." A guy in a platform about fifty yards away from the stage waved. "I'm your sound guy."

Robert shaded his eyes and squinted out into the stadium. "All the way out there?"

"That's right. I can communicate with you through this mike. You need anything? More volume?"

"I ain't deaf," Robert said, wringing a finger into his ear.

"Could you play a little so I can get a level?"

Robert strummed his guitar and listened while the sound man and his assistants adjusted the battered old acoustic until it sounded like a whole rock band. They placed a tiny contact mike inside the sound hole and put another down near the bridge. Robert tried his bottleneck slide; it skimmed across the strings like a banshee. He sang a few phlegmy notes and stomped his foot. The sound filled the empty stadium like a Santa Ana wind. It swirled up in the upper levels and startled hundreds of seagulls.

"OK, let's hear the whole band!"

Slim leaned over to Robert. "How about 'Crossroads'?"

Robert nodded and started the guitar riff. The band fell in behind him, tentatively at first, then with more confidence. By the second verse the harp and drums had jelled nicely with Robert's guitar, but Beau still seemed unsure of what to play on bass. Robert's guitar took up all the spaces. It was lead, rhythm, percussion, and bass all in one. Anything Beau played seemed to get in the way.

Slim came over and shouted at him. "Just play the root notes! Stay with the chords! Keep it simple! And loosen up, damn it!"

Beau adjusted by watching Robert Johnson. He marveled at the old man's sense of timing. It was as if he'd always had a band. The guitar riffs that had once hung out alone like a cappella solos now had a home. And then he started singing.

The high, keening wail floated into the microphones and out through the speakers, amplified beyond human logic. It sounded otherworldly. Workers stopped what they were doing and looked up. Robert's voice, a grainy falsetto, attacked the senses like fingernails on a chalkboard. It compelled you to listen. The sound of suffering and pain in that voice fueled a thousand dark nights of the soul. The words soared above the music.

Robert Johnson's chilling narrative of his night at the crossroads with the devil carried the absolute sting of firsthand experience.

The song ended to utter silence. Beau stood on the stage looking dumbly around at the other musicians. They all shared the same feeling of manifest musical destiny. Slim alone smiled. He winked at Beau. "I can't wait for tonight," he said. "Still nervous?"

Beau nodded.

"Look at Robert. He doesn't seem worried."

True to form, Robert shifted in his seat and farted loudly.

After a gust of hot wind blew the odor away, Slim came over next to Robert, leaned into his mike, and asked the legend whether he thought he'd be able to move the crowd, come showtime. "How about it, Robert? You think the audience is gonna dig it?"

Then, at a decibel level close to that of a jet plane, his voice amplified beyond reason so that it reverberated to every corner of that huge stadium, Robert Johnson answered with perfect Zen-like blues logic. "I don't give a shit."

Slim shot a glance at Beau. "See? That's his secret. He just doesn't care." Slim turned back to Robert and asked, "Well, Mr. Johnson, what exactly do you care about?"

Robert looked back at the musicians in the band, a slightly confused look on his ancient sepia face. "The music. What else is there?"

✋ TWENTY-SIX ✋

Vince's hospital room was still. The smell of disinfectant and alcohol filled his nose and stung like an unexpected whiff of danger. From somewhere deep in his coma, a glimmer of cognition stirred. Vince knew where he was—the hospital—and why he was there—he'd been shot; but he didn't know why he couldn't move. Frustration, greater than his twisted inner world had ever known, flowed through his arteries like bad dope.

Ida John slipped into the room. No one gave her a second glance as she rode the elevator to the third floor. She was just another old woman in the hospital. She waited until the guard outside Vince's door had gone for a cup of coffee, then walked into Vince's room as if she owned it. In the few minutes before he returned, Ida would complete her mission.

She approached the unmoving form of Vincent, her large crochet pocketbook clutched tightly in her fingers. Monitors beeped discreetly on a rolling table beside the bed, and the sound of Vince's breathing filled the air. She slipped her hand into the bag and removed the Mojo Hand. It rustled against the fabric of her dress as she brought it up and held it before his face. Vince did not stir. She raised the sheet and blanket covering him and slid the Mojo underneath, placing it over his groin.

She reached into her purse again and pulled out a pouch of Most High Gris-Gris and the tiny bottle containing the piece of

Robert Johnson's soul. She dabbed her finger in the gris-gris and swabbed it inside Vince's mouth. Then she uncorked the bottle and put it to Vince's lips. She smacked the back of it and saw the miniature cloud roll down Vince's throat. She leaned over him and, in a move that looked like she was administering mouth-to-mouth resuscitation, blew the cloud into Vince's lungs. She held his nose and mouth shut for a moment. Vince bucked, then relaxed. After affectionately touching his forehead for a moment, Ida withdrew, disappearing out the door and down the empty hallway as if she'd never been there at all.

The dripping IV hovered over his arm, slow and sticky sweet, filling him with sugar. In Vince's mind, he was the king, the undisputed king of all the blues. *The king is dead. Long live the king.* If Vince wanted to die, he would die and all their bullshit science wouldn't be able to do a thing about it. But it wasn't time yet.

He had unfinished business.

His eyes opened a slit, letting in a flood of light. He could only force the lids upward a fraction of the way, but through the brush of his lashes he could see the clock on the wall. In his dreams, time had become meaningless. He had no idea if it was day or night.

Vince wanted to move. His brain refused to send the orders down to his limbs.

The effort needed to keep his eyes open exhausted him. He fell asleep again, sliding away on a tide of swirling emotions and painkillers.

In his dream, Ida John came to him, her face materializing out of the mental fog. Vince smiled. He had never noticed it before, but Ida was not a bad-looking woman. She was not nearly as old as he had thought. Her bony hands, dark and leathery, had something else about them, a sensuality of which he hadn't been aware. The more he thought about it, the more he wanted to be touched by those hands. He longed for her aged fingers to stroke him. Her face, weathered and haggish a short time ago, now seemed to glow mysteriously. The ghost of youth hid there among the wrinkles. It was as if the face she wore were a mask, and under that mask existed a beautiful, young, desirable woman. While Vince watched, the mask seemed to dissolve, revealing the real woman beneath. He could feel his organ begin to stiffen.

He wanted to be her slave. He wanted to give himself completely to her, as he had been born to do. That thought excited him. He longed to be dominated by her, to serve her. He wanted to be beaten by her. He yearned to be forced into all manner of disgusting, depraved acts to satisfy her desires. He waited for her command, but none came. His penis ached. Something beneath the sheets fondled it, gently masturbating him with the rhythm of his dream.

He began to fantasize about Ida. The sour perfume of her forbidden body flirted with his senses. Oh, the things she could teach him! Vince felt the rapture build like jungle drums. He knew she was near. Light streamed into his room, shimmering and divine, and Vince began to breathe more deeply.

She appeared next to his bed as a young woman, ripe and beautiful, and Vince forgot the other Ida. The aged crone ceased to exist. Had she ever been that?

Look at her now.

Her lips, full and ruby red, parted, and the pink tip of her tongue flicked wetly at him. Vince did a slow burn. His body, though immobile, strained at its paralysis. His stiff penis twitched against the sheets, and he felt moisture return to his mouth. Inside his chest, a heart asleep began to pound anew. It awakened sharply, springing to life fully dilated and vigorous.

He felt his head throb. Somewhere inside that black and endless universe, the galaxy was expanding. It moved and spun and flexed and flowed. Vince felt as if a worm were wriggling beneath his bandages. A vein pulsed and shifted as blood began to change course. A reservoir of pressure started to drain.

Ida pointed.

What did she mean? Then Vince followed her finger, his eyes as clear and focused as binoculars, and saw what she meant. He was floating.

He could see the white bulk of his body below him. He seemed to be hovering above himself, out of his body, looking down at the hospital bed. His useless shell remained tucked into the white sheets. He saw the bulge of his erection.

He looked back at Ida.

She smiled and pursed her lips. The sweet stench of her breath blew into his face and filled his lungs. He sucked it in hungrily. Inside, it burned his mucous membranes. A revolution began in his lungs. He felt as if he'd inhaled fragrant steam. The pain stirred him; below, he saw the body move.

Looking back at Ida, he heard her say, "Rise."

Annie Sweeny had finished her check of the ASCAP records department in Los Angeles, California. The American Society of Composers, Authors and Publishers kept records of every song they licensed in the United States. They collected and dispensed royalties based on airplay. They knew who wrote what, who published what, and where the royalty checks went. She had checked the publishing history of all the songs recorded by the murder victims. It had taken days.

Her notebook was aglow with information. But none of it mattered now. Searching through her mail-order records, she discovered that Vincent Shives had purchased every record available by the murder victims. The dates matched the deaths. She put Vince's invoices in a folder, and made a mental note to pass it along to George.

Vincent Shives had been captured. Still, she continued her research. She wanted to understand what had happened. Perhaps she did it to satisfy her own curiosity, or perhaps to please Beau. She had said she'd do it. *He probably expects it,* she thought. She'd give him the notebook at the gig.

Fans began lining up for the Crawlin' Kingsnakes concert the night before. It was "festival seating," meaning first come, first served, and people began jockeying for position as early as possible. When the doors opened and the multitude rushed in, Beau watched from his backstage vantage point.

The huge structure filled up in less than two hours. It was a raucous, happy crowd, here to see their heroes perform live. The Greatest Rock Band in the World had come to town. Drop what you're doing and run!

Beau drank a beer and talked to some stagehands. He ate the crew meal, watched the place fill up, and waited for Annie to arrive.

Slim appeared out of nowhere and stood next to him. He looked as if he had something to say.

"What is it?" Beau asked.

Slim looked him in the eyes with such conviction it disconcerted Beau. Something was wrong. Slim sighed and put a hand on Beau's shoulder. "I got some bad news, man. Elvis is dead."

"What?"

"Elvis Presley, dead in Memphis. I heard it on the news."

"How did he die?"

Slim cocked his head to the side. "You're thinkin' what I'm thinkin', aren't you? The guy on the news said it was a heart attack. Thank God."

Relief showed on Beau's face. "Jesus."

"Yes," Slim said. "To a lot of people Elvis was Jesus. At any rate, the king is dead."

Beau finished the sentence for him. "Long live the king."

Slim took his hand away and looked at the floor. "But who is the king?"

Vincent Shives opened his eyes to darkness. The hospital air felt cold but good. He emerged from his coma like a moth from a cocoon, slowly and carefully.

He could turn his head from side to side. His hands worked—he clenched his fists. The IV swung askew as he moved his hand across his chest to feel his head. The bandage there was thick and tight. Something tumbled from his lap onto the floor. *The Mojo Hand!* His heart leapt. *A miracle!* The hand had come to him, to save him. *I knew it wouldn't let me down!* Strength began to return to him as he absorbed the magic of the Mojo. Nothing seemed to be beyond its power. Vince felt invincible.

He sat up and listened.

The corridors were quiet. He pulled the needles out of his arm and sat on the edge of the bed. A trickle of blood ran from the holes in his vein. It ran down to his ivory wrist in a thin crimson ribbon.

Vince looked around for a weapon, but there appeared to be nothing in the room that would serve him. He tested his legs. They were rubbery, but functional. He let them acclimate themselves to the weight of his body for a moment before attempting to walk.

Something shiny in the trash can by the door caught his eye. He peered in and saw an empty, used syringe. The stainless-steel spike glinted in the half-light. He bent over and picked it up. It looked sharp.

He stepped into the bathroom and looked in the mirror. The face looking back at him was pale and haggard, as gaunt as a cadaver's. The bandage on his head formed a cosmic turban, but he didn't remove it. The stitches underneath were still tender, and he could feel the pulse of his blood beneath them.

His eye fell upon a white plastic bottle of industrial-strength cleaning solution and disinfectant. He opened the bottle and smelled. A powerful chemical aroma, as sharp as ammonia, hit him and made his eyes water. A skull-and-crossbones poison warning grinned at him from the label. He took the syringe and filled it with the solution.

The ridiculous hospital gown he was wearing was open in the back, and his ass was freezing. Vince wondered why they would make a man wear such a stupid thing. His own clothes were missing. He crept back out into his room and eased the door open a crack to see outside.

A few feet down the hall, a uniformed policeman was dozing in a chair. His arms were folded across his chest and he leaned back against the wall in an awkward, vulnerable position. Vince grinned demonically.

He stepped into the hall, checked both directions, and slid up next to the policeman.

With one hand he held the man's head, and with the other he plunged the syringe into the sleeping cop's neck and pushed down on the plunger. The cleaning solution hit the cop's carotid artery like molten lava.

His head snapped up, his eyes opened, but the needle stayed in, rocking back and forth, spitting poison into his body. The cop tried to move, to stand up, but a second later his eyes rolled back and he slumped back against the wall.

Vince pulled him into the room and exchanged clothes. He laid the cop out on the bed in the hospital gown, stuck the IV in his arm, and wrapped some gauze around his head. He might not be discovered for hours. Vince put on the uniform. It was baggy but wearable. The gun hung low and heavy from the holster. He checked the loaded chamber, took off the safety, and posed in front of the mirror. *Gotcha!* He slipped the Mojo Hand in his pocket and put the cop's hat over his bandages. Done. *Now to walk out as if nothing's wrong.* Ida's image stayed in his mind, telling him what to do, showing him the way.

He refilled the syringe with solution and put it in his pocket, although now, with the Mojo Hand and the cop's gun, he feared nothing.

Satisfied that the coast was clear, he walked away.

Back stage at the Oakland Coliseum, Oakland Slim and Robert Johnson shared some Tennessee sippin' whiskey and wished each other a long life. The sun had gone down. Bands had been playing all day. It was almost showtime for Robert Johnson. King Washington made a cameo appearance to tell Robert he'd already collected the money in advance. In cash.

Slim scowled at him. "You ain't gonna do to him what you did to me. I won't let it happen."

"Kiss my ass, Jerome. You never were much of a businessman. If I were you I'd shut up and play the gig."

Robert raised a hand. "Y'all want to still be workin' for me in forty minutes, y'all better stop right now. You forgettin' why we're here?"

Heath Pritchard appeared from behind a phalanx of security guards. His leopard-skin pants seemed to hang halfway off his butt. His rail thin body was hung with jewels and scarves. His hair was screwed up like a rooster's comb and sported streaks of pink. He angled through the crowd and grasped Robert Johnson's hand. A cigarette dangled from his lip, ashes falling on Robert's brown wing tips. "'Ave they been treatin' ya right, mate?"

Robert smiled. "Right as rain."

"You hear about Elvis?"

Robert shook his head. "What about him?"

"He died a few hours ago. We're all shocked."

"Elvis Presley died today? Lord have mercy. Today is August six-teenth— that's the same day I died the first time."

Heath kept his cool. "Well, Elvis exits the stage, Robert Johnson steps in. I can't tell you what an honor it is for me to introduce you back to the world. You're a god, man." Heath hugged Robert warmly.

"God man," Robert murmured. "God damn."

Heath broke away and peeled off one of his many scarves, a sil-ver-and-gold Moroccan number with tassels. Arabic writing adorned the edges. He held the scarf out to Robert. "'Ere, man. Take this. It's for luck. Got it in Marrakech, I did. Supposed to have magic in it. Go on, take it. I want you to have it. You're a beautiful cat, man. Really."

Robert looked Heath up and down inquisitively. For a moment no one spoke. The backstage hubbub had come to a standstill. The world seemed to revolve around Heath and Robert. Cameras began to click, their flashes adding a surreal touch to an already Felliniesque atmosphere. "What the hell are you talkin' about?"

Heath laughed. "The scarf, man. It's yours." He continued to hold it out.

Robert eyed the scarf and slowly reached out and took it. Applause broke out among the stage crew and media. Heath started nodding vigorously and saying, "All right. All right."

And then he was gone. The circus moved on.

Robert was left holding the scarf like a shitty diaper on a hot August night. He turned to Slim. "Did you catch that?"

"Somethin' about a scarf."

Beau still felt nervous. Slim tried to calm him. "Hey man, what's the worst that could happen? So you blow a few notes, who cares? They can't hear you anyway."

Beau was about to answer when suddenly the house lights went down. A roar of humanity rose up until it shook the concrete columns of the immense structure. It was the most frightening sound Beau had ever heard, a sound of unbelievable power. The sonic tidal wave washed over him. Eighty thousand people screamed at the top of their lungs in one great rush.

Beau's heart began to race. *Be cool,* he told himself, *be cool.* The sound of the multitude rumbled the floor beneath him, and Beau felt an adrenaline rush the size of Godzilla's pancreas. His knees felt weak. In the sea of darkness before them, thousands of tiny lights flickered on. *Lighters!*

Slim knew it was a waste of time trying to assuage Beau's fears at this point. Whatever would happen would happen. Slim put a hand on his shoulder. A man with a flashlight mustered them together. He led them through the darkness toward the stage.

Beau moved as if in a dream. He fumbled with his cigarettes and lit one hastily. It fell from his fingers so he lit another.

As they mounted the metal steps and looked out at the sea of upturned faces, Robert whistled and said to Slim, "Ain't that the damnedest thing you ever saw?"

Slim smiled back and used his standard line. "Looks like every peckerhead in town is out there."

Robert laughed, but it sounded like he was underwater. The big stage seemed to be affecting them all, even if Beau was the only one to show it. Pressure weighed down on them like an iron harness. The flashlights lit the way.

In the eye of the storm, Robert moved slowly. A stagehand put him in his chair and adjusted his mikes. Oakland Slim stood nearby. "Ain't you gonna use that scarf?"

Robert wiped his hands with it and threw it at Slim. "Take this damn thing. Looks like somethin' my mother would wear."

"Kinda becomes you, Robert."

"Don't push it."

Walking out there, with all those eyes boring into them, they felt the temperature rise. Beau thought about how the Crawlin' Kingsnakes must feel, night after night. Seemed like a lot of work putting up with this kind of stress. To them it was probably easy.

That thought soothed him. It *was* easy. As easy as you could make it. The only thing that mattered was how you thought about it. *Everything is inside you.* He spent the next minute telling himself not to think about it, that people did this sort of thing all the time.

Slim tapped him on the shoulder as they walked out and said, "Remember, play it like it was a small club, OK?"

Beau nodded.

"And let's have some fun!"

Fun?

In front of all these people?

It was at that moment that Beau's tension broke. Yeah. This could be a lot of fun if he let it. He realized that he would remember this gig for the rest of his life and he might as well have fond memories. Beau smiled, and a strange thing happened: the world smiled back.

Robert Johnson made no apologies or excuses for anything. He took his good, sweet time, as if he couldn't care less. He was looking around for the guitar cord to plug into his guitar when a roadie ran out and frantically plugged it in for him. The roadie's eyes were wild and his hands were moving too fast, fumbling with the cord.

"Relax, son, you're making me nervous," Robert said with a wink. The roadie looked up, then scanned the crowd and said, "Good luck, Pops."

"I don't need no luck, boy, just get the hell off the stage and let a man work."

The roadie scurried off without looking back. Robert strummed a chord. It blasted through the sound system like thunder, and the crowd erupted into a cheer.

It dawned on Beau that nobody had discussed the introduction. Should they just start playing? He assumed that most people knew who Robert Johnson was. Or maybe they didn't. What would they think?

The amplifiers stood outlined against the backdrop like an electronic version of Stonehenge. The red standby lights glinted like demon eyes.

Beau fiddled with the dials on his Fender Bassman amp and wondered what song was first. The big electric Jazz bass felt alien in his hands. Slim tapped his harmonica against his leg. Robert had also neglected to make a set list. The old man seemed to not have a care in the world and was about to start the first song spontaneously when Heath Pritchard appeared next to him onstage.

As soon as the crowd saw Heath, it exploded into a mighty primal roar. The sound of the audience was frightening from where Beau stood. It washed over them like a sonic tidal wave.

The five tiny figures at center stage faced the eighty thousand people in front of them. Heath leaned into the mike and said, "I want to introduce the man who had the most effect on my music when I was growing up in England. The world thought he was dead, but he's back! Back from the grave!"

Another roar.

"Let's here it for Robert Johnson, the undisputed king of the blues!"

The crowd shouted together as one, and the noise seemed to vibrate the stage itself. Beau's internal organs vibrated with the sound.

"This is for Elvis," Robert said.

Heath turned and walked off, and without a moment's hesitation, Robert launched into his timeless classic, "Crossroads." There was no count, no "one-two-three-*four!*" He just started playing. Beau and the drummer waited a few bars, then fell in behind him. Beau tentatively picked the root note of each chord, staying on the one and four beat. Slim wailed a harp riff, and they were off.

Robert's guitar, thick as honey, poured the famous riff over the audience like a musical communion. The groove unwound, raw and primitive. People stood as one and acknowledged the sacred notes like pilgrims before Mecca. In five seconds Robert Johnson had won them over.

His high, plaintive voice bisected the night. "I went down to the crossroads . . . tried to flag a ride. . . ."

Vincent Shives didn't know where to go, but he felt himself being guided by Ida John's will. It was almost as if she were inside his head, telling him exactly what to do. *Look for a sign,* he told himself.

He looked up into the sky. A small plane crossed the cloudless, darkening sky, trailing an advertisement. Vince squinted, reading the sign silently to himself. It read: TODAY ONLY! THE CRAWLIN' KINGSNAKES AT DAY ON THE GREEN WITH ROBERT JOHNSON!

He had no idea where Day on the Green was or how he was

going to get there, but he knew that when he got there he was going to kill somebody.

He didn't care much beyond that. Like a robot, he walked the streets of Berkeley in a trance, seemingly controlled by an old woman he couldn't see.

The hand shifted in his pocket. *See?* it seemed to say. *See? I didn't let you down. They shot you but you didn't die, they put you in a hospital but you got away. I am the magic that makes you invincible, Vincent Shives. Nothing can hurt you now.*

He walked on, oblivious of the universe around him.

Twenty blocks later, another cop shouted to him, and when Vince didn't respond the cop ordered him to stop. Something about the way Vince looked was not quite right. He turned to face him. The other cop saw the bandage under Vince's hat and was about to ask him if he was all right when Vince whipped the syringe out of his pocket and jabbed it directly into the man's neck. He depressed the plunger and pushed it in even further. Vince could actually feel the solution being pumped into the man's body. He heard a soft hiss and bubble, then watched the color drain from the cop's face.

The cop gasped, reached out for Vince, then rolled his eyes back up into his head and collapsed. He tumbled forward, already dead as Vince caught him gently and laid him on the concrete.

Vince looked around; miraculously, no one had seen. He walked on briskly, leaving the body, with the syringe still embedded in it, facedown on the sidewalk. *Fool,* he thought. *Only a fool would try and stop me now.*

Vince looked down Telegraph Avenue and saw Ida John pointing. He walked in that direction. A few blocks later he saw her again, this time pointing down a side street. He followed her directions until he came to a BART station. Vince walked in and caught the first train to Oakland.

He heard the announcer call the Oakland Coliseum station and got off. He followed the crowd down the steps and through the ticket gate. A BART police officer spotted Vince's uniform and automatically opened the gate. Vince strolled through and became swept up in the mass of late-arriving people heading for the coliseum entrance.

When he got near the gate he heard something that made him

smile. Music. Beautiful music. It was "Crossroads," one of his all-time favorite songs. Robert Johnson's voice knifed through the night air like a laser. *Robert Johnson, alive.*

A security guard saw Vince walking toward him, assumed that the uniformed officer was one of the many who were patrolling the event, and let him by without a check.

He walked through the gate and into the arena without pause. There were people everywhere and it was impossible to move quickly through the dense throng. It was the largest crowd Vince had ever been in.

The music played. Robert Johnson played a new original composition. A harmonica wailed. Vince looked up at the gargantuan video screen. *Oakland Slim!*

The hand twitched anxiously in his pocket.

Vince casually made his way toward the stage. People got out of his path as soon as they saw the uniform. He enjoyed the respect he was getting as hippies, young girls and their drunken teenage boyfriends, scrambled to remove themselves from his gaze.

Had they looked closely and seen the madness in his eyes, they would have moved even faster.

Onstage, Robert Johnson stomped his way through "Sweet Home Chicago," "Terraplane Blues," and "Travelin' Riverside Blues," to the delight of eighty thousand rock and roll animals.

The song "Kind Hearted Woman" ended with Robert doing an impromptu rap about how the blues gets in his pants and starts tuning his "low-down guitar." The audience loved it. Heath Pritchard and the rest of the Snakes watched from the side of the stage, enjoying this virtuoso performance by the all-time master. Time seemed to slow down while the old man played; everything else became insignificant. The sound of the music became all that mattered. The sound of Robert's voice, the high lonesome wail, compelled you to listen. Intricate guitar lines punctuated the dark lyrics he sang. The devil lurked behind every riff.

Robert's frenzied vocal on "If I Had Possession Over Judgement Day" raised hackles three hundred rows back, up in the nosebleed seats. His voice whipped around the bowl of the stadium. "If I had possession over Judgement Day, then the woman that I'm lovin', she wouldn't have no right to pray."

Slim and Beau fell in behind the songs effortlessly. By the third song it became the easiest thing Beau had ever done, as natural as pissing in the ocean. He laughed when he thought of his earlier fear. *What was I thinking?*

Vince could feel the Mojo Hand getting frantic in his pocket. He knew the time had come to release it into the world. He stood in the midst of a crowd of people so densely packed as to allow no movement in any direction. They pushed against one another, straining to get closer to the stage, swaying with the common energy. Vince, in his desire to reach the stage himself, had somehow gotten caught up in the enthusiasm of the first hundred rows of standing patrons.

They jostled against him, too close to see that he was wearing a policeman's uniform. Vince kept his eyes on the stage, relentlessly moving closer.

George Jones stood in the backstage area with Annie Sweeny. The press section afforded a limited view of the stage, and she couldn't actually see Robert Johnson from where she sat. She could, however, see Beau.

She proudly watched her man perform. He was part of a spectacle involving tens of thousands of people, and it excited her. He was near the vortex of all that power, all that frenzied energy. Her heart was pounding just as if she were onstage herself. Robert's music triumphed. She wished her father could have seen it.

George kept looking around, not sure what he was looking for. He had that antsy feeling, like a prickling in his scalp, that something was about to happen. His sixth sense was percolating like an espresso machine. *Why?* he wondered. Vincent Shives lay comatose. *It's over.*

He scanned the backstage area constantly. The collection of groupies, celebrities, local dignitaries, media people, crew, hangers-on, and other musicians amused him. The Crawlin' Kingsnakes were the hottest band on the planet. They seemed to draw every weirdo out of the closet, into his or her most outlandish costume and into the circus. Backstage at a rock show is like another world, but backstage at a Kingsnakes show was another universe. It fascinated George. Who were these people? Where did they go during the day?

The swirl of attention at a gig like this was off the scale. Everybody tried to make the scene.

Annie said, "Let's go down closer to the stage. I want to see better."

Vince entered the backstage area. He walked through the checkpoint easily—the uniformed security guard there took one look at the badge on his shirt and the gun on his hip and stood aside. Vince sauntered past him without so much as a nod. He kept looking up at the stage, his eyes stuck on Robert Johnson.

He needed to get closer.

He edged his way between the people, shoving and pushing, moving relentlessly toward his goal.

On the stage, Heath Pritchard had joined Robert Johnson for the classic "Love in Vain." It mesmerized the crowd. Heath's guitar complemented Robert's, and they traded leads as easily as passing a joint. The combined charisma of these two men seemed incandescent.

Robert used his slide technique to create mysterious tonalities. As the song ended, Heath threw his hands in the air and clapped over his head.

"Let's hear it for 'im! Robert Johnson!" Another wave of adulation washed ashore.

Robert nodded. "Thank y'all. Thank y'all. So good."

He began the haunting guitar riff for "Hell Hound on My Trail," and Heath joined in. The sound system seemed to be made for Robert's guitar alone, accenting just the right frequencies and transforming the unassuming organic instrument into a veritable orchestra. The bass and drums filled in the backbeat's subtle pathos. Heath's presence onstage made these two songs an event.

Slim howled into his harmonica, bending and torturing the notes until they wrapped seamlessly around Robert's vocals. Slim and Beau had been an inspired choice as backup musicians. They created a solid wall of sound behind him, never intruding on the melody or what he played. The rhythm section stayed in sync, locked in there like a clockwork human machine. They complemented each other; Slim and Beau seemed to know exactly what, and what not, to play.

This was the kind of music that needed no rehearsal. It already existed, floating in the air, and Robert just seemed to be able to reach out and grab it, pull it down, and channel it into his guitar.

It moved Vince as he inched closer. Robert sang about a hellhound on his trail, following him everywhere he went. Vince could appreciate that.

The Mojo Hand squirmed desperately in his pocket. Suddenly, it clambered out and jumped away. Vince shouted and watched it disappear between people's legs.

George noticed a uniformed officer pass by and thought it odd. There weren't supposed to be any uniforms backstage, were there? He seemed to remember that stipulation from somewhere. He watched the cop move closer to the stage.

What gives?

If this guy was on duty, then why was he watching the show so intently, and why was he here, in an area where everything was under control? Private security guards patrolled these spaces.

George swung around to his left in order to get a better look at the guy. Something about the cop was making him nervous. His inner alarms were ringing so loudly that he could hardly hear the music.

George instinctively moved closer.

He noticed how pale the side of the guy's face was and how odd his movements were. The cop moved like a sleepwalker. He thought he saw a hint of bandage hanging out from under his hat. *Strange.*

Vince was only a stone's throw from the stage now. He slowly withdrew the patrolman's pistol from its belt, flicked off the safety, and brought the gun up level with his line of sight.

Holding it out in front of him with both hands, he took aim at the old black man singing onstage. With virtually every eye on Robert, Vince felt nearly alone in the crowd. Alone except for George Jones.

He sighted down the barrel and prepared to pull the trigger. One shot was all it would take, and he was almost close enough to Robert Johnson to spit on him.

George reached inside his coat and jerked the gun from his holster. He saw people gasp as they noticed the assassin in their midst. They shrank away from him, forming a circle of damnation. The gun seemed to glow with an ever increasing field of negative energy that could not be ignored. Somebody screamed.

Then George saw the assassin clearly. *Vincent Shives! Jesus Christ! It's not possible! Vincent Shives is lying comatose in Alta Bates Hospital!* Yet here he stood, back from the gates of hell, trying one more time to kill.

"Drop it!" George shouted, his voice nearly lost in the loud music that engulfed them all. "Drop it now!"

Vince felt, rather than heard, George through the confusion. He swung his gun around to aim it into the crew-cut detective's face.

Vince fired as George went into a crouch. George felt the bullet whiz past his ear. Somebody behind him screamed.

"I'm hit!" George heard a woman's voice shout.

George kept his gun in front of him, standing up to the fire. As time slowed down to a dreamlike slow motion, George sighted down on Vince. He brought the big .357 Smith & Wesson to bear between those frenzied pink eyes.

Incredibly, Vince turned away. He put his focus back on the stage and pulled back the hammer for his next shot. All distractions aside now, it was time to take care of business. He was about to realize his destiny.

He aimed, waiting for Beau to move aside for a clear shot. After a second or two, which seemed like an eternity to Vince, Robert Johnson's face came into his sight. He focused on the side of the old man's head. His mind sent the message to pull the trigger, but his finger never received it.

George fired twice in the space of one and a half seconds, hitting Vince in the neck and temple. His skull exploded like a watermelon. Vince's near-headless body danced away, hit the ground, and shivered spasmodically in a rapidly growing pool of rich, red blood. Then the screaming began.

Robert Johnson never missed a beat.

Heath's two-song cameo appearance ended Robert's set. The audience stood as one and lit their lighters. Robert stood and bowed to the field of humanity. No one onstage or in the audience knew shots had been fired. The noise was smothered by the massive sound system. Only the people backstage were aware.

George Jones stood at the center of a circle of people, holding his badge out and shouting for a medic. Event security moved in to secure the area. They summoned the in-house emergency medical team. Dozens of cameras clicked.

The musicians stood together, arm in arm, and walked to the lip of the stage. Robert thanked everyone profusely.

Heath Pritchard held his beautiful Gibson Hummingbird Sunburst acoustic guitar aloft. "I'll never play this guitar again!" he barked into the microphone.

He gripped the neck with two hands and brought it down like an ax onto the stage, smashing the body in the best Pete Townshend tradition. It splintered like kindling across the hard vinyl stage blanket.

Robert Johnson looked aghast. The other musicians stepped back. Heath seemed possessed. He kept smashing the guitar until all that was left was the neck. Then he kicked the pieces into the crowd and left the stage.

Robert grabbed a mike and shouted, "That boy's crazy!"

✋ TWENTY-SEVEN ✋

Robert Johnson slumped in his old couch and sipped a glass of whiskey. George Jones sat next to him, nursing his own drink. "I owe you my life," Robert told the world-weary detective.

Beau, Annie, and Slim found places to sit in the crowded living room.

"Me too," said Slim.

George looked down and mumbled. "I can't be sure of that. We'll never know who he was aiming at on that stage. It could have been any one of you. I just did what any cop would do. He *had* just fired at me, you know. Nobody shoots at me and gets away with it."

"Are you sure he's dead?" Annie asked, half serious.

"This time, yes," George replied. "I made sure of it. The death certificate has been signed."

Robert laughed. "That don't meant nothin'. I got mine in the cupboard."

They laughed together, relieved to be out of the Crawlin' Kingsnakes' circus.

"I propose a toast," Slim said loudly. "Here's to the blues!" He raised his glass.

"The blues!" they echoed. Glasses clinked. Each person drank in silence, contemplating the incredible events of the past few weeks.

"And here's to Elvis," George muttered. He took another swig of his drink, then put the glass down on the scuffed coffee table.

Beau put his arm around Annie and said, "Annie's got a hell of a story to write, and George here says he wants to start working on a book."

"A book?" Slim snorted. "Is that right, George?"

George grinned. "Yeah, I guess I'm gettin' sick of bein' shot at. I'll sit back and write about some of my cases, like this last one, and probably live a lot longer."

"What about you, Robert?" Annie inquired.

Robert looked at her with large brown eyes as deep and reflective as pools of night. "I never want to go through that shit again. I'm too old for it. It ain't natural to play for so many people," Robert answered. "That last gig cured me."

"Cured you, Robert?" Slim asked. "You mean you're givin' up playin' music?"

"Hell no, I didn't say that." He grinned, flashing yellow teeth. "Don't go puttin' no words in my mouth, Jerome. I'll keep playin' my guitar, it's just that I'll be sittin' alone in my kitchen. It scares me, all that money. It changes folks. Look what it did to Leeland. He was a fine boy until King Washington put all that greed in his head."

"Money does bad things to good people," said George, sipping his drink again. "It's evil stuff."

Robert Johnson cleared his ancient throat, wiped his mouth with a dingy handkerchief, and looked across the room. "You know, I guess I've been living on rice and beans for so long that I just couldn't take no steak. I'm happy with what I got—it's far more than I ever had before. Hell, I don't want to push fate. I cheated the devil enough for one lifetime."

"Such a sweet man," Annie said softly. "All you ever wanted was to play your music and be left alone. None of this would've happened if I'd had the good sense to let things be."

Robert slapped the table, grabbing their attention, "Hey, quit talkin' about me like I wasn't here, OK? I can still play music any old time I want to. I got my guitar. I got my fingers. What the hell else do I need? I'd rather play for myself, ain't that right, Jerome?"

Slim nodded, "Damn right, Robert. You just go on playin' that guitar wherever you want."

"Such a sweet man," Annie repeated.

"Well, he's gonna be a sweet rich man as soon as the lawyers get everything figured out," Slim continued.

Robert flashed a smile as warm as coffee. "If I live that long. I do believe there's still evil out to get me."

"How so?" Slim asked.

Robert cleared his throat. "Well, remember I told you about bein' poisoned back in '38?"

"Yeah?"

"People thought I was dead. Well, there's a story attached to this. You might have trouble believin' it. You see, I *was* dead for a short time."

Beau looked puzzled; he and Annie exchanged glances. Robert continued.

"They gave me the zombie poison, put it in my whiskey at a gig I was playin'."

Slim put his glass down and penetrated Robert with a sobering stare. "Zombie poison? What are you talkin' about, Robert?"

"Ida John was a witch," Robert said. "She did that Haitian voodoo, and believe me, that stuff is bad. She knew all the tricks. I ought to know." He paused, and nodded sagely. "I was her lover. Her husband found out about it and started makin' noise."

Robert looked at the faces around the table. Each one was fully absorbed by the story he told. If they didn't believe what he said, it didn't show. Even George Jones leaned forward on his elbows, his eyes locked on the old bluesman's face.

Every facial tic, every expression seemed to carry twice its weight. Robert Johnson, a man with a past as big as the ocean, told the story every blues fan wanted to hear. The truth.

He rocked in his chair, warming to the tale. "Back in those days, you slept with a man's wife, he was liable to kill you, expected to, even. If he didn't do something, people thought he wasn't much of a man. Now, you got to realize that Ida's mama was a very powerful woman around Greenwood, and she figured Ida should have things her way."

"You mean have you and her husband too?" Annie asked. "How?"

"Voodoo," he said, his voice as dark and smoky as a double shot of sour mash. "The woman was a witch. Course, I knew that, but I didn't care. It never bothered me. Hell, I had already met the devil face-to-face and made a deal with him, so one little ole witch didn't scare me none. She was a tiny thing, slim and beautiful. Her skin was Creole mocha. Her lips burned when you kissed 'em. I couldn't get enough of her. I didn't care about nothin'."

"When you're young, you don't worry," Slim mused.

Robert nodded. "I was either really brave or as thick as a plank. More like the plank, I suppose." He chuckled, then returned to his story. "Ida knew how to make the zombie poison. She knew lots of things. Learned it all from her mama. She gave the poison to her husband to give to me. Course, *he* thought it was gonna kill me, but *she* knew that it was just gonna make me look like I was dead.

"Some white man from the plantation signed the death certificate, pronounced me dead as a rock. They put me in a shed. I stayed there for a while. Funny thing was, I knew what was goin' on around me. I thought they was gonna bury me alive, but they were tryin' to get ahold of my family, and that took a couple of days.

"It's a good thing too. I woulda been put in the ground before my time. That's a hell of a thought, ain't it, Jerome?"

Slim nodded. The others in the room exchanged glances, but no one spoke. Robert took a deep breath and continued.

"After the second day, Ida broke into the shed and gave me the antidote. It revived me pretty quick. Then she led me away. She kept me chained up in a shack out in the woods. Ida said it was for my own good. She said I was a zombie now.

"And I believed it. That was the worst thing I ever lived through, or died through, seein' how you look at it.

"She visited me there a couple times, brought me food and nursed me back to health. It was like I had no mind of my own. I was like her slave. I was in a damn daze. I couldn't wipe my own ass. Couple of weeks later, I got my sense back and made a break for it.

"I went to see Carrie Harris over in Memphis, a relative of mine, and she helped me get away. From there I made my way down to New Orleans, then Texas, and finally all the way out to California. Believe me, I couldn't get far enough away from that woman.

"I met a fine woman out in Hayward and that's where I stopped runnin'."

His story nearly finished, Robert looked around the room again and saw the astonishment in the eyes of his friends.

"So if anybody ever asks you if zombies are real, you know what to say. You just been talkin' to one."

"Christ, Robert," Slim said. "That's a hell of a story. You sure you ain't been drinkin' too much tonight?"

Robert laughed. "Ain't got enough whiskey in this house to slow me down. But the story's true."

"I believe it," Slim said. "God knows I do."

Robert took another swallow of the honey-colored fluid and whistled softly. "There's more, though. Ida John was only sixteen." Robert sighed. "Her family didn't like her bein' married so young. And they sure as hell didn't like me. And back in that part of the country, they hold grudges for a long, long time."

"She could still be alive," Slim said.

Robert nodded. "Yep. She'd be about fifty-five now. Probably mean as a billy goat."

"Wait a second. Are you sayin' she could be behind all this?" George asked.

"Damn right. And I'm scared. That's why I'm gonna crawl back under a rock. That's why I got this." Robert reached in his shirt and withdrew a small leather packet on a string. "It's gris-gris powder, keep them evil spirits away." He tucked the pouch back in his shirt and smiled.

"What's in it?" Beau asked.

"I don't know, but I know it works, because so far I ain't dead."

George Jones leaned forward and said, "I've heard of something like that. It's supposed to be like a magic charm that keeps you safe from harm. I don't believe in it myself, but that doesn't matter. What matters, Mr. Johnson, is that you believe in it."

"You ever hear anything about Ida?"

Robert shook his head. "Nope, but now that I'm front-page news I reckon I'll find out pretty soon."

Slim leaned back. He took a large sip of whiskey and winked at

Robert. "You know, I do believe you're gonna make enough money to move somewhere else."

"I been runnin' my whole life, Jerome. I'm tired."

Annie cleared her throat. "I have an announcement to make. I was saving it until we were alone but I guess it doesn't matter now. I talked to the lawyers today. Seems that Robert Johnson was arrested for assault in 1934." She nodded at Robert. "He was fingerprinted by the Leflore County Sheriff's Department. Served thirty days in jail. The fingerprints match the one's the lawyer took last week."

Slim turned to Robert. "You got arrested?"

Robert shook his head. "Damn. I forgot all about that. It's been a long time. But that's right, I remember now. I got in a fight with a fellah on Mr. Dockery's plantation once. Cops came and took me away."

Annie said, "Well it's a good thing, too. That's what makes your case stand up. Also, because the death certificate was made out by an informant, and signed by the county registrar and not a state health officer, as the law provides, it may have been illegally filed."

"You mean it's no good?" Robert said.

"Might not be."

"Then that means I'm still alive. Hot damn."

"What do you do next, George?" Beau asked. "Is this case closed?"

George rubbed his forehead as if he had a headache, which he did. He just wanted this case to go away and leave him alone, but in his heart he knew it wouldn't. There were still questions to ask, leads to follow up. George's gut feeling wouldn't let him go.

"That's hard to say." He excused himself and went to the bathroom. A few moments later, Beau followed. As they met in the hallway, Beau asked the same question.

George said, "What do *you* think I should do?"

"I think you should talk to King Washington," Beau replied.

George looked surprised. "You think he had something to do with this? Why? You know something?"

"Me and Annie have turned up some information about Washington. He stands to make a lot of money from the victims' publishing and the record catalogs, both of which he owns."

"Is that so?"

"Yeah, the trail leads right through Royal Records, Mambo Music, M. Leveau, and ultimately King Washington. Annie knows the guy is a crook, she deals with him for her mail-order business. Slim's been after him for years for back royalties. The way he swooped in on Robert Johnson and just took over . . . And for chump change! That guy sucks."

George nodded. "Yeah, but the fact remains. Vincent Shives had the murder weapon on him, he was in the act of trying to kill Slim when you shot him, and tonight he tried to kill Robert Johnson. Explain that."

"I don't know. Maybe he was set up."

"By Washington?"

"Vince could just be the tip of the iceberg."

Oakland Slim wandered into the tiny hallway, making it suddenly very crowded. "What're you talkin' about in here? What is it you want to keep so private?"

"Nothing."

"Bullshit. I saw you follow George out here."

"We're talkin' about King Washington," Beau admitted.

Slim looked George right in the eye. "Washington's an asshole. I got a lawsuit going right now with him."

George nodded. "Yeah, I know. You were once on Royal Records."

"Royal Records ripped off musicians like it was goin' out of style. Mambo Music too."

Beau's ears prickled. "Mambo Music? What do you know about Mambo Music?"

"Everything," Slim replied. "I didn't know you were investigating Mambo. Nobody tells me doodly-squat."

"Why didn't you say so before?" Beau wanted to know.

"You didn't ask me. What am I, a mind reader?"

Beau began to talk excitedly, explaining what he and Annie had found. "There's a link between all the victims, including you, Slim. Royal, Mambo, and somebody named M. Leveau."

Slim's mouth hung open.

George could see the sudden change in his demeanor. "What is it, man?"

Slim's voice was dry. He swallowed hard and looked down at his hands, then back into George's face.

"M. Leveau is King Washington. It's a pseudonym he uses when he lists himself as writer."

Ida John stood defiantly at King Washington's hotel-suite door. She'd rung the bell several times.

For King Washington, things were improving. Vince was dead and the advance orders for Robert Johnson albums were pouring in. The Guppi family had been patient and he'd promised full payment in a few weeks. The old mobster, always a businessman, had gone for the deal immediately and apologized for the rash behavior of his underlings. Money talks, he said over the phone, bovine fecal matter walks.

King assured him that the money would be forthcoming, no need to use any strong-arm tactics.

Now, with a fire burning in the fireplace of his suite at the hotel and whiskey warming his gut, King felt relaxed for the first time in months. Leeland and the two hookers chopped up another line of coke. King didn't care for blow himself, but it always made a great party favor for his guests. He'd been celebrating with Leeland all night. Clothes were strewn about the floor.

He closed his eyes and sank deeper into the big easy chair, a contented smile on his wide brown face. How long he stayed in that position he did not know, but it must have been long enough for his cigar to burn down about an inch and go out. It lay across the ashtray like a tiny log, the ash undisturbed. An empty glass sat next to it. King rubbed his eyes, wondering if he'd drifted off to sleep for a moment. The doorbell brought him back to reality.

Leeland and the two hookers were still gathered around the big mirror doing lines.

"Get in the other room," King growled. "And take that shit with you."

They left the room in a hurry, suddenly paranoid. King slipped his gun into the pocket of his sport coat. The doorbell rang again. King squinted through the peephole. He was astonished to see Ida John there. He opened the door. They stood facing each other for at least twenty seconds, saying nothing. Then Ida broke the silence using her warmest voice.

"Well, aren't you going to invite me in?"

King stammered. "Y-yeah, sure, come in . . ."

She entered the suite, looking around and nodding. "Well, it looks like you've done all right for yourself."

King shook off the weirdness of their meeting and within a few seconds became suspicious.

"What do you want?"

Ida raised an eyebrow. "I want to make peace. It's not right to be enemies with your own son."

King shook his head. "That never bothered you before, did it, Mother?"

"We weren't enemies before."

"You left me when I was only three years old. If it wasn't for all the aunts and uncles I would have been out on the street. You abandoned me like I didn't exist, never sent a penny, never even wrote a letter. Why? So you could be a swamp witch down in Louisiana? So you could be a whore and not have to worry about little King findin' out? Well, after I grew up I did find out. I found out everything. You thought voodoo was more important than me, didn't you? You thought I was just some little piece of crap you could forget about!"

Ida looked him in the eyes, her face etched in stone. The power and pride in her demeanor held firm. "That's not true, son. I loved you, but I couldn't take you with me because it was too dangerous. Once I started using the voodoo, I couldn't back out. The power I was summoning would have killed you. I know this is hard to understand, but they would have used you against me."

King slammed his hand against the wall. "That's the biggest load of crap I've ever heard."

"I was protecting you from the dark forces."

King laughed sardonically. "You expect me to believe that? The only dark force around here is your rotten soul."

"Don't insult me, son. I've come here to make peace."

King looked at her suspiciously. "You want to make peace? After all these years?"

Ida nodded.

"What are you up to?"

"This Robert Johnson thing has weighed heavily on my mind."

King reluctantly led her into the sitting room. Clothes were still strewn about on the floor.

"You got company?"

King shouted into the other room. "OK, everybody out! Let's go! Party's over!"

Leeland and the two hookers emerged sheepishly from the bedroom. They gathered their things and left, never looking at Ida John. King stood at the door, handing out money. The door closed and King turned back to the room.

A fire crackled in the hearth and a bottle of whiskey stood open. They both took seats in easy chairs opposite each other.

"I don't feel any need to be civil with you, not after our last conversation," King said flatly. His hand wrapped around the whiskey glass and brought it to his lips.

She wanted to slap him, but instead calmed herself. "The only time you come to me is when you want something," she said softly. "This Robert Johnson . . . I know you want to protect him, but you put your own greed before family honor. That's wrong."

"You're crazy. I knew you'd want to kill him as soon as you found out he was still alive. Then you sent that poor, dumb albino to do it, and look what happened."

Ida let silence frame her next words, adding its small dignity and weight to her proposition. After a dozen heartbeats, she said, "Let's make a deal. Mother to son. Let me take this old man, you don't need him. I'll make you rich in other ways."

King shook his head. "It won't work, Mother. I don't believe in your magic, it won't work on me. This is what kills people." He drew the gun out of his pocket and laid it on the table. "Not some old potions and chants, but bullets." He unbuttoned the middle buttons of his shirt and pulled a tiny rawhide pouch free. He held it up for her to see. "Even if your power was real, which it ain't, it wouldn't work on me because I'm protected, see? This is my gris-

gris. Got some of your nappy old hair in it. If the forces you say you can summon show up here looking for me, they'll smell this"—he shook the pouch—"and think it's you. You see, I did learn something about the black arts."

"But how? From who?"

"Auntie Virgie. She raised me, remember? Oh, and by the way, I made one of these for Robert Johnson and told him it would protect him from evil." King laughed sharply. "He swore he'd wear it day and night forever." He dangled the pouch in her face.

Ida's temper began to rise. She looked at King with venomous viper eyes. "You're messin' with things you know nothing about," she hissed at him, the fine spray of her spittle striking his hot face in a dozen places. She reached into her handbag and pulled forth the Mojo Hand. King recognized it immediately. She thrust it forward. "What about this?" she asked.

He looked at it disdainfully and shook his head. She was about to say something more, but he didn't give her the chance.

"What about it? The Mojo Hand is nothing but a dead man's paw! Can't you see that? It's not alive! Not now, not ever! It's what I used to fool that idiot Shives, but I'm not as gullible as he was, Mother!"

"But the murders—"

"You don't think Vince was smart enough to pull them off?"

"It was the Mojo Hand," she repeated.

"No, it wasn't," he said softly. "It was all in Vincent's mind. Shives was the one who believed it, nobody else. I killed those people, Mother."

He paused and saw the shock on her face, admiring it. "It wasn't the Mojo Hand or old pink eyes, it was me!"

"No!" she gasped, waving the Mojo Hand as if to brush away the words he was saying. She stood, unsure of what to do next.

He saw her revulsion and pressed on. "Why do you think I gave the claw to Vince? Huh? For a souvenir? I wanted him to get rid of Oakland Slim for me so he could get blamed for all the murders. I knew the fool would get caught."

"I could always go to the police," she said suddenly, without thinking.

"Go ahead, go! Who's gonna believe a crazy old bitch with a dead hand? It would be worse for you than me, wouldn't it? How are you gonna explain your relationship with Vince? All the voodoo?"

Ida drew back. The son spoke blasphemy. She realized she was losing her grasp on the situation. "I had no idea," she said in a whisper. "No idea at all." She paused, eyeing him. "You? My own son?"

"Yes, Mother," King said, the satisfaction fat on his face.

"You . . . murdered them all?"

"Yes," he hissed. "For money."

They stared at each other for a few moments. Tension built. Ida shook her head. "Let's put it all behind us," she said. "I propose a toast."

King thought he could feel the strength of her resolve erode. "Yes, I think that would be good," he said. "A drink, Mother. A drink to bury the past."

King had been waiting for this all his life. He'd won. The taste of victory would be so sweet. He could barely contain his glee.

"You're smarter than I thought," she said, watching him pour the whiskey.

"Let's face it," King replied, "this is the modern world. Witchcraft has no place anymore. We're both businessmen, we both know that money makes the world go round."

Ida nodded. She looked away from King's thick face. His self-satisfied smirk cut her deep. She stared into the fire.

King pushed one of the glasses of whiskey toward her. "Here, Mother, drink up. Nothing like the taste of whiskey to wash down humble pie."

Her eyes were still fixed on the fire, the flames reflected in her eye. Suddenly, a small explosion burst forth from the fireplace, and a piece of burning wood came spinning out of the fire. It landed on the rug. The fire spat and crackled angrily.

"Shit!" King shouted, and he moved to kick the errant piece of burning material back onto the bricks. Just as he did so, another pop sent more embers onto the rug.

Ida's hands moved with unreal swiftness. To anyone watching, they would have been a blur. Her gnarled fingers were preternaturally energetic as they went about their deadly task. The large ring on the middle finger of her left hand came open. From the hidden space inside, a measure of white powder fell into a glass. She stirred it with her finger. She moved the other glass a fraction of an inch toward his side.

King Washington finished his job on the floor and turned back to Ida. He sat back down in his chair and eyed the glasses suspiciously. "Did you move this glass?" he asked.

Ida shook her head.

"It didn't move itself," he grumbled.

"Well, I didn't touch it," she answered indignantly.

King's eyes slitted. He picked the glass up and, holding it into the light, examined it carefully. "What have you been up to, old woman?"

"Nothing," she replied.

"You put something in my glass!" he accused.

Ida smiled. "You're too suspicious, son. I never touched your glass, I swear it," she said truthfully.

"Well, then, why was it moved?"

"You moved it yourself, before you got up."

King scrutinized the glass again. This time he thought he saw a layer of fine white particles suspended near the bottom. King looked her in the eye. "I don't believe you."

He stood up, his huge frame dwarfing her, and smiled sardonically. He thrust his own glass at his mother and said, "Then drink, drink from my glass, dear Mother, and we will see what we will see."

Ida stammered. "But—"

"A toast, between mother and son, a toast to your good health!" he bellowed. Ida hesitated. He pushed the glass into her hand. She took it, looked at him scornfully, and began to raise it to her lips.

"Wait a second," he said, and raised the other glass.

Ida waited. King raised a brow. "What is it? Are you afraid of something? Why are you hesitating?"

Ida looked at the glass, swirled the contents in her hand, and watched the thick amber fluid's ebb and flow. She took a breath and raised it to her lips. And drank.

King watched. He saw her down the whiskey in one motion, her wrinkled throat undulating like a mambo snake. When he was sure she had drunk it all he raised his own glass and knocked it back.

Their eyes locked. King smiled. "Good, OK, now let's just sit here and wait."

"For what?" she asked.

King chuckled and said nothing.

He lit a cigar and relaxed. He turned on his stereo and began to play a tape of Robert Johnson's album. The music slid around the room, making King daydream about all the money he was about to make.

Five minutes passed, then ten. King yawned. *This is getting tedious,* he thought. His eyes were drawn to the fire. He let himself be sucked into it, the orange flames shifting and flaring. He watched it undulate. He kept waiting for a change in the old woman's demeanor, half expecting her to keel over any moment. Nothing happened.

"How do you feel?" he asked.

"Fine."

"You look a little pale," he said. His gaze went back to the fire. A warmth spread quietly over him, a pleasant feeling of well-being, and he sighed deeply.

Ida remained upright. "It must be the fire," she said. "It's making the air so dry, so hot, I can hardly breathe."

"I know what you mean," he replied.

"Just look at it," she whispered.

He did. It filled his vision with beautiful shapes and colors. He imagined he could see faces looking back out at him from deep within the flames. He saw Vince, his wild eyes glistening, the impossible whiteness of his skin so strange, like death. Vince's face faded, and King watched as darker shapes came together in the blaze. Art Spivey smiled through the inferno. King blinked. *What's going on here?*

The face did not disappear. Art's eyes held him in their burning grasp, accusing him of all the horrible things he'd done. Then the other faces came forward, swirling together like melting wax. Ed Green, Red Tunney, and B. Bobby Bostic. Like a jury of the damned, they silently indicted him with their unblinking gaze.

"What do you see?" Ida's voice seemed to come from a thousand miles away. He had forgotten all about her. Was she still here? What was happening to him?

"I see faces," he said hoarsely. "Faces in the fire."

King tried to swallow but his throat was too dry. He reached for his glass and realized it was empty. He looked at Ida. The room began a gentle spin.

"Oh . . . no . . ."

Ida leaned closer to him, her breath moist and bitter. "Are you all right?"

King's eyes became unfocused. He swayed in his chair. He gripped the armrests to keep from tilting. "You! You poisoned me!" King said with alarm. His lips were growing numb. He tried to stand but his legs betrayed him and he fell to the floor. The full horror of what was happening swept over him with a wave of panic. The old witch had tricked him!

King was gasping for breath. "You poisoned me. . . . How?"

"That's right, son, I poisoned you. It was in the whiskey just like it was for Robert Johnson. Whiskey works best because it masks the taste. I used your own suspicious nature against you. I knew you'd suspect me, so I put it in my glass. You switched it yourself, you fool. Your own distrust was your undoing. Of course, I have the antidote."

King began to feel light-headed. His stomach turned over. He wanted to get up and run to the bathroom, but he was unable to makes his limbs work. "Damn you!" he rasped.

"You have a place in hell," Ida whispered. "It's waiting for you."

King began to gag. Somewhere inside he realized that his only chance at survival was to vomit, but nothing would come up. He rolled onto his side and tried to catch his breath.

Ida knelt over him and felt his forehead. "Yes, that's good. It won't be long now."

He looked up at her, his eyes pleading.

She smiled. "I know what you're thinkin'," she said. "You're wonderin' if it's the zombie poison, the datura. You're wonderin' if I'll bring you back."

Ida laughed softly, almost girlishly. She leaned down and put her face in front of his. When they were nose to nose, she said, "I guess you'll be finding out real soon, son, real soon. I wouldn't wait up, though."

King opened his mouth and moaned. The sound was pitiful. He struggled to get up, but it was useless. Ida stood up, took the Mojo Hand off the table, and threw it on his chest.

"Noooooooooo!" he groaned.

In his oxygen-starved mind, King began to hallucinate. He felt the hand come alive. It crawled toward his face.

King watched in horror as it placed one finger after another in his mouth. They wriggled against his tongue. King wanted to scream but his throat was too constricted. The Mojo Hand seemed to be trying to crawl down his gullet. King moved his leaden hands to his face and fumbled in vain against the monster hand. His mind began to snap, shredding apart his sanity in jagged, uneven strips. Ida looked down at him and shook her head.

Using a tissue, she reached for the gun on the table and checked to make sure a bullet was in the chamber. *King was right,* she thought. *Bullets kill people, not voodoo.* She knelt next to him, gently placed the gun in his hand, and guided it to his temple. "Here."

The explosion shattered the calm night like a thundercrack. King's body jerked back as the blood fanned out from his skull. His body contorted into the shape of a question mark as it came to rest for the final time.

"The joke's on you," Ida said. "It was the datura. I would've brought you back."

George Jones decided to question King Washington. Suddenly it seemed important. There were too many unanswered questions in George's notebook. His senses tingled. Beau was right, Washington had too much to gain. All roads led through either his record company, his publishing companies, or his acquisition companies. King had been buying up old catalogs for quite some time. He'd licensed the stuff around the world five times over. Directly or indirectly, it looked as if he owned it all. And now he was M. Leveau.

Beau and Slim insisted on coming along, and George reluctantly agreed. They promised to shut up and let George do the talking. George thought their presence would disorient King, maybe make him slip up.

They took George's car. Robert gave them the name of King's hotel.

George approached the door to the suite cautiously.

He prepared himself for the confrontation. He reached out to ring the doorbell. The pressure of his finger on the door swung it inward. "It's open," whispered George. "I'm going in. You stay here."

He slid into the vestibule and smelled cordite—a gun had been fired here recently. George drew his own weapon and inched along the wall until he could see into the living room. He felt a chill.

There was a puddle of blood in the middle of the floor.

King Washington had blown his brains out. The gun was still in his hand. A swath of gore led away from his face, trailing across the floor toward the far wall. George looked around the room, searching for a clue or a hint of explanation. He was careful not to touch anything.

"Jesus Christ!" Beau said from the doorway, a few steps behind him. George looked up and scowled.

"I thought I told you to stay outside," he said.

Beau and Slim stepped closer and peered into what was left of King Washington's face. "Holy shit! He did this himself?"

"Looks that way. Don't touch anything!" George barked.

A shiver ran up George's spine as he bent over the body. An icy, inexplicable feeling of evil passed through him. He stood up, put his gun away, and went looking for the house phone.

George was struck by an acrid smell of smoke in the air, different from the cordite. Then George recognized the appalling stench of burnt human flesh. His eyes were automatically drawn to the fireplace, where he saw the remains of something that he would have nightmares about for years to come.

He approached and squatted before it. A few lazy tendrils of smoke still rose from the ashes. Beau and Slim were right behind him, peering over his shoulder.

"What the hell is that?" he heard Beau ask.

It was a charred human hand, burnt to a crisp. The blackened skeleton was all that remained. It looked like a huge black spider dead on its back. The fingers were splayed apart, as if reaching for something? . . .

"It's the Mojo Hand," George whispered. "I wonder how it got in here."

George stared at it for a long time, trying in vain to find an explanation that made sense. His skin itched and prickled. A light sheen of perspiration expanded over him. Every psychic sense in his body was ringing like a fire alarm.

"Was King Washington the blues killer?" Beau asked.

"I guess we'll never know," George answered.

"Well, if he was, he was duped, 'cause no one man can kill the blues," Slim said.

They stared at what was left of the Mojo Hand.

Beau added the obvious. "The blues is a feeling, an idea. You can't kill an idea. And you can't kill the blues."

"It will never die," Slim whispered.

Not now.

Not ever.

✋ EPILOGUE ✋

Two figures walked down the two-lane blacktop. They'd parked their car a few yards up the road and proceeded on foot.

Robert Johnson whistled. "This must be the place . . . but it sure has changed. Used to be a dirt road."

Beau looked ahead, into the Mississippi night. A gas station and a minimart loomed up ahead. "Looks like civilization took over."

Robert stopped and turned 360 degrees, scanning the entire area. "I coulda sworn this was the place."

Beau pointed at the gas station. "There?"

Robert nodded. "Yep . . . I don't know what to say. I was sure I would meet the devil here, just like I did in 1934."

Beau looked at the brightly illuminated pumps and the signs advertising New Orleans Saints coffee mugs, only seventy-nine cents with each purchase. Moths flew frantically into the fluorescent lights. A truck whizzed past, blasting them with fumes. Garbage swirled. Robert pushed his hat down tighter on his head.

Beau said, "Take a look, Robert. There's your devil."

The gas station gleamed in the night.

·